Fran O'Brien and Arthur McGuinness
established McGuinness Books
to publish Fran's novels to raise funds
for LauraLynn Children's Hospice.

Fran's novels, *The Married Woman*,
The Liberated Woman, *The Passionate Woman*,
Odds on Love, Who is Faye? The Red Carpet,
Fairfields, The Pact, 1916, Love of her Life,
and *Rose Cottage Years* have raised
over €500,000.00 in sales and
donations for LauraLynn House.

Fran and Arthur hope that *Ballystrand*
will raise even more funds for LauraLynn.

www.franobrien.net

Also by Fran O'Brien

The Married Woman
The Liberated Woman
The Passionate Woman
Odds on Love
Who is Faye?
The Red Carpet
Fairfields
The Pact
1916
Love of her Life
Rose Cottage Years

Buy now online www.franobrien.net

Ballystrand

FRAN O'BRIEN

To Dave,
with many thanks
for all you do for us!
Fran & Arthur.

McGuinness Books

McGuinness Books

Ballystrand

This book is a work of fiction and any resemblance
to actual persons, living or dead, is purely coincidental.

Published by McGuinness Books,
15 Glenvara Park, Ballycullen Road,
Templeogue, Dublin 16.

A catalogue record for this book
is available from the British Library.

ISBN 978-0-9954698-2-2

Typeset by Martone Design & Print,
Celbridge Industrial Estate, Celbridge, Co. Kildare.

Printed and bound in Great Britain by
CPI Group (UK) Ltd, Croydon, CR04YY.

www.franobrien.net

This novel is dedicated to Jane and Brendan McKenna,
and in memory of their daughters Laura and Lynn.

And for all our family, friends and clients who support our
efforts to raise funds for LauraLynn Children's Hospice,
Leopardstown Road, Dublin 18.

Jane and Brendan have been through every parent's worst
nightmare – the tragic loss of their only two children.

Laura died, just four years old, following surgery to repair a
heart defect. Her big sister, Lynn, died, aged fifteen, less than
two years later, having lost her battle against Leukaemia –
diagnosed on the day of Laura's surgery.

Having dealt personally with such serious illness, Jane and
Brendan's one wish was to establish a children's hospice
in memory of their girls.

Now LauraLynn House has become a reality
and their dream has come true.

LauraLynn Children's Hospice offers community based
paediatric palliative, respite, end-of-life care, and the
LauraLynn@home Programme.

At LauraLynn House there is an eight bed unit, a residential
unit for families, support and comfort for parents and siblings
for whom life can be extremely difficult.

Putting Life into a Child's Day
Not Days into a Child's Life

Chapter One

Slowly he closes the book he has just finished. It is a favourite, *The Pickwick Papers,* by Charles Dickens. He has re-read the book many times over the years, and will miss its company. He caresses the dark green hard cover with the name embossed in gold, loving that smooth leathery feel. He opens the pages and presses his face into the spine breathing in the musky aroma of paper and ink.

Everything about this place is a neutral grey white. Lives bounded by routine. Broken only by sudden eruptions of violence.

He has been waiting for this day to arrive for ever. But like a child longing for Santa Claus to come on Christmas Eve, the length of time seems never-ending.

Soon he will walk out of here into the world again. A strange alien place. He wonders how it will feel, look, smell. And can't imagine. It is a blank canvas. Like those images he sees on the television. Flat. Two-dimensional. Terror sweeps through him. Terror of the unknown.

Chapter Two

Zoe walked along the pathway and her eyes drifted left and right. As always she noticed names on headstones. Loving messages carved in memory of a darling wife, a dearest husband. Rain drenched teddies remind of the tragic loss of a child. She passed a grave with pink flowers growing in a pot on sparkling white gravel. On another, a cheerful yellow budded plant grew in profusion, challenging the sadness of this place. But here lay the forgotten ones too where weeds reached up through concrete or hardened earth.

She stood in front of their own grave, blessed herself, and murmured a prayer for her grandparents and mother. She had felt guilty that she hadn't been here for a couple of months, and now made a promise that she would come more often, and make the time regardless of what she was doing. She reached to pull a few weeds which had poked their heads up between the grey gravel. Then she stepped across, and opened the bottle of water she carried with her. A few red Geraniums still bloomed. She poured water into the earth in the flowerpot, soaking it. Then she dead-headed the flowers. Took a tissue and wiped it over the black marble headstone, removing any dust which had gathered. She read the inscriptions particularly that of her mother …

Treasured memories of Rachel Sutherland.
Beloved wife and mother.

Tears moistened her eyes, and the words became indistinct.

'*Happy Birthday*', she whispered, put out her hand and gripped the imaginary hand of her mother. She always did that. Hating the thought of leaving her in this place.

She checked the time and then left the cemetery as quickly as she could. In the car, her phone beeped. A text. It was Russell.
'*Where are you?*'
Immediately her heart started to thump, and she texted back.
'*On my way.*'
'*Eta?*'
'*Meet at hotel.*'
She had misjudged the time and had forgotten they had decided to have a meeting before dinner with the clients. Now she sat into the car, put her foot down on the accelerator, and pulled out into the road, praying that she would get back on time.

In the bar, Russell was in deep conversation with the two clients. A man and a woman.
'I'm sorry to be late,' she said, smiling at them.
'Would you like a drink?' the woman asked.
'No thank you …' she declined.
'We'll be going in now …' Russell said.
The waiter approached them. 'Sir, your table is ready.'

They went into the restaurant, and sat down. The clients were good company and while they didn't discuss business as such, their conversation was of life in general and Zoe was very interested to hear how they lived. The man was particularly attentive to her, although she noticed that Russell hardly passed a comment. Never once meeting her eyes, or even smiling. He was like that. He hated anyone to be late. Business always came first with him. She said a silent prayer hoping that the meeting would prove to be successful, and he would be in good humour when they went home.

3

Their company *RZ Gaming* had been established for the last seven years, and she often wondered if it was a good idea for them to work and live so closely together. They were very successful, although both of them were workaholics. There was very little opportunity for a social life except at the weekends and even then it was difficult to make the time to meet with friends. But they had recently become engaged and planned to get married on New Year's Eve, so she hoped that would make a difference.

The meeting over, they headed home, each driving their own car, and as she drove into the underground carpark she saw the lift door close as he went on ahead. That didn't auger well. She could tell he was angry.

She walked into the apartment a few minutes later, went across the room and kissed him. 'Love you.'

He didn't reply, picked up a bottle of whiskey and poured a glass.

'The meeting went well,' she said in a light-hearted manner determined not to be swept up into his darker mood.

'You being late didn't help matters.'

'They seemed very pleasant,' she ignored the remark.

'You can never tell what they're thinking. What kept you anyway?'

'I had something to do.'

'Something more important?' he barked.

'Yes, actually.'

'And what was that?'

She didn't want to tell him, but had to. 'It was my mother's birthday and I went to Ballystrand.'

'For God's sakes,' he exploded. 'And you had me hanging around the hotel waiting for you. Really, Zoe …'

'I'm sorry, I didn't realise how late it was.'

'You know how important this contract is to us?'

'Of course I do.'

'The company are really interested in our virtual reality games, and our hardware for bio-sensing. *VR* is a new world and it's already taking our business to another level. But there are changes at the top in their company and we could be the first casualty if they decide to do business with someone else and dump us.'

'Any games we've designed have been exactly what they need, and they've done very well in the market. There's a big demand.'

'You can never be sure, there's stiff competition out there.'

'I know.' She picked up her handbag and went towards the bedroom. 'I'm for bed, are you coming?'

'No, not yet, I'm going through the documents on this quotation we're doing for the Australian company.'

'Don't be long.'

'No.' He didn't look at her.

She sighed, wondering how much time it would take him to get over this particular annoyance. She showered and climbed into bed, checking what was in the diary for tomorrow. It was a very full day, the most important item being a meeting with the wedding planner. She had wanted Russell to come along with her but now it was doubtful. She looked at her engagement ring and twirled it around, the large diamond glittering.

Time passed and there was no sign of him, so she decided to see if she could coax him into a better mood. She slipped on her black satin dressing gown and tiptoed along the corridor. 'Russell?'

He was working on his laptop.

'Yeah?'

She felt a sense of relief, at least he had replied, that was something. She made coffee and brought it in.

'Thanks.'

She sat down beside him.

'Do you think we're in with a chance?'

'Hope so, we need to expand in that area, there are huge opportunities for our new games, the young people are looking for anything novel.'

'And our teams are particularly innovative in the e-sports market. The US is growing all the time.'

'Our sales people must have their targets increased.'

'We need to make sure they have plenty of perks,' Zoe said.

'Are many people availing of the help of a counsellor?'

'According to her, they are.'

'Then it's worth the investment.'

'But …there is another side to it.'

'What's that?' He looked at her, peevish.

'Because they're using the counselling service, maybe there's too much stress on them.' Zoe pointed out. 'If they were all happy campers then why would they need to see a counsellor?'

'People will use anything that comes free, there doesn't always have to be a reason.'

'Of course, they may have personal problems and the service gives them a chance to talk to someone in confidence,' she mused, staring vaguely into space.

'There are probably numerous reasons why.'

'I hope they're not overworked and under too much pressure.'

'We work just as hard, harder in fact.'

'It's different for us, we have a choice.'

'We're committed to ensuring that our company is profitable. Keeping people in jobs. Well paid jobs. Probably earning the highest salaries in the country.'

'I'm tired, pet, it's late, let's go to bed.' She kissed him.

'I'll be there in a minute.'

'Don't delay,' she smiled. And to her surprise, for once he didn't. As he showered, she slipped off her dressing gown, sprayed just a hint of *Poison*, and lay waiting in the bed for him only partially covered by the satin sheet.

His lithe muscular body was still slightly damp as he threw off the towel and let it fall to the floor. She watched him as he rolled on to the bed. His arms embraced, and they clung together, his lips soft, moving across hers, his moist tongue sending her into heights of pleasure.

'I love you, Zoe, I'm sorry I was sharp earlier, but …'

'Don't worry, my love, it was all my fault, I have to apologise for being late anyway,' she whispered, running her fingers over his chest, tickling his smooth skin.

'I'm too impatient, you'll have to scold me next time,' he laughed.

'I'll be like a teacher.' She wagged her finger.

'Or my mother.'

'Your mother scares me,' she laughed.

'She scares me too.' He pulled closer. 'Come here to me.'

There was no more talk for a while, other than intimate whispers between them as they made love. Russell wasn't the most exciting of lovers, always keeping to his usual missionary position, disinclined to try anything new. But she loved him. He loved her. And that was everything.

Chapter Three

'Gail, this designer is fantastic according to Sylvia. Many of her clients grace the red carpet at the *Oscars*,' Zoe smiled at her younger sister and pressed the bell on the door of the large Georgian house.

After a moment or two a girl opened the door, dressed in a chic black number. 'Zoe and Gail?' she asked immediately with a smile.

They nodded.

'I'm Orla,' she extended her hand. 'It's lovely to meet you both. Sylvia has told us all about you. Will she be joining us today?'

'No, not at this point,' Zoe said. Sylvia was the wedding planner involved in the various arrangements. Zoe hadn't really wanted anyone to plan her wedding, but Sylvia was a friend of Russell's mother so she was forced to accept her.

They shook hands with Orla, and she ushered them through into the reception area.

'Would you like a cup of coffee or tea, girls, before you browse through the range?'

Zoe looked at Gail.

'Not for me thanks.' Gail shook her head.

'Me neither, we don't have a lot of time,' Zoe said.

'I'll bring you through to the Bridal Salon.' She led the way upstairs to where the display of bridal gowns extended through the first floor.

'Wow,' Zoe was amazed.

'As you can see, the whites are all on this side, and at the end we have ivory and creams ...colours are over here in the adjoining area.

We have the veils and accessories in another salon through there.' She waved towards a half open door dressed with a heavy damask curtain which was swept back with a sparkling bejewelled hold-back.

'I think we're going to need more time,' Zoe laughed. 'I don't think I could possibly make a decision today, there's just so much.'

'Overwhelming,' Gail added. 'And where are the bridesmaid's dresses?'

'They're on the next floor. But, usually brides decide on their wedding gown first …' Orla said.

'Let's get on then,' Zoe smiled. 'We'll try and do as much as we can today. I presume that Sylvia told you we only have two months to the wedding?'

'We can order a custom-made gown in that time but there will be an extra fee …' Orla explained.

'That's all right.'

'Right, would you like me to take a few details and I'll be able to help you?' she asked.

They nodded and she led them to an ornate antique table and pulled out grey velvet upholstered chairs for them. They sat down. 'Now first, what colour would you like?' Her fingers were poised over the keyboard of her laptop.

'How about bright red?' Gail giggled.

'Imagine what Russell would think of that?' Zoe laughed.

'If you're an Indian bride it means purity and most wear red saris,' Orla said.

'I think I'll stick with plain old ivory. I just want something simple.'

'Would you like a train?' Orla asked.

'No.'

'Sleeves?'

'Maybe, not sure ...what do you think, Gail?'

'Sleeveless could look sexy.'

'I don't want to be sexy in the church, the priest will have a fit. Not to mention Russell's mother. No, we will have sleeves. It is winter after all.'

'Full length, or ballet?'

'Full,' they spoke together, and laughed.

'Right, that's given me an idea.' Orla led the way across the room. 'This section here has quite a number of gowns which may suit you. And each one swings out on its own hanger.' She gave them an example. 'Now I'll leave you to it, let me know if you want any help.'

Gail took one out and they looked at it.

'No,' Zoe said firmly. 'Too much lace.'

'And this?' she asked.

'No.'

They went through them one by one. 'There's a lot of lace.'

'*Kate and William* style.'

'That's old hat now. I'd like something plain like *Meghan's* wedding dress. Maybe a very fine fabric with just a little bit of detail,' Zoe explained

'What about this one?'

'It's nice …' Zoe said slowly.

'Might be a possibility?'

'What do you think?'

'I like the delicate silk fabric,' Gail mused.

'And the design of pearls around the neckline is unusual.'

'It's lovely.'

'Do you like the square neckline?'

'I love it, but it's sleeveless?' Gail pointed out.

'I might get a jacket to wear over it, anyway leave that dress out so we can go back to it again. We'll continue on. What time is it?' She pulled her phone from her pocket and glanced at it. 'I've booked a table at Amalfi's for one, so we've plenty of time.'

'Thank you, sis. I'm looking forward to that.'

'Now back to business, here's another nice one, somewhat similar to the first.' Gail flicked through the dresses. 'How about this Cinderella creation, all frills and flounces?'

'I'd look well in that, all I need is my carriage and white horses, made out of a pumpkin and four mice,' Zoe retorted with a wide grin.

'And a fairy godmother?'

'Imagine being able to call on a godmother who has a magic wand,' Zoe giggled.

'Reminds me of Mum ...' Gail was suddenly pensive.

'She would loved to be here,' Zoe was wistful.

'To see her eldest daughter get married.'

Zoe fitted on six different dresses. 'They're all lovely, but I particularly like this first one. It has a lovely clinging line, although I hope my bum doesn't stick out too much.' She twirled in front of the mirrored wall.

'You look perfect. It was made for you,' Orla admired. 'What colour would you like for the bridesmaids?' she asked.

'There's only one and this is she. I haven't really had time to think about that. Have you any ideas, Gail?' Zoe asked.

'I think it should be something delicate. Very pale. With just a suggestion of colour.'

'Let's have a look in the showroom on the second floor,' Orla said. They followed her upstairs.

'There's every colour under the sun,' Gail gasped.

'Fantastic.'

'We start with the subtle hues in this section,' Orla explained.

'I love this.' Zoe brushed her hand against the fabric of one of the dresses, and pulled it out to have a closer look. It had a similar cut to the one she had chosen herself.

'It's gorgeous,' Gail whispered. 'And I love that hint of pale pink.'

They continued looking at various colours and designs, but decided to leave the final decision to their next appointment. 'And we'll choose the accessories and the jacket then as well, no time now.'

'I'll make a note of the design numbers and you can always look through them again,' Orla said. 'I have to say you've made a very quick decision. That's a first in here, brides usually take a long time to decide, particularly when the whole family come in. And there are lots of arguments,' she smiled in a confidential manner.

'This is my family and there will be no arguments.' Zoe put her arm around Gail's shoulders and kissed her on the cheek.

'We're sisters,' she said, smiling.

'Who better to help you decide on which wedding gown to choose.'

'You're exactly right. And I've got amazing taste. Come on girl,' she took Zoe's arm. 'Let's go and eat. I'm starving.'

'I can't afford to eat too much, I've to watch my weight and if I don't then I'll never get into that dress.'

'Sure you will.'

'I don't want to be neither one size or the other. Normally I'm ten but if I put on weight I'll be edging to twelve but then neither size is right and I'll be a sight. No, a careful diet is my plan from now on until the wedding. No alcohol, no chocolates, biscuits, cake, takeaways. I hate the thought of it, you know how much I love my food.'

'And you'll have to cook for Russell which won't be easy when you can't eat it yourself.'

'I'll just have to be strong and disciplined.'

'And it'll pay off in the end, you'll look a million dollars.'

'But it's so hard to actually cook when you get in at eleven.'

'Prepare some dishes at the weekend and freeze them.'

'Good idea, I'll take your advice on that.'

'I'm so happy for you, my sister is finally settling down to domesticity.'

Zoe scanned the menu.

'You've done well, even without me. Never thought you'd even think of getting married.'

'I'm going to have pasta with shrimps, I love the sauce,' Zoe decided. 'Oh no, I can't, it's too fattening.'

'Pizza, and a glass of white wine for me.'

'It will have to be salad and water, how boring.'

'Start tomorrow.'

'And then it will be the next day and the next while I grow bigger and bigger.'

They laughed and ordered.

'I have to say it's so good to have you back, it's been too long,' Zoe said.

'It's lovely to be home.' Gail had a wide grin on her face.

'Do you miss London?' Zoe asked. Gail had been living in England for a number of years and now to have her back meant everything.

'I suppose …' She was suddenly downcast.

'Has Pierre been in touch?'

She shook her head.

'Sorry, we won't talk about that.' Zoe sipped her water and took a few seconds to think of something else to say. 'Any response from your job applications?'

'Not yet, but I'm hoping.'

'You'll find something in the same field. Get on to any contacts you have in event management, you've a lot of experience.'

'I've already sent out a few emails.'

'Will you buy a house or an apartment?'

'I haven't a lot of money. We were renting in London so there wasn't a chance to build up much savings.'

'You can stay at home.'

'I hope Dad won't get too tired of me hanging around the place.'

'I know he's delighted you're here. He's lonely.'

'I'll keep him company.'

'Is there a new person in your life that you haven't mentioned?' Zoe asked, teasing.

'No, I've had enough of men for now.'

'Was there another woman involved with Pierre? Sorry, I shouldn't have asked that.'

'Don't worry,' Gail sighed. 'Of course there was, a right bitch in Paris.'

'Bastard,' Zoe said, her voice scathing. 'How have you dealt with that?'

'It hasn't been easy.'

'You poor thing, it's very hard to get used to being without the man you love.'

'And missing all those little intimacies,' Gail smiled and shrugged. 'But I've decided now that life is going to be fantastic, and I'm really looking forward to your wedding.'

'So am I, but work is hectic, and while we've booked our honeymoon I hope it actually happens.'

'You're going to love Vietnam.'

'I've always wanted to go to that part of the world.'

'You'll have to get some nice clothes.'

'I've every intention.'

'We'll go out some day and shop until we drop.'

'I'm looking forward to it.' She took a sip of water. 'I went down to Ballystrand the other day and visited the grave …' She bent her head to hide the rush of tears in her eyes. 'And I thought it would be wonderful if Mum was here.'

'I don't know how you can go, I just couldn't.'

'Someone has to look after it.'

'You could pay someone to do that.'

'No, I prefer to go myself and say a prayer. I think about her a lot.'

'Does Dad go?'

'No.'

'He may be like me and just finds it too hard.'

'Matt will be out soon,' Zoe murmured.

'He should be kept in for the rest of his life,' Gail said, angry.

'There's time off for good behaviour.'

'Good behaviour, my eye, that bastard doesn't deserve it. He disgraced the family. And Dad won't want to see him again either.'

Chapter Four

'You will have to come in to meet me once a week, Matt.' Tom Sheridan, the Probation Officer, pushed a sheet of paper across the desk towards him. 'Sign there.' He pointed to the line at the end of the page and handed him a pen.

Matt wrote his name.

'And the date,' Tom said.

Matt inserted that. It was the nineteenth of November. A date carved in his mind for the last few weeks since the Governor had told him when he was going to be released.

'Right, now here is your certificate.' He handed it to him. 'And a list of the addresses and phone numbers of the various departments you will need. You have your Birth Certificate and PPS number?'

He nodded, having already obtained both.

'That's it.' Tom stood up. 'How are you feeling?'

'I don't know,' he muttered.

'It may be hard for you to get used to being on the outside, but give me a call if you need any help. I'll do what I can.' He handed him a card with his mobile phone number on it. 'Is there someone meeting you?'

He shook his head. 'I'll make my own way.'

'One of the officers will sort you out with money. There's an amount which roughly equates to one week's dole, and also a clothes allowance. But you've saved a good lot out of your pay for working in the gym so you should be able to manage.'

'I hope so.'

'Although you will be entitled to supplementary welfare payment after a while, so apply immediately, and make an application for a medical card too.' He looked down at the various sheets of paper in front of him, picked one up and handed it to him. 'Make contact with the *CAP* people, you know, *Care after Prison.* They can help in various ways in the first few weeks.'

Matt stood outside the prison. The street was busy with pedestrians and traffic passing by. As he looked around, a terrible sense of agoraphobia swept over him, and a cold sweat studded his skin. For one crazy moment, he wanted to run back inside the prison and hide away in his cell but instead he stood there, gripping his fists, trying to control the anxiety. He felt like a child who didn't know what to do.

The officer at the gate had directed him to the nearest bus-stop and he walked that way, but there was a woman with a child already standing there and he felt reluctant to go any closer. So he stood a distance away, hoping he'd manage to get to the bus in time. He held tight on to the backpack which held his few possessions. A spare set of clothes, *The Pickwick Papers* which had been given to him by the librarian, and his laptop which he bought himself from the wages he had received while working in the gym.

Matt Sutherland was a thin wiry man of thirty-one. His dark hair was cut tight, and he was very fit. During those first months of his incarceration, it was such a shock to his system that he literally followed every order of the prison officers without question. Got up in the morning. Ate his meals. Spent as much time as he could in the gym. But spoke little to any of the other prisoners except the men who shared the cell with him in the early years. Later he was given a job serving in the canteen which helped pass the time and he earned some money doing that.

He had managed to come off drugs while on remand, although there was tremendous temptation to take up the habit again as they were freely available, but he managed to keep to himself and didn't succumb. As an alternative, he smoked cigarettes heavily, as did many of the men in prison, but managed to give them up too.

Into his second year, he was encouraged to take some of the courses available to prisoners and decided to do his Leaving Cert. School had been cut short and he had never finished. He worked hard and managed to complete it in two years and went on to do a degree course in computer studies.

The bus approached and he ran to the stop. The woman and child got on. He followed and told the driver where he was going, put the money in the coin box and tore off the paper ticket. He stuffed it into his pocket and walked down the bus, but was taken aback when he faced the passengers who all seemed to be staring at him. He cringed, sure that they knew where he was coming from. There were a couple of seats free but he turned back towards the front of the bus and stood there holding on to a bar praying the journey would be quick and he could get off the bus soon. He was surprised to hear a recording of a woman's voice telling him where he was going, each street mentioned in both English and Irish.

He looked out through the window of the bus to see where he was. He inched closer to the door and watched the readout telling him he was on O'Connell Street. Then, as there were quite a few people getting off, he went with them and stepped down. There were crowds on the street, and he noticed that many were talking on their mobile phones as they walked along. He was self-conscious and felt everyone knew who he was. He stopped near the GPO and wondered about going home to Ballystrand to visit the grave of his mother and grandparents. It was something he had wanted to do for a long time. At the next junction he stood waiting among people gathered at the kerb.

He was nervous. Afraid to put out his foot on to the road in case a vehicle came too close. The *Luas* tram trundled past and it was only when the rest of the people crossed that he followed, relieved to get to the other side. It was nerve wracking for him as he walked towards the corner and turned left along the quay.

At the bus station, he had to wait over an hour for the bus to Dungarvan and this time chose a seat at the back, thankful that he didn't have to stare into people's faces. Even then he still felt ill at ease and looked out the window at the city scape which slowly changed into a country scene, making a mental note of any landmarks which he recognised on the journey.

Chapter Five

Matt's father, Feargal, sat in his study in front of a large heavy mahogany desk. It was littered with papers and books. Scattered untidily. His fingers scrabbled, joints swollen with arthritis. He lifted. Peered. Discarded. Muttered to himself. He wore dark trousers, a blue shirt, and a striped tie, but he needed a shave, a white fuzz of stubble growing around his narrow chin.

He pulled a photograph from underneath a large heavy dictionary. Dusted it off with the cuff of his sleeve and went over to the window, peering intently at the detail in daylight, holding it at various angles. It was a close-up of a man dressed in dark uniform standing outside a lighthouse. He smiled. Then went to the mirror over the fireplace, stood on the tiles and held the photo up beside his face. He stared intently at his own reflection and that of the man in the photo. He did this for a time and then returned to the desk where he put it away again under the dictionary.

Then he found a notebook in an overflowing drawer and sat down. Flicking through the pages he reached a point three quarters way through, picked up a pen and began to write. His fingers held it awkwardly because of the influence of the arthritis, but he continued on, filling the pages with surprisingly clear sentences. With deep concentration he leaned his forehead on his other hand as he wrote. Every now and then he stopped and stared into space, trying to think of a particular word. Shadows began to gather in the room and it grew dark. He switched on a lamp.

His eyes peered at the page and he scribbled intently. Caught in the glow of golden light which shone down on his shiny bald pate, glimmering on the white hairs which grew each side of his head.

Suddenly he was reminded of his wife who had died at the time of which he wrote. He shook his head. He didn't wish these memories to force their way into his mind. He stopped writing. Raised his pen from the page, but still gripped it tightly. Her loss had cut deep into his heart. He had known what it was to love and when he had lost her his heart was black with misery. He still longed for the intimacy of their life together. The touch of her hand on his. Soft like the downy fur on a new born kitten. Thinking of it, his skin tingled and he raised his own hand to his lips and pressed gently in an effort to feel again her lips on his. Imagining how it was when he first knew her, and she had given herself to him on their wedding night.

As a lighthouse keeper he was away from home a lot and he missed her keenly. During those long lonely hours he was driven with jealousy that she would look at another man with her large dark eyes and be drawn to him leaving Feargal out on the edge of her mind. A lost soul. Unable to hold on to her. He telephoned as often as he could, anxious to let her know that she was in his thoughts. But she wasn't good on the phone. Unable to show emotion. Always talking of the practical things in her day. The children's activities. Where they went. Who they met. What news locally. This endless litany of minutiae drove him crazy at times.

He always longed for a lighthouse posting in Ballystrand. He had requested that more than once. It eventually happened, but within a couple of years, the lighthouse was fully automated and unmanned and Feargal was forced to take early retirement.

Chapter Six

Zoe and Gail met with Sylvia, the wedding planner, the following week.

'We're going to have to keep her at bay, she wants to arrange every detail of my wedding,' Zoe laughed as they took the lift up to the office.

'Don't worry, I'm on your side,' Gail said, with a wide grin.

'The first evening event will be a dinner for the two families. I've been thinking of booking a group of classical musicians to play at the reception beforehand. And I've got various menus for the dinner which you can peruse.' Sylvia handed them to Zoe.

'They're very predictable,' she said after a moment.

'Russell's mother doesn't want anything too unusual for the guests.'

'I think possibly this second one seems the best of them,' Zoe said.

'Go for that then,' Gail agreed.

'Now for the wedding banquet …' Sylvia pulled out another file.

'Banquet?' Zoe asked. 'Sounds like we're all going to be in medieval costume,' she giggled.

'Yes, why don't we do that? *Robin Hood and Maid Marian*,' Gail added.

'And *Friar Tuck* can marry us.'

They burst out laughing.

'We have already booked the marquee which will be erected on the back lawn off the conservatory at Langton House,' Sylvia continued, her face slightly flushed.

Zoe nodded, trying to stifle the awful temptation to laugh again. Sylvia was so serious as she went through the details of the flower arrangements. The band for later in the evening, and the DJ for the disco. The menus which were provided by a catering company weren't very different to those for the family dinner.

'The starters seem to be more interesting than the mains.' Zoe looked down the list of dishes.

'It's always difficult when you're catering for this number of people,' explained Sylvia.

'I understand that, but can we chop and change?' Gail asked.

'I'm sure we could if you really want.'

'Right, let's see ...that smoked salmon terrine with prawns sounds nice, let's put that down as a possible.' Zoe made a note.

'How many choices?'

'There are four.'

'Let's take one from each menu and include that cold almond and garlic soup, sounds lovely.'

'That will affect the price,' Sylvia sounded uncertain. 'Each menu is priced individually.'

'It can't make that much difference.'

'I'm not sure.'

'Discuss it with the caterers.'

She nodded.

'Also, how about some alternatives like a Thai dish and an Indian, just to give people a choice. Most of the menus have various meat and fish dishes but they're not very exciting.'

'Thai? Indian?' Sylvia seemed taken aback by Zoe's suggestion.

'I think that's a great idea,' Gail agreed.

'So for mains we'll have a regular fish dish, and perhaps a beef dish.'

'And then a Thai and an Indian, one of which could be vegetarian.'

'So that will cover everyone's taste.'

'That's four choices,' Sylvia pointed out. 'A lot more than usual.'

'Yes, why not?'

They laughed, and continued on with the dessert dish which was a combination plate of fruits, and finished up that part of the menu fairly quickly.

'Now, how about transport?' Sylvia opened another file. 'I was thinking about vintage, perhaps a white Rolls?'

'That's a bit over the top,' Zoe immediately objected.

'I thought you'd go for a stretch limo,' Gail said with a broad grin.

'I'm not going on my Debs, Gail,' Zoe responded, laughing.

'What about Bentley then?' suggested Sylvia. 'We'll need three or four.'

'Why?'

'One for the wedding party, the bridesmaid, the groom and best man.'

'But one car can be used a few times, back and forth to the church.' Zoe was firm. 'It's no distance from Russell's house. I don't mind spending extra on the food, but four cars are far too much.'

Sylvia crossed out the number on her page.

'Is that it?' Zoe asked, glancing at her phone.

'We have to decide on the musicians for the Mass.'

'Can't we have the same classical group as on the night of the family dinner? They can play to one side of the altar.'

'I suppose, but I was thinking of a soprano and a cellist who would be up in the gallery, and maybe a violinist as well.'

'Sylvia, the group will be fine.'

'And we don't need a soprano,' added Gail.

'Russell's mother is very keen on having a singer.'

'I'll have a chat with her, I don't want it to be like a funeral.'

Gail burst out laughing again.

'Now, have you decided who will be your flower girls and page boys?' Sylvia asked.

Zoe look at her, puzzled. 'We're not having any, just Gail.'

'Jean would like to have some of her grand nieces and nephews take part.'

'I'll talk to her about that as well,' Zoe said immediately.

It seemed to her that Russell's mother, Jean, was taking over her wedding. Jean and Clive were offering them the opportunity to have their wedding at their home in Enniskerry and because of that Russell's mother had arranged a lot of things with Sylvia and Zoe had just let it happen. She really hadn't time to get involved. But as it was, she and Russell were paying for it and had to have an input, although he had no interest at all.

'I think Sylvia was a bit disappointed that we didn't agree with all of her ideas,' Gail said as they climbed into the car.

'Or Russell's mother, although I suppose I can't expect her to be anything other than conservative. She's thinking of all her posh friends and their opinions.'

'You seem …' Gail hesitated.

'What?' Zoe asked, her eyes on the street ahead.

'A bit disinterested in the whole thing.'

'It's not my idea of the ideal wedding, you know.'

'It's more than that. When we've been together you don't call or text Russell or he you. I'd have imagined you'd be on to each other all the time, texting *I love you* or *see you later* or whatever.' Gail had a teasing grin on her face.

'Both of us are so busy all the time he wouldn't appreciate being interrupted in the middle of a meeting.'

'But he must be finished work by now, yet he never called.'

'He doesn't ever really finish work,' Zoe said slowly.

'Workaholic?'

Zoe nodded.

'When do you spend time together?'

'Usually at the weekend, on Saturdays we sometimes meet friends for a drink and go to a club.'

'His friends or yours?'

'His, I suppose, I've lost touch with some of my more recent friends with the pace of work. But there is a group of school friends I still see occasionally.'

'You should never lose touch with friends. Why did you let that happen?'

'Most of them are in relationships now and some have children, so they don't have much time to meet me.'

'That's such a pity.' Gail seemed really quite upset for her.

'I'm so busy all the time I don't notice it.'

'Maybe your life will change after you get married and there will be the patter of tiny feet around the apartment?'

'I don't think so, Russell isn't keen on having a family.'

'What about you?' Gail was surprised.

'Well, I'd like children at some stage, but there's no hurry.'

'Are you sure you'll be able to change his mind then?'

'I hope so …' Zoe wasn't certain about that.

'Ever heard about the leopard?'

'What do you mean?'

'Never changes his spots.'

'You could be right.'

'Did you propose to him or he to you?'

'He made a big thing of it. Champagne. Roses. It was difficult to say no. I was completely taken aback.'

'Is he usually a romantic at heart?'

'Not really.'

'When I met him first he seemed really nice, although it was only in your office and he didn't say very much.'

'He's not always in such good form,' Zoe had to admit.

'Who is? We can't all be the same every minute of the day.'

'I suppose not.'

'You sound like you might be having serious doubts about him?' Gail asked, her pretty face full of concern.

Zoe stared at her. It was a shock to hear her sister put it so succinctly.

'No, of course not. Anyway, I'm committed now. So much has been arranged. To back out at this stage would cause a lot of trouble, especially with Russell's parents. I can't imagine how Jean might react.'

'Don't marry him if you are unsure of how you feel. It's crazy if you don't love him enough.'

'But …' Zoe immediately protested. 'I do love him.'

'What's he like at home?'

'I suppose he can be a bit moody. It's the stress of work.'

'Which one do you love?'

'What do you mean?'

'The house devil or the street angel? You know that old saying?'

She couldn't answer.

Chapter Seven

The bus dropped Matt off in Dungarvan, and he made his way out of the town towards Ballystrand. He held his hand out hoping he might get a lift, but no car stopped. The sky darkened and it began to rain. He pulled up his collar, but still kept his hand out in the hope that someone would stop. Unexpectedly a car pulled up on to the kerb. He wasn't sure whether this person was going to offer him a lift but he moved slightly closer. Matt noticed that he was taking a call on his phone so he moved away again.

Just then, he noticed that the passenger door window had been lowered. A middle-aged man looked towards Matt. 'Need a lift?'

Matt went over. 'Yes please.'

'Where are you going?'

'Ballystrand.'

'I'm going that way, hop in.'

'Thank you.' Matt was really grateful.

'It's turning out to be a bit miserable,' the man smiled as Matt climbed into the car, putting his back-pack down between his legs.

'Take off your anorak before you put on your seat belt, it's soaked,' the man suggested.

Matt nodded and struggled out of it.

'Throw it on the back seat.'

'Thanks.'

'Right, let's get going.'

He started the car, and pulled out into the road. There was a sudden beeping sound. 'Put your seat belt on.'

Matt looked around, unsure where exactly it was in this car.

'There it is on your left.'

He found it.

'All safe now,' the man grinned at him. 'What's bringing you to Ballystrand?'

'Just visiting.'

'I'll be staying at the Abbey for a week. I need some time out.'

'It's a lovely place ...' Matt said.

'Peaceful,' the man added.

Matt said no more. They drove along at a steady pace. Matt felt a little under pressure to speak to him. But what was he going to say, he wondered. He couldn't talk about his life and what he had been doing for the last few years. He couldn't talk about his family. He couldn't say anything at all. Nervously, he compressed his lips, and stared out the window. It had been a long time since he had been in a car. There was something about it that was strangely comforting, the enclosed space reminding him of his cell in prison.

He began to notice familiar landmarks, taking him back in time to when he lived here. These last years spent incarcerated had meant that he had expunged most of his childhood memories, terrified of unlocking the emotions which had been sealed away. But now since he had arrived in this place they were forcing their way into his consciousness with an unexpected wildness and he seemed to have no control over them.

Half an hour later the man dropped him in Ballystrand. 'Thank you very much for the lift,' he said, reached for his jacket which was on the back seat and picking up his backpack.

He looked at the passenger door but found it difficult to find the handle. His hand moved over the door in a frantic search for some raised section. He felt a fool when he couldn't find it.

'There you are.' The man pressed some part of the door and it clicked open. 'One of those new-fangled handles,' he said by way of explanation. Matt was embarrassed and stepped out. He turned back and stretched out his hand to the man. 'Thanks for giving me a lift.'

'No trouble at all, look forward to meeting you again.'

He nodded. But didn't think there was any chance of that happening. He couldn't make friends with people. Couldn't draw them into his past knowing that anyone who heard what he had done would immediately turn against him. It painted a very bleak future.

Chapter Eight

'Mother has invited us down at the weekend ...' Russell said after they had finished dinner one evening and both were working on their laptops.

Zoe looked up. 'Can we manage it? What about the German buyers who are coming in?'

'We'll have completed our business with them by Saturday evening and we can head down afterwards. She's keen to hear what progress we've made.'

'Progress?'

'Wedding plans.'

'You haven't made any.' She couldn't resist.

'Well, you have and so has mother. She's very excited.'

'I wasn't that keen on some of her ideas,' Zoe had to admit.

'What do you mean?' His tone was sharp.

She cringed, hoping he wasn't going to fly into a sudden rage.

'She wants a very conservative wedding. Pretty ordinary to tell you the truth.'

'What do we care. It's just a wedding.'

'Just a wedding? What a way to describe what is supposed to be the happiest day of our lives?'

'I don't mean it like that, but to be honest I'm just looking forward to getting away.'

'I've been wondering if we'll even manage to go for three weeks.'

'We'll keep in touch with the office by email and text.'

'But then we won't switch off completely,' Zoe pointed out. 'What if we cut it short and made no contact with anyone? Let the heads of departments handle everything and instruct them to make contact with us only in a major emergency?'

'Impossible,' he dismissed it out of hand.

'Maybe we should defer until things are less busy?' she suggested.

'I want to get the whole thing over and done with,' he flashed.

'Sometimes I wonder do you want to get married at all?' Zoe remarked.

'We're engaged, aren't we? Didn't that show my intentions? And you know I love you.' He leaned towards her, his lips gripping hers, his body close.

She responded immediately. It wasn't often Russell made love to her spontaneously and now she wound her arms around him and held tight. She opened the buttons on his shirt and slipped her hand inside, caressed his chest and then moved down to his flat muscular stomach. Then she kissed his smooth skin here and there teasingly.

'Zoe …' he protested.

'What?' she giggled.

'I'm in the middle of something,' he said.

'I know and it's wonderful.' She played with his belt trying to unbuckle it.

'Not now.'

'Come on, we've time for a quick one.' She kissed him hungrily.

'No, later.' He moved away from her.

'The mood will be gone. Let's get down on the rug, it's so sensual, I love you when you're all dishevelled.' She began to unzip his trousers. For a moment, he responded and embraced her. They clung together and she pressed her lips on his again.

But suddenly he rolled away from her, stood up abruptly and fixed his clothes.

'Russell, don't I excite you anymore?' she teased.

'Of course you do, but the time has to be right. I've to call New York

31

before they close up for the day.'

'So if you didn't call them on the dot, would it be the end of the world?'

'I suppose not, but it's not the way to do business.'

Zoe sighed. Disappointed. She understood where he was coming from but felt life shouldn't be so organised. There had to be room for doing something on impulse, without it love had no chance and it would be erased by the everyday business which always had to come first.

'You've just made it on time, dinner is almost ready.' Russell's mother, Jean, embraced them both with enthusiasm.

'Sorry but we're very busy at the moment,' Zoe apologised.

'You're always the same, you two.'

'It's life these days,' Russell said.

Jean was an effusive person and now swept them through the hall. 'Go on up to your rooms and freshen up. I'll ask Kitty to hold on for a short while.'

'We won't be long,' Russell lifted both bags and ushered Zoe up ahead of him.

Jean was very conservative in every way, insisting that Zoe and Russell slept in separate bedrooms when they came to stay at Langton. But it was only one night and Zoe had to put up with it.

'Sneak into my room later, love.' Zoe kissed him. 'I'll miss you.'

'Don't be so childish,' he said, returning her kiss with an air of disinterest. 'See you in ten minutes? Can you be ready by then? Although you normally take ages, so speed it up this time.'

'Sure …' she agreed with a sense of acceptance. There was no point arguing with him, she was beginning to realise that lately.

Dinner was formal. Served by the live-in housekeeper, Kitty, who had worked with the family at Langton since Russell was a boy. His father Clive was a pleasant man and Zoe got on very well with him, as he was Chairman of the Board at their company, *RZ Gaming*. They sat

32

down and were just finished their starters when there was a ring on the doorbell.

'That must be Sylvia,' Jean said. 'Russell, will you get the door. I'm delighted she's come.' She seemed really pleased.

Zoe wasn't sure whether she was happy to see the woman or not. But maybe her presence would be a distraction, too much of Jean over the evening might be just that, too much. She smiled to herself.

Sylvia came in, wearing black, very chic as usual. 'How lovely to see you all.' She floated across the room, air-kissing all of them.

'Thanks so much for coming down on a Saturday, we do appreciate that,' Jean gushed.

'A glass of wine, Sylvia?' Russell asked, lifting the crystal decanter.

'No thank you, I'm driving. Something soft will be fine.'

'You could stay here, there's plenty of space, and then you could enjoy a drink,' Jean suggested.

'Thanks for the offer but I must get back tonight, I'm busy.'

'That's a pity.'

'No such thing as weekends when I'm in the middle of arranging a wedding.'

'I'll get you that drink,' Russell smiled at her.

'Tonic water would be fine.'

'No trouble.'

He can be so charming, thought Zoe, remembering Gail's remark about *street angel* and *house devil*. They finished dinner. Kitty served coffee in the drawing room and Sylvia kept them entertained with anecdotes of her clients' weddings. The highs, lows and the catastrophes. So much so, Zoe thought if she heard the word *wedding* once more she would scream.

'You two men can take yourselves off somewhere else, we have a lot of talking to do,' Jean said.

'I've to work anyway,' Russell stood up. 'So excuse me.'

Did that mean he was gone for the night? wondered Zoe. She had hoped that they might have spent some time together this evening, but now that chance was gone.

'Clive, you go and look at the television,' Jean dismissed her husband too.

'I don't suppose you'll want my opinion anyway,' he pushed himself out of the chair. His eyes twinkled across at Zoe as he smiled. She had a sudden feeling that he understood how she felt whenever she visited this house. And she could sympathise with him too. Jean was a very controlling woman and seemed to make all the decisions.

'No, we don't. Your tuppence halfpenny wouldn't be worth even that. We'll see you later.'

'I've got my marching orders,' Clive said, and his fingers brushed gently across Zoe's shoulder as he passed.

'We shouldn't be too long,' Zoe smiled, trying to diminish the hurt he must feel at being excluded.

'It will take as long as it takes,' Jean said. 'Now Sylvia, where are we?'

Clive raised his eyebrows and grinned at Zoe as he opened the door and disappeared.

Sylvia went to get her briefcase from the hall and took out a sheaf of papers and photographs.

'Jean, we were discussing menus with Zoe and Gail, and have come up with an interesting combination of dishes.' She handed each of them the menus, and opened her iPad.

'But we did mention that we would like to include alternatives of Thai and Indian the last time we met, Sylvia,' Zoe said. 'As you know, we'd like to offer our guests something different, wedding menus can be very boring. Don't you remember?'

'I wasn't sure if Jean would be agreeable with that, so I thought I'd wait until she has had a chance to consider your suggestion,' she said slowly.

'Thai and Indian, is that what you said?' Jean exclaimed.

'Yes, just to give people a different option.'

'None of my family or friends would be bothered eating that sort of food,' she snapped.

'It's just another choice, along with the usual meat or fish,' explained Zoe.

'It lowers the tone.' Jean pouted. 'And it would be more expensive too no doubt.'

'Russell and I are paying for this.' Zoe pointed out.

'And we are providing the venue and all that goes with it. We must have a say in it.'

'I'm particularly keen,' insisted Zoe.

'What does Russell think?' Jean asked.

'I haven't really discussed it with him,' Zoe had to admit. Reluctant to tell Russell's mother that he had very little interest in the finer details of the wedding.

'Let's get him in here then.' Jean went out into the hall. 'Russell, I need you,' she called.

There was no reply.

'He's probably in the bedroom.' Jean came back in. 'Zoe, go fetch him,' she ordered.

The word *fetch* echoed in Zoe's mind. The idea of grabbing Russell and dragging him down was ludicrous.

She knocked gently on his door. 'Russell?'

'Yeah?'

'We need you.' She went in.

'I'll be down in a minute, I've to finish this email.'

She stood beside him and kissed him. 'Don't be too long. Your mother is anxious to have your opinion. If we can get through the wedding details soon, then we'll have some time to ourselves.' She was persuasive and put her arm around his shoulders.

'Why do you need me anyway?' He looked up at her, his expression cross.

'We're talking about the menus.'

'I don't care what we eat. It will probably be the usual anyway, nothing very exciting,' he grumbled.

'Come on down as soon as you're finished.'

He did come down later but by then they had gone on to the flower arrangements.

'Russell, it took you long enough, you've held us up,' his mother said sharply.

'I'll show you the menus, Russell.' Sylvia picked up the cards and handed them to him.

He glanced, without much interest.

'Love, I want to include a Thai dish and …' Zoe explained.

'Include them if you want, I don't mind. You brought me down for that?'

'I don't want this type of food, it's just not the sort of thing we eat ourselves. I've told Zoe that already, Russell, but she just doesn't listen to me.' Jean waved her hands in the air.

'It's just to have something different, Russell. We enjoy Thai and Indian food ourselves as do a lot of our friends …'

'Go with that, but don't bother me again.' He threw down the menus.

'But Russell?' Jean was obviously very annoyed. She sat there, disgruntled, and said nothing.

'Decision made,' Zoe smiled.

'Shall we go on?' Sylvia asked.

'I suppose,' Jean agreed.

'Papers …' Sylvia went to another item on her list.

'Yes, I was talking to Fr. Nolan and he will need your papers, Zoe, letter of freedom, birth and baptismal certs.'

'I'll get them.' She made a note.

'Music for the evening,' Sylvia announced.

'I hate that part of it,' Jean groaned

'You probably won't be around at that stage,' Sylvia said.

'We've booked the band and the DJ for later, they're friends of ours,' explained Zoe.

'That's great, I'll tick that off my list.' Sylvia looked at her iPad. 'Now I'd better be off.'

'Would you like tea or coffee before you go?'

'No thank you, Jean.' Sylvia stood up.

'We're staying. Shall I ask Clive to come back in?' Zoe suggested.

'Yes do, that's if he hasn't fallen asleep. If he has, leave him there,' Jean said tiredly. 'But ask Russell to come down, I haven't had a chance to see him lately, he's a workaholic you know.' She turned to Sylvia by way of explanation.

'Could be worse, he mightn't want to work at all,' Sylvia laughed.

'All our family are hard workers,' Jean said.

'It's the way things are these days. If you don't work hard then you will fail.' Sylvia put her papers and iPad away.

'Look at Clive, he's still working,' Jean remarked.

'Most men and women share everything these days. They both work. Look after the children, do the housework, and cooking …everything. It's a joint partnership isn't it, Zoe?'

'Yes, very much so,' she agreed

'It's been good to see you, Zoe, keep in touch.' Sylvia hugged her and then Jean. 'Thanks so much for a delicious dinner, Jean, and Kitty too. And thank Clive, you're such lovely hosts, it's a pleasure to be invited down to Langton House at any time.'

Upstairs, Zoe went straight into Russell's room without even knocking.

'Hi love, all finished?' She leaned over him and kissed his ear, hoping that they could spend some time together now. 'Please tell me you are.'

'Not yet, I've still some more work to do.'

'Are you coming down, your mother is wondering?'

'Not yet.'

'Can't you do it tomorrow?'

'There's nobody working on a Sunday. Tell her I'll be there soon.'

'But I want to see you …'

He shrugged her off. 'Let me work, Zoe, please?'
'Can I help you with it?' she offered.
'No, you keep mother happy.'
'Come down soon, love.'
He nodded.

She stopped on the stairs and looked back up, wondering why Russell was so cold towards her. She sighed. Maybe it was all the fuss about getting married? Maybe he didn't want to get married at all? But yet he had proposed, and presented her with a beautiful diamond ring. What was going on with him?

Chapter Nine

Ballystrand had changed a lot since Matt had last been here. He passed a supermarket which had replaced the butchers, vegetable shop, and the bookmakers. The old bank building was closed. But there were a couple of new shops, and a café. The village was carefully tended. Although it was very late in the year, there were still some flowers blooming in containers at the edge of the pavement, and even on the small side streets. The houses were all painted in pastel colours, and the place had an air of gaiety about it. He came into the square, which had a fountain in the centre surrounded by a black wrought-iron railing. The rain had stopped and water sprang up into the air and sparkled in the sunlight which had just come out from behind the clouds. To his surprise, there wasn't a car to be seen there. It had always been full of cars but now obviously there was somewhere else to park. A couple of women wearing yellow *hi-vis* jackets picked up rubbish off the street and put it in black plastic bags. A man weeded a flower bed. There was obviously a sense of community among the people who were anxious to keep their village looking as beautiful as possible.

Matt felt at home immediately, slung his backpack over his shoulder and began to walk towards the beach. But he kept his head down, hoping that he wouldn't be recognised by anyone who knew him when he was young. He came out at the head of the beach, looking over the arc of the bay stretching in front of him. Winter sunshine sparkled on the waves which crashed on to the shingle.

He sat down on the sand at the head of the dunes, and stared out to sea. It was a beautiful place and almost deserted today except for a couple of people walking their dogs in the distance. His eyes misted over. He hadn't realised how much he had missed it. After a short while he ran down the incline, and stopped for a moment to take off his socks and trainers, and roll up his jeans. The wind whirled around him and he breathed in great gulps of sea air. He would have loved to dive in but without swimming trunks that wasn't possible. He strode through the waves even though the water splashed up and the legs of his jeans became increasingly wet. But he hardly noticed, reminded of his own early boyhood when he and his friends ran along the shore after school.

'I got a right whack from Baldy,' he could hear himself say one particular day.

'Not as bad as I got from Skinner yesterday, look, my hand is still purple.' His best friend held out the offended palm.

'They're all old bastards,' someone else grumbled.

'I won't be able to write.' Matt licked his hand.

'That's your excuse for not doing your *ekker*,' the others laughed.

'Are you coming to football practice?'

'If my Dad lets me.'

'But there's a big match on next Sunday, we have to train.'

'I don't know whether I'll be on the team or not.'

'You won't be if you don't do the training,' someone else reminded.

'He's always on at me about homework,' Matt muttered.

'So is mine.'

They groused as all twelve-year-old boys did.

'My Dad's taking me fishing, do you want to come?' one of the others asked.

There was an immediate chorus of enthusiasm, and they began to plan excitedly. The idea of going fishing was always very attractive.

Many an afternoon was spent on the river casting flies, something Matt always enjoyed hugely. Those days came back to him now. Setting up their fishing gear on the bank, hoping it would be cloudy. If the sun shone brightly then the fish didn't bite. Pascal's father had hip high waders and stood midstream. A big man, he was well able to walk along in the swirls of dark green water. The boys wore wellies, and he insisted they stayed in the shallows among the reeds, although the water sloshed over the tops of the boots and soaked their feet anyway. Sometimes the lines caught in rocks or branches floating along and they had to be hauled in to start all over again. Still, the elation of those days was never to be forgotten.

He came to a rocky outcrop. Clambering up, he sat and put on his socks and shoes, and remembered how the simplicity of life gradually changed as he grew into his teens. Back then he awoke in the morning filled with anger. Resented being told what to do by his Dad who had big plans for him. He would go to college. Get a degree. Have a successful career. But he became friendly with some older boys in school. Gave up the football. The fishing. His childhood friends. With those other boys he was introduced to his first can of beer. Then he tried spirits. And that led on in time to hash and cocaine.

His father became very angry when he discovered that Matt was stealing money from his mother's purse or his own wallet. Rows erupted. Physical. Violent. Although he held himself back from ever hitting his father and took the beatings. His mother intervened, protesting at Feargal's treatment of their son. Matt remembered his scathing rebuttal, shouting that she should mind her own business and keep out of it, and he had a sudden recollection of his sisters' fearful eyes as they ran to their rooms to avoid the controversy. His memory of that time was dominated by rage until that last final day which was still a blank. He knew what had happened now. But it was the barristers and the judge who created the version of events which he had eventually accepted.

Matt climbed over the rocks. Suddenly in his head the mournful sound of the foghorn echoed and he could see the lighthouse etched against the sky, banded red and white. He walked down on to the rocks thinking that all of the lighthouses had been automated by now, and that even the foghorn itself was no longer used because of advances in technology. But he had read that there were still calls from owners of smaller craft for the foghorn to be reintroduced and warn of danger when fog cloaked the land and sea in coastal areas.

Matt stared back to see the house in which he had grown up. His eyes misted. He could hear his Mum's voice telling him to come in for his tea, the exited screams of his sisters as they played on the swing in the back garden, the gruff voice of his father warning him to stop kicking his football up against the side of the house and marking it with mud, and the excited barking of his dog Rex. He smiled at the memories, but hesitated taking that last walk down the road from the lighthouse for a few moments. But short though it was each step took him closer.

He walked past the houses. Able to put the family name on each one. Their own house stood apart on a slight incline among a grove of tall trees and he wondered who was living there now.

His footsteps became even slower as he approached. *'Seaview'* was a white dormer bungalow, the front door was now painted black, and the brasses shone brightly. White blinds hung in the windows. Matt stopped, fighting against the urge to go up the path and knock on the door. Imagining his mother opening it, smiling at him and welcoming him home.

Suddenly a few young boys appeared around the side, waving hurleys, their bright faces shining with enthusiasm. They stopped at the gate and stared at him. Eyes curious.

'Hello Mister?' the biggest said.

'Hello Mister?' the others chorused and then all of them laughed.

'Who are you?' one asked.

'Are you lads on the mitch?' he replied with another question.

They looked embarrassed.

'You won't tell?' one asked.

'No,' he grinned.

Their smiles were wide as they ran out the gate past him. He stood watching. He had been so like them. He glanced quickly up at the house again, and headed off in the other direction to the boys. He had read enough to know how it was these days. Everyone was so suspicious. And he didn't want to meet anyone who might have known him. That most of all.

There weren't many people around, and with his head down he turned out of the village towards the church. It had started to rain again, and he pulled up the hood of the anorak and was glad that it gave him some protection from curious eyes. The cemetery was at the back of the church. He remembered where the grave of his grandparents was situated and quickly made his way around to that corner. But he wasn't prepared for the shock which hit him when he saw the black marble headstone with the names of his grandparents and his mother carved there in memoriam. In front was placed a red Geranium in a pot, and he was surprised to see that some blossoms were still in bloom even though it was so late in the year.

He knelt down in a torment of guilt and love. Images of his mother flashed through his mind. She was such a beautiful woman. Dark eyed. Always smiling, warm and loving. Tears clouded his eyes. Why had he made life so painful for her?

He prayed then for each of the souls interred in this place, and for his mother he whispered words of apology. 'Mum, I'm so sorry for everything. I didn't mean it. Please forgive me.' He leaned forward and kissed the headstone where her name was carved. And his Gran and Grandad too. Regretting then that he hadn't thought of bringing some flowers to put on the grave. He stayed there for a while, whispering a decade of the Rosary for their souls, and prayed that they were in Heaven.

He jogged back to Dungarvan, glad of the opportunity to run. It got his heart pounding. His emotions churning. When he arrived, he went into a chipper and bought himself a large bag of chips. It tasted good with plenty of salt and vinegar. Eating as he wandered the streets, he made his way back to where the bus had dropped him off earlier in the day. It was growing dark now, and he sat in the shelter waiting for the

Dublin bus to arrive hoping that there was one scheduled.

Another man stood under the shelter. But Matt was too scared to ask him if he knew the time of the next bus.

He waited a while and then decided to hitch a lift instead.

He went out to the Dublin Road, put up his hand, and to his delight it didn't take long before a lorry pulled up ahead of him. 'Where are you going?' The driver leaned down and asked.

'Dublin.'

'I can take you some of the way, hop up.'

'Thanks.' He climbed into the cab, and travelled with the man who let him off outside Naas. But it took a while to get another lift and it was late that night when he arrived on the outskirts of Dublin. He was relieved to be back in a place where no-one knew him. He needed to eat something but had been very grateful to the first man who had shared his sandwich with him in the evening. He walked through Inchicore, looking out for somewhere to stay for the night, but didn't see any *B & B's* or hotels.

He continued along the canal and into the city. There was a hotel on Camden Street and he asked the man at the reception desk how much it would be for a room but he told him that they were full. He continued on down into Georges Street and crossed over into Temple Bar. There were quite a few people drinking in the pubs and a lot of tourists around. He saw another hotel, but it looked very expensive. Still he went in and enquired if they had a room. It was the same story. Eventually he wandered into O'Connell Street and as he passed the GPO he saw a group of homeless men being handed food.

A woman looked keenly at him as he approached. 'Soup?' she asked.

'Thank you.'

'Sandwich?'

He nodded, very grateful.

She handed them to him.

'Have you somewhere to stay tonight?'

He shook his head.

'Do you want to call some of the hostels, I could give you the numbers.'

'I don't have a phone.'

She seemed surprised.

'I'll go to a phone box.'

'Very few of them left now, I don't know where you'd find one. I'll call for you. Eat that over there and when we're finished I'll check the situation.'

'Thank you, it's very good of you.'

The food was tasty and he felt a lot better when she waved him over.

She took a pen and a notepad. 'What's your name?'

He hesitated, and didn't know what to say, nervous about giving his true name.

'We're completely confidential, but I need a name, any name, to book you in if there is room.'

'Eh …Matthew …Smith,' he blurted.

She wrote it down.

He had made it up. He simply couldn't give his real name and would have to use *Smith* for the foreseeable future. As he waited while she made a few phone calls, he helped the other people hand out tea and sandwiches.

'Matthew, you're in luck, I've got you a bed.'

Chapter Ten

'Zoe, you must bring your family down to stay, we haven't met them yet,' Jean said.

'Thank you,' Zoe took a sip of chilled white wine.

'There's just your father and sister, isn't that right?'

She nodded, feeling very awkward. She hadn't thought this through. Had only imagined them all meeting just before the wedding. But a weekend at *Langton House* was something else entirely. She would have to decline the invitation. Her father wasn't a very social person. Since his retirement he had become somewhat of a recluse. Immersed in his book collection on the history of lighthouses.

'My father is very reserved, it would be hard to persuade him to visit,' Zoe explained.

'But surely a pleasant evening here would appeal to him. It would do him good,' Jean persuaded.

'Perhaps,' she admitted.

'And Russell tells me that your sister has come home from London, so she must come too, we'll make it a party.'

'Yes, she has.'

'Isn't that very nice for you all. Sad though that your mother is no longer with you.'

Zoe nodded, inwardly emotional, and wishing Jean would stop talking.

'I'll have a look at the diary.' Jean stood up and left the room.

Zoe went over to Russell who sat reading the newspaper.

'What time do you think we should leave?' she whispered, pressing his shoulder.

He didn't reply at first.

She sat beside him on the couch.

'When will we head back?'

'Soon.'

Relief flooded through her.

'Here we are now.' Jean came back into the room. 'Let's see if we can decide on a date.' She turned the pages, but then hesitated. 'It looks as if I'm very busy coming up to Christmas, I'll have to get back to you.'

'I'm not sure either. It will be hectic before the wedding.'

'Russell?' Jean spoke sharply to him.

He grunted.

'Have you been listening?' Jean asked.

'No mother, I'm reading the paper.'

'Put it down and listen to me.'

'Give me a minute.' He continued on.

She stared at Zoe, and with an air of exasperation raised her eyebrows up into her perfectly coiffured grey-blue hair. 'He's no better than his father.' She looked at her husband, Clive, who sat on the other side of the room reading a newspaper as well.

'What is it?' Russell asked, a hint of boredom in his voice.

'We're trying to arrange a weekend for Zoe's family to come down.'

'I'll leave that up to you.' He picked up the paper again.

For once, Zoe didn't feel like forcing him to make a decision. The frustration she often felt when he wouldn't commit didn't happen. Now the longer he procrastinated suited her. She didn't want to invite her father down. She couldn't imagine how he would fit in here. She had introduced Russell to him briefly, but they hadn't had much of a conversation. Gail had only met him on one occasion and Zoe was planning an evening out soon. She wanted her to get to know Russell, and decided to get together, just the three of them, sometime the following week.

They left shortly after that and Zoe was glad. There was no more talk about the visit. As they drove back to Dublin, she realised that even persuading her father to attend the wedding might be difficult. It was only as the plans had become more definite that she could see that aspects of her life might conflict. 'How about meeting Gail for dinner on Wednesday?' she asked.

'Sure, just organise it.' He shrugged.

That was it. Typical Russell. Short and to the point.

On Wednesday evening, she went into his office. 'Ready?' she asked.

'I'll need a bit more time,' he said, looking at the computer screen.

'We have a booking at the restaurant for eight.'

'You go on ahead and I'll follow.'

'I'd prefer us to go together.'

'Then Gail will be waiting on her own,' he said.

'All right, but don't be long, love, I'm looking forward to a very enjoyable evening, just the three of us together.'

'So am I.' He didn't raise his eyes.

Zoe arrived at a new restaurant in Ballsbridge, and was there just a few minutes before Gail. Immediately she saw her come in, she stood up and waved.

'Where is Russell?' Gail looked around.

'Held up at the office.'

'Hope he won't be long.'

'He said it would only be a few minutes so he should be here soon.'

A waiter came over. 'Would you like an aperitif?' he asked.

'I'll have a gin and tonic,' Gail said.

'And I'll have the same,' Zoe giggled. 'Neither of us are driving so we can enjoy a couple of drinks. We took a taxi in this morning. And I'll skip the diet for tonight. Tell us, how's the job hunting going?'

'I've made contact with a few employment agencies but no joy yet.'

Her expression was disgruntled.

'You're only home a few weeks.'

'I know, but I hope that I find a job soon. I particularly want something in the event field, it's my thing. And I'm not keen to go back to London.'

'And we don't want you to go back either, you know that.'

The waiter arrived with their drinks and handed them the menus.

'We'll hold on for a bit,' explained Zoe. 'We're expecting someone else. Sorry, Gail, I don't want to order if Russell isn't here.'

'Course not. How did the weekend go with the parents?'

'It was all right. While I've been down before, it was interesting to see how Russell interacted with his mother this time. He was very cranky. Anyway, she wants you and Dad to come down for a weekend.'

'I wouldn't mind, their place is fabulous, isn't it?'

'But what about Dad, I've been having sleepless nights at the thought. How is he this week? I haven't had a chance to get over.'

'I can't get much out of him. I've tried.'

'Do you think he's glad that you're home again?'

'He hasn't said.'

'I'm sure he must be.'

'To be honest, I want to get my own place as soon as I have a job though I'm not keen to tell him that.'

'Bet he enjoys your cooking.' Zoe sipped her drink.

'I have to stick with his conservative taste, meat, two veg.'

'It's his age. And he's not a bad cook himself.'

'That's why I was really looking forward to tonight.'

'Where is Russell?' Zoe looked in the direction of the front door.

'He'll be here soon, don't worry.'

'It's annoying, sometimes he can be very unreliable.'

'Once he turns up at the church,' Gail giggled and raised her glass.

'Zoe?' Russell appeared. 'Sorry, it took longer than I expected.'

'Don't worry. You know Gail.'

'Lovely to meet you again.' He kissed her on the cheek.

'Would you like a drink, sir?' the waiter asked.

'No thank you, I'll just have wine with the meal. It's so nice to finally get a chance to meet you properly,' he smiled at Gail.

He's very charming this evening, Zoe thought. Putting his good side out. But she had to admit that he looked attractive dressed in his dark suit, white shirt and lemon tie, every bit the successful executive. She could see that Gail seemed to like him and Zoe was glad.

The evening was a great success. The meal was delicious and they were all impressed and agreed that they would definitely come back to this restaurant. Gail and Russell got on very well, in fact the conversation was mostly between the two of them, chatting and laughing. But Zoe was relieved about that, sat back and relaxed. Watching how pleasant he was towards Gail she wished she could see that side of him more often.

As she often did, Zoe called around to see her father during the week, always glad to see him, and Gail too since she had come home.

Gail was a very good cook and served up a delicious dinner this evening. They chatted enthusiastically about everything and anything, but there was something Zoe wanted to discuss with her sister and as they cleared up in the kitchen, and Dad had gone into his study, she took a chance and broached the subject.

'Remember I told you Matt is being released from prison.' She rinsed the plates and put them into the dishwasher.

'I haven't been keeping a note of it.' There was heavy sarcasm in Gail's voice.

Zoe understood how her sister felt about Matt, but had hoped that this might have changed over time. While she had visited her brother in prison twice, she felt a certain responsibility to him knowing that he would be free soon.

'He isn't going to be part of our lives, so it hardly matters,' Gail snapped.

'He may want to come home.'

'What?' Gail turned to her.

'We can't hide his existence.'

'He doesn't even know this address, he probably thinks we still live in Ballystrand.'

'I felt I had to tell him.'

Gail dropped a bowl and it crashed in smithereens on the tiled floor. They stared silently at each other for a moment.

'Did I hear you correctly?' she demanded, a shocked expression on her face.

'Yes.' Zoe went into the utility room.

'You mean he could just knock on the door at any time?'

'I suppose.' Zoe came back with a dustpan, bending to brush up the broken pieces.

'He's not entitled.'

'I don't know his situation now that we've moved. This could still be his family home. We're his family.'

'What will Dad say?'

'I don't know.'

'Has he ever mentioned Matt to you,' Gail asked.

'No, and I've never told him that I visited him in prison.'

'I thought he was out of our lives. Now suddenly he's back. Anyway, didn't he get fourteen years?'

'Yes, but he got time off his sentence for good behaviour.'

'And here I am hoping to make a new life for myself and I have to deal with this,' Gail said furiously. 'What chance have I of getting a good job with a jailbird for a brother?'

Zoe emptied the broken crockery into a sheet of newspaper.

'I had put it all out of my mind, well, tried to. No wonder I could never have a successful relationship, I'm all twisted inside, it's probably never going to happen.' Gail was angry.

'Girls, what's going on? I heard a crash.' Feargal appeared in the doorway. He had once been a tall strong man but was now bent over, a back condition causing an obvious hump and he looked every bit his years. 'You're arguing,' he accused.

'I dropped a bowl on the floor,' Gail explained.

He stared at the floor. 'I don't see it.'

'We've swept it up, don't worry,' Zoe said.

Their father could get very aggravated when he didn't know what was happening around him.

'Hope that's all it was.' His blue eyes watched them keenly for a moment and then he went out of the room.

They continued cleaning the kitchen and then Gail asked. 'How are we going to deal with this?'

'I don't know.'

'We'll have to make a plan. Be prepared for that day. And more than anything, how will Dad react? God only knows what he'll say if he sees Matt. And we probably won't even recognise him anyway.' Gail put away the pots and pans in the press.

Zoe sat at the table. 'You're not the only one who has to deal with this situation. I still have to tell Russell about Matt and I'm not looking forward to it.'

'He seemed an easy-going man, he probably won't care. It's got nothing to do with him.'

'It's his mother. She's so concerned about her social status.'

'You would marry money,' Gail laughed.

'But if her only son marries someone who has a brother with a criminal record it might be just too much for her.'

'So we're all affected by that bastard.'

'Don't say that.'

Will any of us be able to get through life normally? Are we even normal people? This thing has been hanging over us for all these years.'

'We've done well career-wise. We both moved on. Put it behind us.'

'That's because we refuse to be broken down by it. We're going to win in spite of him. I've had a lot of relationships but not one of them lasted except Pierre and look what happened with him.'

'I know quite a few people who are in the same situation. At least I'm with Russell now but there are girls in work who go out every weekend in the hope of meeting someone but have no luck. They spend all their time on those dating websites, and while they do meet guys, most of them turn out to be non-starters. The men just fly from girl to girl, get the best they can out of them and off they go to the next one.'

'I've known some girls and guys who have settled down and have families and they met on the internet but they're the rare couples.' Finished cleaning, Gail sat opposite Zoe.

'In the meantime, we'll have to deal with this as it happens,' Zoe said.

'What about Dad?'

'I don't know how he's going to react.'

'Why not get in touch with Matt and tell him not to come.'

'I can't, I don't have a number for him.'

'So any minute …?' Gail had a horrified expression on her face.

Chapter Eleven

That first night spent at the hostel was a learning experience for Matt. He was so relieved that he had somewhere to sleep he immediately threw himself into the bottom bunk which he had been allocated. The room was full of men. The stench of unwashed bodies, and dirty feet, the noise of loud snoring and muttering. They coughed, and spat, and the man in the bunk above him rolled about caught in some nightmare, every now and then wailing so loud Matt awoke with a jerk. But in spite of that it wasn't long before he dozed off again. Although he never slept very well he did manage a few hours.

In the morning, he went to the showers and hung his clothes on the hooks at the back of the cubicle door. He stood under the hot water until he felt refreshed, and then he dressed himself and went out again. But as he walked into the noisy canteen he put his hand into the inside pocket of his jacket and suddenly realised that he couldn't feel the plastic packet in which he kept his money. He panicked as he searched frantically for it in his other pockets, only able to find the fifteen euro and some silver he had in his jeans. He took off the jacket and went through each pocket again and again, his jeans and backpack too, but couldn't find it.

'Who stole my money?' he yelled, looking around at the other men who sat at tables eating their breakfast. No-one raised their eyes to him and slowly the sound of voices diminished and there was silence. 'Which of you bastards stole my money?'

'What's wrong?' a woman asked, her voice soft.

He turned around to see her standing behind him. 'My money's gone.' With disgust he picked up his jacket from where he had thrown it on the floor.

'Come with me,' she said and led the way out of the canteen, down a corridor and into an office. 'Sit down.' She indicated the chair in front of the desk. 'Tell me your name?'

'Eh …Matthew …Smith.'

'I'm Sr. Teresa.'

'It's nice to meet you.' He extended his hand and took hers.

She looked at him and then wrote his name down. 'Tell me what happened.'

'My money's gone. I was keeping it so that I could get somewhere to live.' He tried to explain but found it hard to hide the emotion he felt.

'Unfortunately, with all the people here it can sometimes happen. It's difficult to control.'

'I understand it's not your fault, I should have been more careful.' He was a little calmer.

'Have you had breakfast?'

He shook his head.

'Go on into the canteen and have some, and come back later to eat as well, you can't be on the streets without sustenance.'

'Thank you, I'm sorry for losing my head.' He felt foolish now.

'How long have you been homeless?' she asked.

'Just one night.'

'Will you be going home?'

He shook his head.

'Have you anywhere else to go?'

'No.'

'It's almost impossible to get accommodation, and it's very expensive. There are queues outside every property,' she said.

'I had heard that.'

'Unfortunately, our numbers here are increasing all the time.'

He nodded.

'I wish you all the best, but be careful of your money,' she advised.

'I will,' he said, despondent.

Later, Matt went to Social Welfare and applied for whatever help to which he was entitled. That took most of the morning, as he waited in various queues and different people questioned him. But there was a problem. He had no address. A particularly friendly man agreed to hold his application until he could supply him with an address before it would be processed. He was grateful to him, but was in a quandary. Where was he going to live? He knew no-one who would give him a room.

He tried to put it out of his head, persuading himself that he would live from day to day. Now he headed out of the city towards Clontarf, suddenly feeling better when he reached the sea, loving the breeze which pushed against him. He didn't care that it was icy cold, it was bracing and he felt good. In prison he spent a lot of his time in the gym and in the last couple of days he missed the opportunity to exercise, so he made the most of his chance to run. It kept him sane.

He returned to the shelter for lunch and dinner, and that night went to the GPO again. 'Thank you so much for getting me into the hostel last night.' Matt was very grateful to the woman who helped him the night before. 'Although I was robbed there.' He told her what happened. 'Maybe I might be better on the streets.'

'Some people prefer to sleep rough,' she said, handing him a sandwich and pouring a cup of tea from a flask. 'The difficulty is that you have to ring the hostels every night to see if there's a bed, you were very lucky last night.'

'I appreciate your help.'

'Unfortunately, I can't be making calls for people.'

'I'm not going to ask you again.'

'Best of luck,' she smiled.

'Thank you.'

That night he had no choice but to go back to the shelter to see if there was a bed. There was an emptiness in his heart. He missed the company of people in prison. At least some of the officers had been pleasant. The man who ran the library was always interested in talking books. The teacher keen to discuss what further courses he might do on the *Open University,* and even encouraged him to do a Masters. The few men he knew well were always friendly.

He hurried to the shelter as quickly as he could, but there were no beds available. They sent him to another hostel but it was the same story there. Returning then to O'Connell Street, he went back to the people at the GPO. They were clearing up by that time, but still had a sleeping bag and ground sheet to give him.

He didn't know where to go. What place he might find shelter. He felt lost in the darkness of this city. It was raining. Cars drove past splashing through puddles, the resultant muddy spray soaking his jeans. Groups of late night revellers, young men and girls came out of pubs, and staggered along under the influence of too much alcohol. Some of their number being supported by others. Streets shone wet under cones of light through which wind-blown particles floated. He was in the heart of this place, and walked vaguely along as a stranger in an alien land.

He turned down into the side streets, and chose to stop eventually at an old building which had a half open gate. Inside, he threw down the ground sheet on the earthy surface and pushed the gate outwards so that he would be protected against unwanted attention by passers-by. He unzipped the sleeping bag and slipped into it, and was glad of the warmth. He closed his eyes, longing to drift off to sleep. Then something moved across the sleeping bag and he jerked upwards, his hands feeling across the wet fabric for whatever it was, hoping that it wasn't a rat. That most of all. He hated rats. Suddenly, he felt a warm furry texture. God, it could be anything, he thought.

The thing squirmed. He shivered. His immediate instinct was to push it off him, but then he heard a sound. A tiny squeal. And hesitated. It squealed again. His thumping heart kept up a mad fearful dance.

He struggled out of the sleeping bag, pushed himself up and stood out on the street nearer the light, staring down at the creature which had followed him. It was a dog. A young animal. Another homeless creature. He lifted it up closer to him, and could feel its sharp claws. 'Hey there?' The dog gripped his chest, and licked his chin. 'Looking for somewhere to lay down your head?' he smiled at it. 'OK, I'll share my sleeping bag with you.'

He went inside the doorway again, lay back down and kept the dog close to him, it's warm body comforting. He slept a little after that. Waking up when the sky brightened, his body was stiff and sore from the hard surface underneath him. To his surprise, the dog was still there. Now he could see it properly. It was a mongrel, its coat being mostly black with a white patch on its forehead. He guessed that it was probably only a few months old and likely to have strayed from home as it had a red collar.

He pushed himself up out of the doorway and noticed only then that the place was derelict, and it was a long time since anyone had opened the door. It still drizzled, and he pulled up the hood on his anorak for more protection. Then he took up his new companion in his arms and headed around to the shelter run by Sr. Teresa for a shower and breakfast. The man at the door insisted that he leave the dog outside, and Matt searched in his backpack and found a length of string. He tied it to the collar, attached it to a pole, and was glad he seemed safe

It was such a relief to go into the shelter. He had a shower, and then went into the canteen which was already packed with people. Breakfast consisted of the full *Irish,* and as much hot toast and coffee as he wanted. He was grateful to the lady behind the counter who gave him some bits of bacon for the dog as well.

He and the dog spent the next night in a shop doorway covered up by some sheets of cardboard which he had found outside. Lying there, he watched feet walk past, terrified that whoever owned those feet would approach and attack him to steal what few possessions he had. But the dog kept him company as he was beginning to understand the world of the homeless. He called him Rex, after a dog he had when he was a boy.

Chapter Twelve

Coming up to Christmas, Zoe was extremely busy at work and they spent long hours in the office or travelling to see their clients. Zoe was in charge of marketing and sales and it took her away from home regularly, flying all over the world. She knew that Matt had already been released, and assumed that he may have left the country to make a new life for himself.

Gail had got a job at last in the field of event management through a contact she had in London. 'I'm really enjoying it. They're such a nice company,' she told her excitedly. 'I'm working on various concerts they have coming up as that's my expertise. And they're glad to have me, I think,' she smiled, delighted.

Zoe hugged her. 'You deserve it.'

'Although I'm not sure if Dad is so pleased that I'm gone all day now and a lot of evenings too. He's got used to me being around.'

'He's in better form. That must be because you're here.'

'We get on well now.'

'Will you stay at home?'

'I don't think so. I'd like to have my own place.'

'He'll miss you then.'

She shrugged. 'I must live my own life, and maybe I'll meet a new guy one of these days.'

'You will of course.' Zoe was confident.

'Hope so.'

'Although I have a problem …'

'What?'

'I still haven't told Russell about Matt. Time is going by so fast.'

'I suppose you should tell him, at least before the wedding.'

'I know, but the thought of it is …'

'What will he say, do you think?'

'God only knows.' Zoe grimaced.

'Forget about him, let's concentrate on your wedding. We've a fitting tomorrow night, haven't we?'

'Yes and I hope I'll get away in time.' Zoe glanced at her phone diary.

'You're so busy all the time, I don't know how you'll ever have a normal married life.'

'We're managing so far,' Zoe said with a rueful smile.

'And you've invited him and his parents up next week?'

'I just had to. It wasn't going to be possible to arrange a night down in Wicklow, so it's much easier to do it here. You know Dad is always uncomfortable eating out.'

'So we'll scrub up the place, make sure it's looking good. Hope I'll be around to help.'

'Thanks.'

'What about the food, will we cook it ourselves?'

'I wondered about arranging caterers, just in case either one of us gets held up.'

'What about that restaurant we went to a while back, they do outside catering.'

'We've used a crowd called *Best Help Yet* for functions in the company, and we know the owner, Lorraine, very well. I'll talk to her, although it's very short notice.'

'Hopefully she'll be able to do it.'

'She's always very accommodating. I'll send an email.'

'We could try the restaurant then if she can't.'

Zoe was a little less apprehensive now about introducing her father and Gail to Russell's parents, particularly his Dad, Clive.

She hoped that the two men might hit it off, both being much the same age and by Friday afternoon, she and Gail had finished the last of the cleaning, and the table in the dining-room was set. The caterer, Lorraine, had been able to fit them in and later she arrived with one of her girls, Suzanne. All the food was in hot containers and they were preparing everything in the kitchen. Zoe prayed that the evening would go well, everything done without fuss to suit her future mother in law's expectations.

The bell rang and Zoe hurried down the hall, delighted to see Russell, Jean and Clive when she opened the door. Relieved too that Russell had actually made it. He seemed to be making an effort these days and she was very grateful for that.

There was much kissing and hugging as she ushered them in. Helping off with coats and bringing them through into the sitting-room which was warmed by the leaping flames of the coal fire.

'Isn't this a lovely room?' Jean exclaimed.

'It's small, but fine for Dad and Gail at the moment,' she explained. 'I'll just tell them you're here. Now who would like an aperitif?'

'I'm always partial to a dry sherry,' Jean said, smiling.

'Whiskey for me,' Clive said.

'Just water, thanks,' Russell added.

'Give me a minute.' Zoe went into the kitchen where the girls were working.

'Aperitifs?' Lorraine asked.

'Dry sherry, whiskey, and a natural water, thanks.'

Zoe went into the study where Feargal sat reading. 'Dad, Russell and his parents have arrived. They're looking forward to meeting you.'

'Give me a hand up,' he said.

She took it. Standing, he dusted himself down. 'Must look my best for the future in-laws,' he said with a grin. 'I put on my best suit.' He patted the lapels.

'Thanks love.' She kissed him.

The evening was very enjoyable. Lorraine and Suzanne served the drinks and food and there was no need for Zoe and Gail to run in and out of the kitchen, and they were free to chat with their guests. Clive and Feargal got on very well, Clive being particularly keen to know all about the history of lighthouses which Dad was very glad to talk about. The food was a great success and even Russell was at his most charming.

Chapter Thirteen

Every Monday, Matt had to report to the Gardai at Store Street and after that, go to see Tom, his Probation Officer. This was his life now. Two appointments every week gave him a reason to go somewhere with a sense of purpose.

'It's good to see you.' Tom was a friendly individual and they had always got on well. 'Have you made any contact with your family yet?'

'I couldn't.' He shook his head.

'That's such a shame.'

'They wouldn't want to see me. I'm sure of that. The only person who came to see me in prison was my sister Zoe and that was only in the last couple of years.'

'That's very unfortunate.'

'I can't blame them.'

'How are you doing for money?'

Matt told him that most of his money had been stolen.

'There is a one-off payment to help you with expenses, it's called an *Exceptional Needs Payment* and you should be able to access that.' He pulled out a few sheets of paper from a drawer in his desk, and handed them to Matt. 'There's the address for accommodation. And the Community Welfare Service has a Homeless Persons Unit. There are various voluntary organisations listed there as well.'

'I'm hoping to get a job.'

'If I hear of anyone needing a programmer I'll mention you.'

'Thanks.' He was grateful to the man. 'Although I'm sure when they hear of my background they won't be inclined to offer me a job.'

'You've got a very good degree and you'll be a big asset to some company.'

Matt grimaced.

'Have you got a mobile phone?' Tom asked.

'I must get one.'

'While you're waiting for accommodation, you'll need a phone to try the various hostels. A cheap one, *Pay as you go.*'

'I've been calling around every night but it's hard to get a bed so I've been on the streets with the dog, and showering and eating at Sr. Teresa's Shelter. They're very kind to me.'

'I know Sr. Teresa, she's a good woman. But …did you say that you've got a dog?'

'A stray. But he's company until I get somewhere to live. Although I don't feel confident about that, there's very little available.' Matt chose not to mention that he had been so used to having people around him in prison, the thought of living alone in a room on his own all the time actually frightened him. And being so fond of Rex, he knew that he wouldn't be able to bring him into any accommodation he might get.

Tom took out his wallet and pulled out four fifty euro notes. 'Here's some money to keep you going. And get yourself a phone.'

Tom hesitated. 'That's too much.'

'I insist.'

'Thank you so much, I'll pay you back when I get money.'

'Don't worry about it, just look after yourself, I'll see you next week.' He shook his hand.

One morning he went to Sr. Teresa's shelter to have a shower. He was very grateful to everyone who worked there, handing out clean clothes, tents and sleeping bags to people living on the streets.

The man on the door sent him through to Mary who gave him towels, soap, shaving cream, razor and brush. 'Fresh clothes, Matt?'

'Thanks Mary, I'd appreciate that.'

She went into the store room and after a while she came back with the clothes. She checked the sizes. 'You're not *extra-large* are you?'

'Not the last time I looked, it might be a bit loose,' he laughed. '*Large* would be better but I really don't mind, it's just good to have something clean to wear.'

'If we could have some way of organising what we have here then it would mean you'd get the right size. Although we've just been given a computer by a local businessman and if we could set up a proper system on it we wouldn't know ourselves, but we have to wait until we find someone to do that.'

Excitement swept through Matt. 'I know a bit about computers, I could have a look at it if you like,' he offered.

'You do?' She looked at him, surprised.

He nodded.

'We'd be delighted if you could. I know a little myself, emails and that sort of thing, but beyond that I'm lost.'

'I'll just shower and change and you can show me.'

'There you are.' She pushed the items across the counter towards him. It always meant a lot to Matt to even touch fresh clean clothes.

He had had to leave Rex outside, but one of the women in the canteen gave him a bowl of leftover chicken and some water for the dog. He went in to Mary who showed him the computer.

'Fancy tea or coffee?' she asked.

'Coffee would be great, thanks,' he smiled at her.

She returned with it and a ham and cheese toasted sandwich.

'Enjoy that, then you can have a look at the computer. We really appreciate your help. We've been waiting for an angel to come along and you're it,' she said, laughing.

He did that, losing track of time, until he heard the noise of a hail shower on the roof and went out to check on Rex but the man on the door had brought him inside.

'Thank you.'

'I'll have to put him out again as soon as it's dry, but we can't have the little mutt drowning, it's miserable out there.'

Matt shook his hand. 'I'm doing some work for Mary but give me a shout if he's a problem.'

The person who had donated the computer was also paying for broadband and Matt played around with it, going through all the systems installed, and the hard drive had plenty of free space on it.

Mary came in later before she finished her shift at two o'clock and introduced him to Sr. Teresa, but they recognised each other immediately.

'You're the man whose money was stolen,' she said.

'Yes, Sister.'

'It's nice to see you again, how have you been getting along?'

'Not so bad, thank you.' He didn't go into detail.

'We're very grateful to you for checking out our computer.'

'I'm trying to work on a system which would keep account of the stock you hold, and make it easy to operate. And maybe after that I might manage to set up a system which would keep a record of the donations.'

'Thank you so much.'

'I'm really enjoying this.' It was true and he had a wide grin on his face.

'Have you been sleeping on the streets?' she asked.

'Sometimes I get a hostel and other nights I sleep rough.'

'Have you been here?'

'If I'm lucky.'

'We're usually overcrowded as you probably know, but always give us a call.'

'I do, but there are a lot of people looking for a bed so I suppose it's *first come first served*,' he admitted. Although of all the places he had stayed in this was the best. He had applied for a special payment which had been suggested by Tom, and had received two hundred and fifty euro to keep him going. He made sure that it wasn't stolen this time, and as he was being fed by the shelter and stayed in the hostels usually, his expenses were kept to a minimum. He had no hope of renting anywhere.

Unfortunately, when he was in a hostel he had to tie up the dog in some doorway nearby, always relieved to find him still in the same place the following morning. But as he rose at four, there were very few people around, and together they ran for five km getting back into the habit of his prison days. He ran everywhere he went, the dog loping along with him, and the glow which permeated through him made him feel like a man again.

As soon as he had set up the computer system to control the stock of clothes donated, he offered to handle that for the shelter. He was the one who gave out the clothes to people, able to find the sizes and colours at the touch of a button on the computer. He had also reorganised the stock room, colour and size coded, and that made things a lot easier. He was so glad to give people choice, for themselves or their children. A lot of the clothes were actually new, and that made all the difference to people. If second-hand, they were washed and pressed free of charge by a local cleaner.

Then he had an idea and told Sr. Teresa what he had in mind.

'If you like I could set up a web site for you. It might mean that you could increase your donations.'

'How wonderful.' Sr. Teresa was delighted.

'We could show everyone what we do here,' Mary agreed.

'Have you thought about Facebook?' asked Matt.

They shook their heads.

'You could actually raise funds that way, and Twitter too.'

'I've heard of that.'

And there's a fundraising site where you can aim for a particular amount of money.'

'How about a million?' Sr. Teresa asked, laughing.

'That might be a bit ambitious. You would be depending on people to pledge lots of small donations and you're allowed a certain length of time in which to reach the figure and if it doesn't come up to the total by then the people don't have to make the donation.'

'How exciting, I'd love to try it. If we increase our donations in that way, goodness knows what we could do for our poor people.' Sr. Teresa was enthusiastic.

Matt took out his new phone and began to ring around the list of hostel numbers he had in the hope of getting a bed for the night. As Christmas approached the weather had become extremely cold, and there was always a high demand. About the sixth call he got lucky and said goodnight to Sr. Teresa who was working late.

'It's a dirty night, Matt, how far have you to go?'

'Dorset Street.'

'That's a bit of a distance.'

'It won't take me long,' he smiled.

'Not at the rate you run I suppose …' she said.

'It's good to keep fit. And the dog enjoys it too.'

The following day after lunch, Sr. Teresa called him into her office.

'Sit down, Matt,' she indicated the chair in front of her desk which was just a simple deal table.

He did as she asked, wondering why she had called him in.

A sense of dread swept through him. What was coming up? Was she going to ask him to leave? Was he no longer any use to them here? The thought of that hurt him, and the image of long days on the streets without anything to do had a nightmarish quality.

'I've been meeting with our Board this morning and I put a suggestion to them about you.'

His heart sank.

'We were thinking of curtaining off a part of the store-room and setting it out as a little bedroom for you, so you won't have to phone around every night to get a bed.'

A surge of emotion and thankfulness spread through him. 'Thank you,' he stuttered. 'You're very generous.'

'You've been very good to us, offering your time and expertise, it's time we repaid you.'

He shook his head, silent now, as tears filled his eyes. But then something occurred to him, an awful thought.

'I think …I should tell you that I've done time,' he said. 'And it was a very serious crime.'

'Don't worry, I know all about it.'

'How?' he asked her.

'Your Probation Officer was in touch. I know Tom Sheridan well. He follows up a lot of the men for whom he has responsibility. He's a very caring person and told me about your background.'

Matt felt ashamed. 'All of it?' He barely managed to get the words out, hoping that Tom hadn't revealed the whole sordid story.

'No, of course not. Just that you had committed a crime and served a long sentence. But don't worry, it won't go any further than myself, and I'm well able to keep a secret,' she smiled at him.

'Thank you,' he whispered.

'And keep your dog out the back. He can be our guard dog when he gets a bit bigger.'

He couldn't believe her generosity.

'I wondered if you will be seeing your family at Christmas?'

He shook his head.

'Why don't you call to them? Christmas is such a nice time of the year, a time for families to get together.'

'I don't know.' He was tortured with indecision, and simply couldn't imagine how he might knock on the door in Donnybrook and expect his family to welcome him in.

'I want you to think about going to visit them. And take as much time as you like when you decide to go. We don't expect you to be here all of the time, you need to live your own life.'

He found it hard to express the gratitude he felt towards her. 'You've saved my life, Sr. Teresa.'

'Not at all.' She dismissed him in that light-hearted way of hers.

Chapter Fourteen

A couple of weeks before Christmas, Zoe brought all her friends out to dinner for a hen night and they ended up in a club until the late hours. There was no time to go away and stay over somewhere, but Russell did manage to have a stag night as well.

Presents arrived every day. An amazing array of stuff mostly from everyone Jean and Clive had invited. They received vouchers and money too from Zoe's family and friends.

On Christmas Eve, Gail and Zoe met together in town to do some last-minute shopping.

'I love Dublin at Christmas.' Gail's eyes were lit up with excitement. 'The lights are fantastic, and the atmosphere is electric.'

'And this is the first time you've been home in years. It's so great to have you.' Zoe put her arm around Gail.

'It will be lovely with just the three of us tomorrow. Next year you'll be with Russell. And I'm so glad you've decided to keep your own name and are not dropping it altogether. You'd lose your identity if you took on Russell's family name.'

'Never, my name is very important to me.'

'Dad doesn't seem to mind that you're getting married, you know, losing a daughter and all that sort of thing.'

'Or gaining a son.'

They stared at each other for a moment in silence, a question between them.

'Do we need anything else for tomorrow?' Gail spoke first.

'I'm sure there are, let's go into *M & S* and have a wander.'

After picking up a few items, they crossed the road and went into *Brown Thomas,* meeting Ciaran and Jim at the front entrance doors where the two men welcomed customers into the store, resplendent in their top hats. Zoe knew them from going in and out and now she introduced Gail, and they wished them a *Happy Christmas*.

Inside it was festive and brightly lit with sparkling Christmas decorations on a silver theme. People chatted and laughed as they crowded around the counters excitedly, putting the sales people under extreme pressure.

'Let's have a look at the handbags.' Gail steered Zoe into the department and they had a pleasant time browsing through the designer bags.

'I love this *Mulberry* satchel,' Gail posed with a large black bag.

'Or this one.' Zoe picked up an *Alexander McQueen*. 'And don't look at the price.'

'I never bother doing that,' Gail laughed.

'Come on, let's look at the shoes …my weakness.' Zoe led the way through the throngs, and they spent more time trying on one pair of shoes after another.

'The *Gucci* are gorgeous.' Gail looked at herself in the mirror, circling on six-inch heels.

'And what do you think of these?' Zoe picked up a pair of silver sandals by *Valentino*. 'And they're my size.' She slipped them on.

'Perfect for a honeymoon,' Gail said with a grin.

'I'll buy them,' Zoe decided immediately. It was in her nature to be spontaneous. 'These are a Christmas present to myself from Santa Claus. And I'd like Santa to bring you those Gucci in his sack.'

'But I'll have to think twice about buying them, my bank account isn't so healthy yet,' Gail admitted.

'I'll buy them for you.'

'What?' Gail was taken aback.

'It's your Christmas present.'

'I can't let you do that, they're far too expensive,' she protested. 'I'll have to pay you back.'

'Don't worry.'

'I love you, and I will pay you back,' She hugged Zoe.

They giggled. It was fun to be together after all the years apart.

Home later, they set about preparing the turkey. Baking the ham. Making stuffing and peeling vegetables. They enjoyed themselves, pouring a glass of wine to celebrate and a whiskey for their Dad.

It was about seven o'clock when the doorbell rang.

'That's Russell, I asked him to call if he could before he went down to his parents.'

'Did you get your present yet?' Gail had an impish grin on her face.

'He's coming up tomorrow evening so we'll give each other our gifts then.'

'What have you bought him?'

'Secret.' She put her finger on her lips and smiled, and then hurried down the hall. She opened the door. '*Happy Christmas*, love …' she stared in shock at the man who stood there.

It was Matt.

'Hi Zoe.' He stood on the doorstep, carrying a red Christmas gift bag. Wearing a dark anorak and jeans. His hair cut short, a neat beard on his chin. He looked much the same as he had when she saw him in prison some months before.

'I'm sorry to come unannounced,' he murmured. 'I left the dog outside, is that all right?'

'Sure, come in,' she said and closed the door behind him. Almost immediately, the doorbell rang again. She froze, knowing it was probably Russell.

'The doorbell is ringing.' Feargal opened the study door.

'It's Matt, Dad,' Zoe said it plainly. There was no other way, but she didn't open the door for Russell.

Feargal stopped in his tracks. 'Who?' he barked, his mouth open, his false teeth loose.

Zoe said nothing.

'The bloody jail-bird?' Feargal growled.

Matt bent his head.

'What are you doing here? he yelled loudly, a terrible anger in his eyes. 'We don't want to see you here, none of us.'

Zoe didn't know what to do.

Gail appeared from the kitchen, the colour in her face draining white as she saw Matt. She took a deep breath, her eyes wide with astonishment.

The doorbell rang again.

'Why doesn't someone answer the door?' she asked and walked down the hall past Zoe and Matt.

'*Happy Christmas*, Gail,' Russell had a broad smile on his face.

'*Many Happy Returns,*' Gail said.

He kissed her on the cheek. 'Santa Claus has left you a present of a dog, he's tied to the gate,' he said.

'Don't know anything about that,' she said, ushering him into the hall and closing the door.

Behind them, Feargal was still yelling at Matt. 'We thought we'd got rid of you altogether and we never wanted to see you again. You disgraced us. We had to move up here to get away from it all.' He spat, almost foaming at the mouth in fury.

Zoe came over to Russell and kissed him.

'What's going on?' he asked, puzzled.

'I'll tell you later …'

'And here you are turning up on Christmas Eve without a thought for our feelings,' Feargal continued to rant. 'And just when we are enjoying ourselves too. Bloody bad egg, always was, always will be.' He turned back into his study and banged the door.

'Matt, how could you come here and upset Dad so much?'

'I'm sorry, Gail.'

'You're just a fucking selfish bastard, I can't believe …' She spluttered.

'I'll go,' Matt said. He put down the red paper bag on the floor and walked back down the hall.

'Isn't anyone going to explain what's happening?' Russell rounded on Zoe.

Matt opened the front door and left, closing it quietly behind him.

'That was my brother Matt,' Zoe said.

'I didn't know you had a brother.'

'He's been away for a long time,' said Gail. 'None of us want to know anything about him now.'

'Let's go inside.' Zoe ushered Russell into the sitting-room, and Gail followed.

'Would you like a drink, or a cup of coffee?' Zoe offered.

'Coffee, thanks.'

'I'll get it.' Gail hurried out.

'Sit down love, I'm glad you could call in,' Zoe said softly

He sat down on the couch. 'I can't stay for long, Mother has friends in to dinner. But before I go I need to know why your father was so angry with your brother?'

'Stuff happened in the past,' Zoe explained as little as she could.

'Why didn't you mention you had a brother?' Russell demanded.

'I meant to but …'

'What does that mean? Next you'll be telling me you've a whole family I never heard about.'

'No …just Matt.'

Gail brought in a tray and put it on the table. She placed the coffee percolator, cups and saucers down with a clatter, milk jug, sugar bowl, and a plate of biscuits. Then she poured.

Zoe stirred her coffee with a spoon. Increasing the pace until the liquid began to spin around. Realising that it was going to slop over she stopped abruptly.

There was a nervous tension in the room, an uneasy silence.

'I'll check on Dad.' Gail left the room.

'Russell, I'm sorry you came in on that row.'

'I don't know what to think. I feel I've been taken in.' He stood up and prowled around the room like a big cat stalking his prey in the jungle.

Zoe felt cornered. In complete confusion. How much should she reveal to Russell?

He stood over her, hands on hips. 'Well?'

'He was in prison,' she whispered, deciding that it was now or never.

Russell stared at her, mouth open, his expression one of complete shock. 'He broke the law?' His voice was guttural.

She nodded. Tears in her eyes.

'What did he do?'

Zoe's mind searched frantically for an explanation, and only then realised that she would have to tell the truth. It was the only option. 'He killed someone.'

'*Jesus Christ,*' he exploded. 'Who did he kill?'

'I can't say who …'

'And you never uttered a word to me. You're supposed to love me. There are to be no secrets between us. I know I'm not perfect but to deceive me …like this is…' he stuttered.

'I didn't mean to deceive you,' she said. 'Believe me.'

'If I didn't call in tonight then I might never have found out, and it's just a week before our wedding too.' He flopped down on the couch, and sat holding his head in his hands.

Zoe went across to him and put her arm around his shoulders. 'This shouldn't come between us. It has nothing to do with us. We haven't seen Matt in a long time, I don't know him at all and as you have already heard he certainly isn't welcome here.'

'It's not so much the fact that he's a criminal, that's bad enough, it's because you didn't tell me. You have a father and a sister and that was your family. And now this skeleton in your cupboard appears. Good

God, I don't know what to think.' Abruptly, he shrugged off her arm, stood up and walked towards the door.

'Don't go, Russell, let's talk,' she begged.

'I can't …not now.'

'Please?'

He shook his head.

She followed him. At the front door, she reached to kiss him goodnight, but he marched down the driveway to his car and drove off.

Chapter Fifteen

Matt jogged along the path with Rex on the lead. His mind was spinning, and he regretted now that he had gone to the house. It had been crazy to arrive without warning and expect anything else. His father's rage had shocked him, as had that of Gail. At the time of the trial and leading up to it, Feargal had never spoken to him, obviously traumatized and unable to deal with the event. Even when Matt was on remand, and struggling to come down off his addictions, no-one had come to see him. It was a terrible shame on the family and he could understand how they felt. It was a surprise to him that Zoe had arrived in to see him just a couple of years ago.

He remembered that first time. He had stared at her, the subdued voices of other prisoners talking with their families were all around him, and he felt like he was under the sea, gasping for breath, his ears filled with the sound of whirling bubbling water. Her lips moved but he couldn't hear what she was saying. He tried to speak but it was like being in one of those nightmares where all physical motion was impossible no matter how hard you tried to move.

Shame had swept through him then. He stared down at his hands which twisted and turned nervously. Tears filled his eyes and dribbled down his cheeks. He was unable to meet her clear blue eyes.

'Matt?'

He heard her voice then. So familiar.

'How are you?'

He shook his head, and rose from the chair, almost knocking it over as he walked hurriedly to where the prison officer stood by the door. The man opened it and he rushed through, his shoulders shaking as he made his way back to his cell where he threw himself on his bed and broke down completely. His face was buried in the pillow, his hands grasped the edge of the mattress, like he was a small child sent to bed for misbehaving.

It took days for him to recover from Zoe's visit. Lashing himself for being unable to show how grateful he was that she came to see him. But the emotion which had dominated him from the first moment he saw her, refused to allow him respond as any normal person would. He should have put his arms around her. Say how sorry he was. How good of her to come. And express his thanks over and over. But his reaction was crass. That first opportunity to meet one of his sisters and he had made a complete mess of it, not asking how she was, or his father or sister Gail either. He wondered was his father even still alive. His one hope during all those years was that he would be accepted back home by his family, but another side of him doubted that it would ever happen. Now at the first opportunity, he had not been able to deal with it. Idiot. He accused himself. Fucking idiot.

It had been very busy leading up to Christmas and it was the first time he had ever been alone at this time of the year. He was very much aware of the happiness and excitement of the city. Children's faces filled with wonder as they stared at the displays in the shop windows, the tall Christmas trees, and the sparkle of the colourful lights which hung above. Now he immediately got involved in helping to make up some more food parcels for the long queue of people which snaked around the building. The parcels contained just basic foodstuffs plus some extra Christmas treats. As he worked, he tried not to think about the fact that he was the same. Lonely. Bereft of a home and family.

On Christmas Day, there was a cheerful atmosphere among all the volunteers who served dinner to the homeless people who packed the big dining room. He found it hard to put a smile on his face after what had happened the evening before. His father's tirade was the first time he had expressed his feelings towards him since that night.

Now he found it difficult to sleep. Nightmares took him back. His father striking out when he refused to behave as he had expected. His mother trying to protect him from his father's violence until she was finally forced to retreat from the situation tearfully, crying piteously, begging him to stop hitting Matt.

The words of his father and sister echoed in his head. B*astard, disgrace, bloody selfish,* and brought back those terrible days, a mix of film cuts swirling in a hazy mist.

Suddenly he had a terrible urge to take something which would ease the hurt. The burning shame within him. His soul was distracted. What was there to live for? He was unloved. A waster. Unwanted. He knew it would be no problem to get any drug he wanted. Then he could drift into a place of peace and know nothing more. That was what he wanted most of all.

Chapter Sixteen

Zoe closed the front door after Russell had left and went in to the sitting-room. It was so Christmassy. The fire brightly lit. The tree sparkling. Presents arranged around it. They had made such an effort, decorating the room in a theme of red and gold. It had promised so much.

She sat by the fire and let the tears flow. What a catastrophe. How could any of them have imagined that if Matt ever came home, the timing would have been so crucial. And what would Russell do, she wondered. Could he ever forgive her? Was that even possible? She took her phone from her jeans pocket and was about to press his number but then hesitated. It was too soon.

She went into the kitchen but it was empty, so she opened her father's study door and looked in to see him sitting there in tears, Gail beside him.

She pulled over a chair, sat beside him and held his hand.

Gail shook her head, eyes worried.

Zoe didn't know what to say. She took the blame for giving Matt the address of this house. Obviously, she shouldn't have done that. Normally Feargal was very quiet, but this incident took her back and reminded of his violent outbursts against Matt when she was young. They sat together, the three of them until slowly he stopped crying and lay back in the chair, his eyes closed. Zoe was afraid to move in case he began to cry again and whispered to Gail that they should just stay there, and she nodded her agreement.

They kept him company for another hour or so and then Zoe stood up. 'Dad, it's late, I think you should go to bed, I'm sure you must be tired.' After a moment he pushed himself into standing position, and they followed him upstairs and into his bedroom.

Gail pulled back the bedclothes and he sat on the edge of the bed.

'There's your pyjamas,' Zoe unfolded them.

'Goodnight, Dad.'

They both kissed him.

Outside the door they stood looking at each other. 'He's in bad shape,' Zoe said.

'And it's all Matt's fault turning up like that. How could you give him our address? It was crazy. You knew he'd probably come back at some point and cause trouble as usual.' She rounded on Zoe.

'I hoped he would have changed by now.'

'Someone like him will never change. At least not for the better.'

'We don't know that,' Zoe objected.

'Bastard.'

Zoe turned away. She couldn't agree with her sister.

They stayed standing in silence outside the door.

'I'm sorry for losing my head like that, how did things go with Russell?' Gail asked softly after a few minutes.

'He wasn't too pleased I didn't tell him about Matt, so he's gone off to think about it.'

'And you're getting married in a week's time?'

'Maybe I am. Maybe I'm not,' Zoe said slowly as tears filled her eyes.

'I'm sure he won't let such a thing come between you. The wedding is all arranged, you couldn't possibly cancel now. Imagine what his mother would say, she'd have a blue fit.'

'If he doesn't want to marry me, then it's all over.'

'Maybe it's just as well it happened. Now he knows about Matt and it will never come between you again and cause a problem. You were intending to tell him anyway, and if you hadn't you never know whether one of our relatives would let it slip at the wedding. Imagine that?'

They went back into the bedroom but their father still sat on the bed staring at the floor, and he had made no effort to undress.

'Dad, aren't you going to put on your pyjamas?' Zoe asked gently.

He made no response.

'We'll help you with your jacket, and trousers ...' She began to take them off.

'And I'll unlace your shoes.' Gail bent down.

They put his pyjamas on over his underwear and tucked him up. They left the bedside lamp on and came back a short time later to check that he was all right, and were happy to see that he was sleeping soundly.

On Christmas morning, to their relief, Feargal seemed to be all right when he came down to breakfast, wishing them both a *Very Happy Christmas.*

Zoe called Russell, but his phone went on to voice mail and she had to leave a message. Then she sent a text as well asking him to call her. But there was no response from him and it didn't bode well.

The girls behaved as if nothing had happened the night before, and put the turkey in the oven to cook. Gail made a sherry trifle and Zoe set the table with the best cutlery and glassware.

Later, they went to Mass with their Dad at the local church. To listen to the children's choir singing the carols that she remembered from her childhood was very special and for Gail to be home for this Christmas meant a lot to both of them and it was lovely to share the celebration together.

They came back and finished the cooking and were ready to sit down and eat about four o'clock. They carved the turkey and ham, served stuffing, roast potatoes, red cabbage, celery, sprouts and delicious gravy. But Zoe was very tense. She hadn't had any response from Russell and kept her phone close to hand in case he rang. But she was hopeful that

84

he would just knock on the door later and everything would be normal. She made an effort to enjoy her Christmas dinner, opened a bottle of wine, laughed, pulled crackers, and made the best of the day. Feargal's mood was still low. A vacancy in his eyes. But they tried to jolly him along. Zoe had bought him a thick coffee table book on lighthouses all over the world which had some wonderful photographs, and Gail had bought him a book on politics he had expressed an interest in recently. He never bought presents so shopping vouchers were his gifts for which the girls were very grateful. After clearing the dishes, they relaxed in the sitting-room. Their Dad browsed through his presents and seemed to have brightened up. The girls sipped another glass of wine and watched some corny films on the small television they had in that room.

'It's strange looking at that tiny screen,' Gail giggled. 'We're so used to the big one inside.'

'Well, it suits the old films.'

They smiled at each other.

'I'm sorry about the row over Matt last night ...' Zoe murmured.

Gail sighed.

As the afternoon darkened into evening, Zoe was all the more conscious that Russell hadn't called until suddenly her phone rang. She grabbed it and hurried out into the hall delighted to see his number come up. 'Hi there, Russell, I hope you're all having a lovely day,' she gabbled excitedly. 'And give my best wishes to your Mum and Dad ...'

'Zoe,' he interrupted her conversation abruptly.

'Yes?' she whispered.

'I'm outside.'

'I'm sorry, I didn't hear the bell, hold on ...' She opened the door, but didn't see him. 'Where are you?' she laughed.

'I'm in the car, come out.'

She ran down the path and he pushed open the passenger door.

'Why don't you come in, it's cold out here,' she asked.

'I want to talk to you.'

'Ok …' She sat into the car, aware of the strong aroma of the leather upholstery which would always remind her of Russell and his love of luxurious cars. '*Happy Christmas*, love.' She leaned towards him but he pulled away.

'It's not a very *Happy Christmas*, is it?' he asked sharply.

'I suppose last night wasn't, but we can't let it affect us surely?' she coaxed.

'Don't be stupid, Zoe. It has affected us, can't you see that?'

She was silenced.

'And I can't marry you,' he said bluntly.

'But we still love each other …' she said hesitantly.

'I don't know whether I do love you or not after this.' He avoided her eyes and stared out through the windscreen.

'I still love you,' she whispered, her voice trembling.

'Don't say any more, Zoe. There's no point. I've made my decision. Our wedding is off. I'll send out emails to everyone and personally talk to the closer family. I presume you will do the same. Mother will speak with Sylvia and everything will be cancelled. There will be a cost for doing that at such short notice but we can split that between us.'

Zoe could only listen in shock.

'As the apartment is mine, I expect you to move out as quickly as you can,' he snapped. 'Remove all your stuff, I don't want to see a trace of it when I get back. In the meantime, I'll stay with my parents and commute up and down from Wicklow. Does that suit you?' He pulled a notebook from his pocket.

'No …I don't want …that.' She was in tears.

'Email me with a note of anything you want me to handle. And we'd better return the gifts which have arrived.' He stared ahead, hands on the steering wheel.

She sat there, unable to believe that this was happening. Eventually, she opened the car door, stepped out and walked away from the sleek shining body of the black Mercedes. She went into the house without looking back.

In the hall, her phone rang and for a crazy moment she wondered if Russell had had second thoughts, but it was his mother Jean. She let the call go on to voicemail knowing she couldn't talk to her now.

Gail came out of the sitting room. 'Where have you been?'

'That was Russell.'

'Where is he?'

'He's gone now.'

'And?'

'It's over,' she said dully. Sitting down listlessly on one of the hall chairs.

'Oh Zoe, that's so awful for you.' Gail put her arms around her sister and hugged. 'Come inside and I'll make you a cup of coffee, or maybe we'll have another glass of wine?'

'Coffee will be fine.'

They went into the kitchen.

'You look as if you're in shock, I'll put in plenty of sugar.'

'Thanks.'

She handed a mug of hot coffee to Zoe, who sat there, hugging it in both hands and sipping slowly.

'Are you warm enough?'

Zoe nodded. Her mind in turmoil. Was this actually happening? Yesterday she was going to be married and twenty-four hours later it was all off.

Chapter Seventeen

On St. Stephen's Day, after breakfast Zoe took a deep breath and sat down opposite her Dad.

He raised his head from the book he was reading and looked at her, his eyes lacklustre.

'There's something I have to tell you and I hope you won't be upset.' She felt guilty having to disappoint him in this way and was concerned that he would react badly.

'What is it?'

'Russell and I have broken up, we won't be getting married,' she said in a nervous rush.

He raised his eyebrows. 'What happened?'

'It's just one of those things, I don't think we were meant to be together.'

'I'm sorry to hear that, you must be very upset.' He reached to pat her hand.

'I am ...' Tears moistened her eyes.

'I wish I could do something for you,' he murmured. 'I wish your mother was here ...'

'So do I.' Zoe felt even worse.

They sat there in silence.

'Would you mind ...if I moved back home for a while?' she asked him.

'I'd be delighted, sure what could be nicer?' he said with a grin.

'Thanks Dad, I appreciate it.'

'Stay as long as you like,' he said gently.

Tears filled her eyes, and she felt emotional. She was so glad her father was there for her. She hugged and kissed him.

There were a lot of calls to make the following morning, and the first was Russell's mother, Jean. She dreaded talking to her as the message she had left on her phone the night before had been positively incoherent.

'Hello Jean …' She didn't know how to start such a conversation.

'Russell has told me that the wedding is off.' The woman sniffled, obviously very upset. 'I haven't stopped crying since. It really is too much, I don't know how you let this happen.' There was a loud sob.

'I'm sorry.' As she didn't know what Russell had told her, she said no more.

'What went wrong, Zoe? I couldn't get a word out of Russell. I thought you loved each other. And now to cancel everything is just too much for me. I can't cope with it. All the plans we've made. The marquee. The flowers. The caterers. I've talked to Sylvia, and she's going to contact people but of course everyone's on holiday. It's a terrible time for you to do such a thing.'

'I'll be sending emails.'

'But some people won't receive them until they're back after New Year.' It was an angry snap. 'What will we do if they turn up, and I have to tell everyone that it's off. I will die, Zoe, I'm telling you, I will die. And then there are the family, the guests, people who have bought new outfits especially for the wedding, it's all so embarrassing. Isn't there some way you could make up with Russell and go along with the wedding as you planned and sort out your differences afterwards. You'll have a wonderful honeymoon and will be so happy then I'm sure. You'll come back like lovebirds. Couldn't you consider it please, Zoe, just for me?' she begged.

'No Jean, that wouldn't be possible.'

After what had happened she couldn't see herself and Russell going ahead. His attitude had been gross to say the least. There he was last night with his list of items telling her to get out of his apartment. Such a cold fish. Some time ago she had her doubts about him but he seemed to make an effort and changed to some extent and she had been reassured, but now, even though she still loved him, she knew that she would never marry him.

'I don't know what I'll do.' Jean went on. 'Clive is distraught too and very disappointed. You know how fond of you he is. And you all work together, what will happen there?'

'Please give him my love,' she said.

Zoe left Jean crying loudly on the phone. That was the worst call she had to make. She felt sorry for both of them. They had put a huge amount into the planning of the wedding. Weeks ago they had even brought in a garden designer to remodel the garden in winter hues. She regretted that particularly, it must have cost an awful lot. And then there was the redecoration of the house, the replacement of furniture, and drapes. Admittedly all that was permanent and not something to be thrown out after the wedding, but came at a heavy price none the less.

Zoe had asked Gail to help her clear her stuff out of the apartment and later they drove over. White marble flooring. Furniture in hues of white with an odd coloured item placed just to create a splash. The large glass windows on all sides allowed an amazing view of the city. Electronically controlled white blinds slid up and down at the press of a switch.

'It's a pity you're leaving such a fabulous apartment,' Gail said, wandering around.

'It's just a box.' Zoe made a dismissive gesture.

'What are you going to take today? There's so much stuff, and I'm sure you bought a lot of it.'

'I did. The blinds are fairly new.'

'Take them,' encouraged Gail.

'That might be a bit much,' she managed a grim laugh.

Gail went into the dressing room, and swished back one of the sliding doors in the wardrobe. 'It will take some time to bring over all of your clothes.'

'I've a lot of stuff,' she said.

'And a huge amount of evening wear too.' Gail ran her hand over a silky full-length dress in bright red chiffon. 'I love this one, I'll have to borrow it if I ever get a chance to wear something like that.'

'You can have it if you want.'

'Thank you,' Gail smiled.

'We'll have to make a few visits back and forth.'

'My God, look at that collection of shoes, I knew you had a lot, but not this much,' she screamed out loud.

'Can't leave these behind.' Zoe picked up a favourite cerise pink stiletto sandal.

'No way, pity you're a thirty-seven and I'm a thirty-nine.'

'Let's get on, I'll have to fold smaller things in black bags and shoes can go in suitcases. Dresses and stuff we can just fold over our arms,' Zoe said firmly. 'And then there are the wedding gifts too, although most of our friends gave us money so that won't be so difficult to return. And Russell can send back the presents we received from his family.'

'You'll have a job to fit all this lot into your bedroom.'

They stared at the suitcases and bags in the hallway.

Zoe tried to keep her emotion under control. She had lived here with Russell, and she considered this apartment to be her home. To be forced to leave cut through her like a knife.

Gail and Zoe spent most of the day taking the rest of the clothes and shoes over to Donnybrook. They went back the following day and managed to clear her personal possessions in a couple of runs in the car.

'I'm glad we didn't actually buy a house,' she said, as they made a final check around the rooms.

'It would have been much more complicated. Is that yours?' Gail pointed to a small bronze sculpture of a horse.

'It is actually, I bought it in the Solomon Gallery at one of their exhibitions.'

'It's so sweet.' She picked it up. 'Don't leave it.'

'Ok, I won't.' Zoe put it in a bag.

'What about the paintings?'

'Some belong to Russell and others we bought together.'

'Fifty-fifty?'

'I'm not going to cut them in half.'

They walked into the dining room and stood in front of a large landscape of the west of Ireland.

'That's really nice.'

'We spent a few euro on that one.'

'Take it,' Gail encouraged.

'No, I won't. I'm only taking my personal stuff, it wouldn't be fair.' Zoe went into the bathroom and cleared the presses. Then took some towels and new bedlinen from the airing cupboard. 'I just bought these recently and I'm going to need them. I'm lucky that Dad doesn't mind my coming home. He seemed very happy about it, and was surprisingly clear, no confusion. I was surprised.'

'Some days he's really good, and on other days he doesn't seem to know where he is.'

'You probably notice it more than I do.'

'It was a shock to find him like that when I came home.'

'Maybe it will be good for him if both of us are home for a while.'

'I've been looking around for an apartment to rent but it's very difficult to get anywhere these days. I've joined a few queues and the agents take the names, but there isn't a hope of getting a place.'

'There just isn't enough property available.'

'It's a complete con. I don't know if I'll ever get a place to live.'

'Remember we were saying we might get an apartment together,' Zoe suggested.

'That would be great but to be honest now I'd feel guilty leaving

Dad on his own even if you're there.' Gail lifted one of the bags. 'Do you think you've got everything?' she asked.

'I'm not sure, I'll come back another time to pick up anything I've forgotten. It's not as if I'll never see Russell again. We'll meet in the office.'

'He'll probably change his mind and want to get back together before you know it.'

'I'm not so sure. Now, I'll take these bags, and can you carry those two over there please, and that's everything.' She walked towards the door with an air of determination, and stood there for a moment trying not to let the tears flow.

'If it hadn't been for that bastard Matt you wouldn't be in this position,' Gail said bitterly.

'Maybe he did me a favour and I saw Russell in his true colours.'

In the kitchen at home, Gail opened a bottle of wine and they enjoyed an Indian takeaway they had ordered.

'Thanks for suggesting that, it's delicious. I don't think I could ever eat turkey and ham again it has so many bad memories.' Zoe broke off a piece of nan bread and dipped it in mango chutney.

'Not at all, we'll be together at Christmas again and all of this will be forgotten. If I could get over Pierre there's hope for you.'

'There's so much to be done,' Zoe sighed. 'I started making a list earlier.'

'We'll do it together. And you'll feel much better tomorrow.'

'I don't think I'll ever feel better.'

'You will.'

'I've just thought of our honeymoon in Vietnam, and all that money down the drain.'

'Can you claim on the travel insurance?' Gail asked.

'I don't think so. I think it has to be illness or death, something really serious.'

'Would they cancel it for now and give you another holiday down the line?'

'I don't know. I'll ask.'

'Or even give you half the value perhaps?'

'That would be great. I'll call when they're open.'

They went through the items Zoe had written on the list, and between the two of them, decided who was going to contact who. It made such a difference to Zoe to have Gail home.

They poured the last of the wine later and sipped it.

'How did you think Matt looked?' asked Zoe.

'Older, I suppose.' Gail fiddled with the screw top of the wine bottle.

'I thought it took a lot of courage to call.' Zoe felt she had to mention him.

'Maybe. But what was he looking for?' Gail's voice was suspicious.

'He brought a present,' Zoe confided.

'Did he?' Gail was surprised.

'I put the bag under the stairs and forgot about it.'

'I don't want any presents from him, that fucker.'

'I'll get it.' Zoe went into the hall and came back with the red bag.

'Better not show it to Dad, he'll throw it at you.'

A flutter of annoyance swept through Zoe as she undid the red satin bow. 'A bottle of wine and a box of chocolates.' She took them out. 'It was thoughtful of him.'

'I won't be drinking that wine, or eating the chocolates,' retorted Gail.

'It can be hard for people when they first come out of prison.'

'You're very sympathetic. I can't believe you feel that way after everything that happened.'

'Someone has to look out for him.'

Gail dismissed that with a grimace. 'It isn't going to be me. I think he should still be doing time.'

'I understand how you feel.' Zoe had to be gentle.

Gail sighed. 'Maybe we should agree not to talk about him anymore, we'll only aggravate ourselves.'

'You're right,' Zoe agreed reluctantly.

Over the next few days, Zoe and Gail spent their time cancelling all wedding arrangements and, of course, there had to be phone contact with Russell, which made it doubly difficult for Zoe. Everyone they talked with were very surprised and upset for them both, particularly Zoe's friends. One of the most awkward aspects was the return of the wedding presents and for Zoe the hardest thing was writing *Thank You* cards, each one intensely personal.

As the week crept up to New Year's Eve, Zoe felt under a lot of pressure, unable to sleep very well, her mind going around in circles as she thought about her wedding and the fact that it wasn't going to happen now.

On the morning of the day she would have been married, Gail knocked on her sister's bedroom door and pushed it open. 'Hi love?'

Zoe pushed herself up with a weak smile.

'How did you sleep?'

'Not very well.'

'Poor thing, I'm so sorry, have a cup of tea and some toast. I didn't think you would want to eat too much, although I could do something else if you like?'

Gail put the tray on her knees, and poured hot tea from the china teapot.

'That's perfect,' Zoe smiled.

'Get that in to you.'

'I will.'

Gail pulled a chair over and sat near the bed.

'This is a tough day but we'll get through it together. I thought we'd go into town, have a long lunch and some retail therapy.'

Zoe nodded.

'We'll go in about twelve, would that be all right for you?'

'Thanks for suggesting it.'

'And the sales are on, we might pick up a few bargains.'

'I don't even know where my clothes are,' Zoe looked across the room to where her bags and suitcases were piled.

'You've some in the wardrobe.' Gail went across the room and opened it. 'You'll be able to find something here, surely? And let's see a bit of glam.'

'I will,' Zoe said vaguely.

'Finish your breakfast. You've plenty of time to get ready, and even make some calls or send emails if you want to.'

Gail managed to cheer Zoe up that day as they strolled around the shops looking at the bargains. But neither of them bought anything. They had a late lunch at *Albaros* and then took a leisurely walk around St. Stephen's Green.

'It turned out to be quite a nice day,' Zoe said softly.

'And with a ring on your finger you might already be regretting it.'

Zoe stared into the distance pensively, and then glanced down at her ring finger. It was bare. She had put her engagement ring back in the box.

'Do you think Russell is the only man in the world you could ever love?'

'I've been asking myself that question all week and I couldn't come up with an answer.'

'I'm sorry, all your plans have come to nothing. It's such a disappointment.' She put her arm through Zoe's and they walked close together.

'Thanks a mill for coming out with me today, love you,' Zoe murmured.

'Come on, let's go and have a drink.'

Later, they sat chatting in *Kielys* and took a taxi home about eight. They went into the house and Gail pushed open the sitting room door. 'I'll make coffee, you go in and flop.' She switched on the light and the room was illuminated. Zoe stared astonished at the group of women who rushed forward and embraced her.

Her five best friends.

She burst into tears and hugged them. 'How did you get in here?'

'Your Dad let us in.'

She searched for a tissue to dry her eyes.

'Here, Zoe.' Gail handed her a box.

'Thanks.' She sniffled.

'That's the first time she cried today. She's been amazing.' Gail hugged Zoe.

'I've been …holding it in.' She bent her head.

'Let it go, cry as much as you like,' Gail said. 'I'm going to open a bottle of champagne. Look after her, girls.'

She left the room, and returned with a chilled bottle of *Bollinger*. 'Right, here we go,' she pulled the cork with a loud pop and the fizzy liquid overflowed.

The girls held up their glasses and Gail filled each one and they raised a toast to Zoe. Then they giggled and laughed. Reminisced. Told jokes. And a few glasses of champagne later even Zoe was enjoying herself. As they wished each other a *Happy New Year* slowly the fact that this should have been her wedding day began to hurt just a little less.

Chapter Eighteen

Matt felt very down that New Year. What should have been a hopeful time was marred by the attitude of his father on Christmas Eve. Even though he knew he deserved every bit of it, he had to accept the fact that no one wanted him and he would never be accepted home.

He was glad to be still working with Sr. Teresa at the homeless shelter and welcomed there by people who cared about him, that most of all. One evening at the end of January he received a call from Tom, his Probation Officer.

'Hi Matt, I've had contact from your sister Zoe and she would like to see you. She gave me her phone number to pass on to you.'

He was stunned and his heart beat so fast he thought Tom would hear it over the phone. 'Zoe?'

'Yes.'

'Give me a minute, I just need to get a piece of paper and a pen.' He picked it up from the desk. 'Go ahead.' He jotted the number down. 'Thanks Tom.'

He sat down. Unable to believe that Zoe wanted to see him after what happened. He saved the number in his phone and was inclined to ring at that very moment, but hesitated. It was nine o'clock and a bit late. He would wait.

In the morning, he finally took courage to tap Zoe's name in his short list of contacts and pressed *call,* but he was disappointed when it went to voicemail.

Zoe Sutherland here, please leave your name and number and I'll call back as soon as I can.

Her voice was sweet and took him right back to when he was young. *Matt, Matt.*

She was always the one sent to get him from the garden for his dinner or tea. Zoe was dogged and she didn't give up. He would hide somewhere and laugh as she searched for him. But she would come back again and again. Whereas if Gail was sent out, she had no patience, and after a moment or two she would immediately complain to their mother that she couldn't find him. But Matt knew just how long to push the situation, particularly if his father was there.

The beep on the phone sounded and now it was his chance to speak. But he couldn't at first. Then, all in a rush. 'Zoe, it's me,' he stuttered. 'I'd love to see you ...' But then the chance of leaving a message ended and he realised she didn't know his number. He wondered if he should call again, but only remembered then that his number would have come up on her phone. All that day he listened for his phone to ring, praying that he would hear it above the noise in the shelter, but it was very busy and there were long queues of people waiting for attention.

Winter was the most difficult time of the year. The cold nights forcing many homeless people to seek shelter in the hostels. For Sr. Teresa, if there were not enough beds, she would still bring in the most pathetic cases and give them a place to sleep. Matt was the person who had taken on the task of keeping watch during the night with the volunteer on the door. The rule was that people had to be in control of themselves and not cause problems. For Matt, he had to insist on this and found that difficult. How to turn someone away into the darkness of an icy night. To force them to try to find somewhere to lie down out of the rain and cold. He could see himself in those begging eyes and that cut through his heart.

It was later that night when his phone rang. 'Excuse me for a moment?' he said to the man in front of him at the counter. Always polite to people no matter what their attitude to him.

'Matt? It's Zoe.'

For a minute he couldn't say anything. His throat constricted. 'Thanks for ringing me,' he managed to blurt out.

'Would you like to meet some time?'

'Yes. I'd love that,' he said, unable to believe this was happening.

There was a bit of fuss among the men who had gathered at the counter. One particularly noisy individual had broken the queue and had pushed the man Matt was dealing with to one side.

'Come on you, get off that phone. We're waiting here.' His voice was thick and he was drunk, holding a bottle of beer in his hand.

'What day would suit you?' Zoe asked.

'Any day.'

'The weekend would be best for me. How about Saturday morning?'

The man was getting very irate with him.

'Can you hold on for a moment?' he said to Zoe and moved towards the man. 'If you don't calm down you'll be put out.' He grabbed the bottle out of his hand. 'Now get back into the queue.'

The man reacted angrily. 'Gimme that.'

The other men behind began to push the inebriated man out of their way.

The porter appeared, a look of concern on his face.

'Put him out,' Matt instructed reluctantly.

Peter was a heavy-set man and well able to handle most of the men who came into the shelter who were only lightweight when compared to him.

'No, please, please, don't put me out …' The angry man suddenly collapsed in tears.

'Come on you.' Peter grabbed him, and forced him to walk through the door.

Matt lifted his phone again, but Zoe had gone.

'Fuck.' He curled his hand into a fist and thumped it angrily on the ledge under the counter. It was painful.

He dealt with the rest of the men who were calm now. All very meek and thankful as they accepted the clothes he had to give them.

Zoe didn't call back that night and when eventually he had allocated the beds and space which were available, he joined the group who were going over to O'Connell Street to hand out food and clothes to those who hadn't got a bed and were going to sleep rough.

He felt guilty that he had had to leave the phone, and now hoped that Zoe hadn't got the impression that he didn't want to meet her. He whispered a prayer to his mother. He sometimes did that. Always feeling that she was looking over him.

His prayer was answered and Zoe rang early the following morning. He was serving breakfasts but just stepped outside into the corridor for a moment.

'I'm sorry about last night, another call came through,' she apologised.

'No problem, it was my fault.'

'I wasn't sure if you'd be up so early, but I took a chance.'

'I'm always up early,' he smiled.

'I suggested Saturday, would that suit?'

'Yes,' he said.

'There's a coffee shop at the top of Grafton Street, it's the first one on the left as you go down. Do you know it?'

'Yes,' he said, but didn't know where it was. He wasn't up that way too often.

'Say eleven o'clock?' she suggested.

Chapter Nineteen

'Gail, would you consider talking with Matt sometime?' Zoe asked gently.

'I don't want to see that shit ever again.'

Zoe ignored her remark and continued. 'It's just …I'm meeting him on Saturday and I'm sure he would like to see you, just to talk, even for a few minutes …it would mean a lot to him,' she said.

'No, I couldn't. I'm busy, I have that big concert in Croke Park, so it will be really crazy for the weekend. It's on for three nights. I could get you tickets for Friday if you want?'

'No thanks, I have to see Russell and finalise things, the office isn't the place to do that so we've arranged to meet at the apartment.'

'I don't know how you put up with meeting him in the office every day.'

'We've both been away on business trips so I've managed to avoid him a lot of the time.'

It had been hard the first couple of weeks after New Year when everyone came back to work and the news that they hadn't got married filtered out. She had to deal with a lot of sympathetic looks and concerned words from her staff and found that very difficult.

Now she had to meet Russell face to face to discuss how they would deal with their personal financial arrangements. She dreaded the thought of it.

Initially they were going to split the expenses for the wedding fifty-

fifty, whatever the costs were now would still be treated like that. Zoe had saved enough money for her half of the wedding and honeymoon. As her father had agreed that she could come home, living there temporarily would ease her financial burden. Although as Gail already shared the expenses at home with her father, now that figure would be divided in three.

They went through the various invoices in silence. It was very awkward, and Zoe found Russell's attitude hostile to say the least.

'I think that we should reimburse your parents for the costs involved at the house,' she suggested.

'No, that's not necessary,' he had immediately snapped. 'They don't expect it.'

'I think it's only fair,' Zoe said.

'I'll deal with all of that.'

'But I'd like to help.'

'We don't want to have anything to do with you again,' Russell retorted, 'And particularly my mother after the way you treated her on the phone.'

Her stomach dropped, and she literally felt sick. But she took a deep breath and tried to hide her upset at his remark. 'How is she now?'

'As you can imagine, her whole life has been turned upside down.' He picked up a sheaf of papers. 'I've just made a note of a few items, but as I wasn't involved in the organisation of it, I've only a vague idea of the final figure.'

Zoe opened up her iPad. 'Some of the companies have been really nice. My friend who was doing the flowers managed to cancel the order so there is no charge there. And the lads in the band have said they won't charge either. My hairdresser and the beautician are the same. Everybody has been so generous.'

He made no comment.

'Most of the people which Sylvia dealt with are making a cancellation charge. The marquee. The caterers. The photographer and various other things. She's very upset that the wedding is off and is doing her best to minimize the loss.'

'She came down to see us,' he said.

'The figure is approximately eighteen thousand euro and that includes your suit, the groomsman, my wedding dress and Gail's dress.'

'Right, that's nine thousand euro each?' he asked.

She nodded.

'I'll transfer that into your bank account,' he said, making a note of the figure. 'Now, I'll see you at our usual meeting on Monday morning, eight o'clock.' He was immediately into business mode.

He did that best, she thought. Even when she had fallen in love with him they had been working together for a number of years and she should have realised what he was like. They were both workaholics, their personal lives pushed aside until business was done and it was convenient. Looking at him now, his dark good looks reminded that perhaps it was a physical attraction. He only had to touch her and she would tingle, longing to be in his arms at the most inappropriate moments. Embrace him in the lift if they happened to be alone. Hold his hand underneath the desk as they sat down to a high-powered meeting or move her thigh against his just to remind him that there was more between them than just business. But Russell couldn't understand that, and never responded. It was a miracle their relationship had ever blossomed and now she felt it had only happened because they were away on business in Paris and he had too many glasses of cognac.

'Is that OK for you?' he asked with a snap of impatience in his voice.

She nodded.

'I've heard from the company in Poland who are interested in our products and licences, and I'll send you their response.'

She looked at him and her pulse raced. How would she live without him, she wondered. Had he really been essential to her existence? Was he part of her? Or was that too dramatic altogether?

'Right.' He stood up.

Their meeting was obviously over.

'Oh, there's something …' She put her hand into her bag, took out a small black ring box and handed it to him. He accepted it in silence. 'And the keys.' She put them on the table.

'That's a marker,' Gail said. 'And it's a good thing. All wrapped up and tied with a bow. The end. Or maybe I'm being harsh?'

'No, I suppose it is an accurate description. I've begun to realise that it really is the end and I'll have to accept it. Like the last chapter in a book.'

'We'll be two old maids,' Gail laughed. 'Going off on holidays with our father.'

'He wouldn't go anywhere with us. Never was a holiday man.'

'And he's become even more of a recluse. Have you noticed he's scribbling away in his notebook all the time these days. Every time I see him he has it with him.'

'I've suggested he should write a book.'

'It would be good for him. But a man who keeps himself to himself like he does will never reveal his deepest thoughts,' Gail said, a serious tone in her voice.

After dinner, they sat together. As usual, their father was writing and took little notice of the programme which was on television. As he turned another page, a piece of paper slipped out and drifted to the floor.

Zoe bent down and picked it up. 'You dropped this, Dad.' She handed it to him but not before she had a chance to notice the wording of the first line.

It read.

'Dear Matt, I am so sorry that I have been so cruel towards you …'

Her father immediately crumpled it in his hand.

She didn't say anything. Why was her father writing to Matt? And why apologise? She couldn't imagine that ever happening, they had always violently disagreed about everything and had seemed to hate each other. After his attitude towards him on Christmas Eve this was the last thing she would have expected him to do.

Zoe arrived at the café on Saturday morning. The place was busy with a warm atmosphere, the aroma of brewed coffee drifting. Matt was already waiting for her. He stood up when he saw her.

She walked through the tables and stretched out her hand to him. He took it, and pressed it gently, but stood awkwardly as if he didn't know her at all.

'Let's sit down,' she said.

The waitress arrived at the table and handed each of them a menu.

'What would you like, Matt? Fancy the full Irish breakfast? They do a good one here.'

'No thanks, just a coffee for me.'

'That's two coffees, *Americano,* Matt?'

He nodded.

'And I'm going to have a fruit scone. Would you like one?'

'No thank you,' he murmured.

'Jam and cream?' the waitress asked.

'Yes, why not? I'll treat myself,' she smiled at Matt and leaned her elbows forward on the table, immediately aware that he had drawn away from her, sitting back fully in the chair. 'Since you came to the house, I've wanted to get in touch and have a talk,' she said gently.

'I timed it very badly,' he said.

'And thank you for the Christmas presents.'

He smiled.

'We enjoyed them.'

'I'm glad.'

She paused for a moment. There was something she wanted to know, and felt reluctant about asking. But she had to. 'Did you have a particular reason for coming over to see us at Christmas?'

'Someone suggested it might be a good time but it didn't turn out like that.'

'So there was nothing special you wanted to say?' Zoe pressed him, suddenly disappointed.

'There are a million things …I wanted to see all of you again, I missed you …it's so lonely …you've no idea.' His eyes were bleak, a darkness in their depths.

The girl brought the coffees and the scone and set it out on the table, with milk, sugar, cream and a little pot of strawberry jam. They busied themselves for a few minutes. She noticed that he didn't take milk or sugar and drank the coffee black as she did herself. And also that he blessed himself before he took that first sip of coffee.

She cut the scone and spread jam and cream. 'Would you fancy half? There's enough …'

'No thanks, the coffee's fine.'

'Your loss,' she laughed and bit into the crumbly scone mixture with relish. 'Delicious.'

'It looks tasty.'

'I only allow myself an occasional sweet treat, otherwise I would be the size of a house.'

'You were always thin as I remember.'

'Tell me, where have you been living since …?'

'In a homeless shelter.'

'How did that happen?'

'I was helped by the nun who runs the place and one thing led to another.'

'Were you living on the street?'

'On and off.'

'You should have let us know,' she said, very concerned.

'I didn't want you to see me like that.'

'I can understand, but I could have helped with money.'

'Thank you, but I've enough now.'

'Are you living on the dole?'

'I get supplementary welfare which is just under two hundred, and I was allowed to use the shelter's address. Sr. Teresa is a very generous person.'

'How can you live on that amount of money?'

'I have very little expenses and I'm trying to save enough for a deposit on a flat, although everyone says it's almost impossible to get a place.' He went on to explain what he did at the shelter.

'You're amazing.' She was astonished.

He shook his head. 'They're very good to me, and I like to help people, anyway it's going to be very hard for me to get a regular job.'

'What was it like …all those years?'

He shrugged.

'What did you do to pass the time?'

'There are jobs and you get paid a small amount.'

'I'm sure it's not very much.'

'No,' he smiled.

She popped the last piece of scone into her mouth, caught her breath on the crumbs and began to cough.

'Try the milk,' he said and handed the jug to her.

She sipped it and after a moment or two managed to get the coughing under control.

'Are you all right?' he asked.

'That's what I get for my greediness.'

It was the first time that an element of relaxation had come between them.

'Another coffee?' she asked. 'I'm going to have one.'

'No thanks.'

She ordered another, but really it was just to give her an opportunity to talk some more with Matt.

'I'm sorry for what happened on Christmas Eve,' she said. 'To be honest, I hadn't told Dad that I had visited you in prison. When I knew you were released I told Gail, but said nothing to Dad so it was a shock to him.'

'I thought he looked frail,' he said.

'He is.'

'I take the blame for that.'

She didn't reply.

'How is he?'

'He's not great.'

'Did he say anything after I had been there on Christmas Eve?'

'No, although he was very upset.'

'And Gail?'

'I have to tell you she doesn't want to meet you again.'

There was a cloud of moisture across his eyes.

Zoe felt for him, aware of how unhappy he must feel about that.

'I went down to Ballystrand,' he told her.

Her eyes brightened. 'I was there myself before Christmas.'

'It was something I had wanted to do for a long time.'

'I like to go to the cemetery occasionally.'

'I went there as well.' He bent his head, and said nothing for a moment or two. 'I'd better be going.'

'I'll get the bill.' She waved to the waitress who brought it over.

He immediately picked it up and handed her twenty euro.

'Let me …' Zoe insisted.

'I want to. This is the first chance I've got to buy my sister a coffee and a scone …' Matt smiled at her.

The waitress took it, returned quickly with the change and put it on the table.

Matt put his hand out to take it, but then hesitated, uncertain. 'How much should I leave for a tip,' he asked Zoe.

'That's enough.' She put the coins in the box.

'There are things I don't know,' he admitted awkwardly.

'Don't worry, you'll pick it up in no time.'

'I feel so stupid.'

'Matt, don't say such a thing.'

He smiled at her. 'What does Gail do?' he asked after a moment.

'She's in event management. Organising concerts.'

'Sounds interesting. I feel really weird that I don't know much about my family.'

'And I'm still in *RZ Gaming,*' she said. 'Remember I told you about that.'

His face lit up. 'I didn't mention this when you came to see me.' He went on to tell her that he had done a degree in computer programming. But suddenly, the excitement of a moment ago had disappeared and was replaced by a look of remorse. 'Although I know it's going to be very hard to get a job with my record.'

She immediately thought of employing him herself but knew that Russell wouldn't tolerate that. 'I have to admire you for getting a degree while in prison. That's some achievement.'

'I had to do something. Otherwise, I could have gone down the drug route again, it's so easy to get them inside.'

She remembered visiting him in prison. Going through those heavy doors. Unlocked by the guards. Searched by them to see what she was carrying. It had been a nightmare experience. And when she saw Matt and realised what he had to endure it broke her heart.

Now she was impressed with him. Particularly how well he looked. Spotlessly clean. Dark hair cut tight. A narrow beard. And wearing a black tee shirt, jeans, and anorak. They walked out together into a busy Grafton Street, full of Saturday morning shoppers.

'Thanks for meeting me.' He held out his hand to her and she took it and held it tight for a moment.

He had a firm handshake, his skin smooth and warm and she felt a rush of emotion. Remembering him as a boy catching her and Gail by the hands and whirling them around, all of them screaming with excitement in the garden in Ballystrand. Now she wanted to put her arms around him, hug him tight and never let him go again, ever. But she hesitated, perhaps it wasn't the time yet. 'Would you meet me again?' she asked.

'Yes, I'd love to.'

'This is for you ...' She pulled an envelope from her pocket and handed it to him. She felt awkward about giving him money, but knew that he needed it.

'Thank you, Zoe, but I'm doing all right …' he seemed embarrassed.

'Matt, it's a gift,' she insisted.

'Thank you so much, you're very generous.'

She smiled up at him. 'It's been really great to see you.'

'And you …'

Then without a thought she threw her arms around him and held him tight.

Chapter Twenty

Matt's meeting with Zoe had a huge effect on him. To have contact with his family after all these years was mind-blowing and he found it difficult to get Zoe out of his head in the following weeks, all the time expecting her to walk in the door.

He realised that she had been shocked to hear he lived in a homeless shelter, and felt ashamed of himself. He had hoped he might be lucky enough to get some sort of job in IT but there was something in Zoe's expression that immediately made him feel that this was probably going to be very unlikely. But her gift of five hundred euro was so generous it really made up for his money which had been stolen. He would be forever grateful to her. Now he had enough money to repay Tom, his Probation Officer.

When Matt met him the following Monday, he offered it to him, but Tom refused. 'Keep it, Matt, you need it more than I do.'

'You're very generous, thank you. Zoe gave me money and I wanted to repay you. Suddenly I can't believe how well off I am.'

'You met Zoe?'

'She's a wonderful person.'

'Is there any chance of you moving home?'

He shook his head. 'My father would be against that.'

'Maybe in time, who knows?'

Matt told Tom about his father and his two sisters. It felt good to talk about his family.

'It's a coincidence that Zoe is in IT. Any chance she might give you a recommendation for a job?'

'No, I knew by her expression.'

'Pity.'

'If it came out that the latest employee had spent all that time in prison it could be the end of her own career, and I can't even bear the thought of what that might mean.'

'I have to say you've done well, Matt, I don't think you'll slip back to where you were …foolish, hot headed …but you've matured and it's good to see you're not a danger to the community any longer,' Tom said with a grin.

'I hope not.' *A danger to the community.* Those words had an ominous ring. Most people were put away because they were exactly that, and only given their freedom again when they had completed the appropriate sentence which had been handed down by the judge. But he knew many were habitual offenders who only played a waiting game in prison, enjoying the benefits of a life without any responsibility. A place where they were fed and clothed. Where they could access drugs if they wanted them. And in many cases could still organise their criminal organisations from inside. Everything could be bought in prison, even the guards, if they played the right game.

He had called Zoe later that day they met and thanked her for meeting him and for giving him so much money. And she definitely seemed enthusiastic about seeing him again and he was glad of that, it was the first step back into his family.

They met again the following week, and the week after that too. It was a gradual growing together. On that first occasion, he had felt very awkward and found it hard to even think of anything to say to her. To sit at a table in a cafe drinking coffee with his sister was something he could never have imagined. When she came to see him in prison he could hardly talk at all. What do you to say to someone you have only met a couple of times in twelve years?

'What about girls, have you met anyone?' she had asked that last time, with a smile.

He shook his head, feeling shy about the whole subject. He remembered how shocked he was to see the beautiful girls and women who walked the streets when he came out of prison at first. He was so attracted to them, and found it hard to handle the sexual desire which swept through him, something which he hadn't experienced since he was a teenager. While a lot of men put posters of women up on the wall around their beds in the cells, he only put up a token one in case the lads thought he was gay.

'No one at all?'

'There are girls around the shelter, the volunteers, but I don't think it would be my place to make a pass at any of them. We're all working and I don't think Sr. Teresa would be too impressed,' he laughed.

'But don't you go out with anyone for a drink?'

'No, I don't drink any more. I did enough of that when I was a teenager. I hope I'm more mature now or should be.' He tried to be honest.

'You're a very different person altogether to the one I remember.'

'We hated each other back then,' he had to admit.

'Sibling rivalry. You were the eldest and seemed to get everything. We felt left behind.'

'Negative attention mostly. Driving the parents mad. Particularly Dad. He was always strict and I resented that. And he was disappointed I had no interest in lighthouses, but I suppose I was only a kid then and it was a bit much to expect.'

'Do you ever think about …' she hesitated, but then continued on. 'What happened at the trial?'

He looked into her blue eyes and was swept back in time to those days in Ballystrand when they played on the beach and swam in the sea. In his memory the sky was always blue and the sun was shining.

He always ran to his Mum if anything went wrong. She was so loving and always came between his father and himself, arms out to protect him.

'To be honest, I can't remember what happened. It's a blank in my mind.'

'Why did you admit guilt in court?'

'They showed me some photographs.' It was very hard for him to even think about that time.

They were quiet for a while.

'Did you get any counselling?' Zoe asked.

'No. But I have a Probation Officer. He's a nice man.'

'I'd like to meet him,' she said.

'Funny,' he smiled. 'He said the same thing.'

'Maybe we could get together?'

'I'll mention it to him.'

Zoe met Matt and Tom Sheridan a couple of weeks later at the usual place on Grafton Street.

'It's good to meet you, Zoe.' He held her hand firmly.

'And you …thanks for everything you've done for Matt,' Zoe wanted to let him see how grateful she was.

'I think very highly of your brother. He's done well in prison and deserves help.' He had deep hazel eyes, and a warm candid look in his expression. 'Is there anyone else in the family who might be sympathetic?'

She shook her head.

'I believe you are in the IT business?'

'Yes, the gaming industry.'

'You might see an opportunity for Matt, he's an excellent computer programmer.'

Zoe felt very uncooperative. And guilty too, knowing she was deliberately refusing to help him. 'Honestly, I don't hold out much hope in our own company.' She looked at Matt with sympathy. 'Sorry.'

'Maybe you might think about it?' Tom suggested.

'I certainly will,' she smiled. Caught in his gaze she was suddenly disarmed.

'Maybe we might meet again?' he asked.

'I'd like that.'

Chapter Twenty-one

Russell's father, Clive, returned to the office. He had taken his wife, Jean, away on an extended holiday because she was so upset about the wedding debacle. Immediately, Zoe went to see him anxious to talk. She knocked on his office door and heard his voice tell her to come in. 'Clive?' She crossed the office to the large heavy mahogany desk behind which he now sat going through his post.

'Zoe?' He immediately rose and came around, his arms wide open in embrace. They stood together for a moment but neither said a word. She could feel tears well up in her eyes as his soft cheek touched hers. Then, he stood back and looked at her. 'How's it going for you?' he whispered.

'Not so bad.' She leaned into his shoulder again and let herself relax. At home, she was keeping up a front, giving the impression that she was holding it all together as she did with her work colleagues and friends, but somehow with Clive, she felt she could be herself.

'Come, let's talk.' With his arm around her shoulders he walked her over to an armchair and sat her down. 'I'll just lock the door, we don't want to be interrupted.' He took the remote control from his drawer, pressed the button and the door locked automatically.

'Tell me what happened?' he asked, and poured two cups of coffee. He handed one to her. Clive always had fresh coffee ready in a percolator, despising what was available in the office.

'Russell didn't tell you?'

'No.'

'You may be shocked.'

'Nothing shocks me nowadays.'

'I know it was a difficult time for Jean …and I feel guilty. I'd like to see her, but wanted to ask your opinion first.'

'I'm sure she'll be happy to meet. But give her some time to settle in back home after the trip.' He patted her hand. 'How have you managed with work. It must have been difficult.'

'I've been on a couple of quick business trips, Paris and Berlin. Fly in, having a meeting, fly out. Two days max in Europe. Almost a week in Japan. But we've nailed that deal with the Japanese which is worth a lot of money.'

'So I heard,' he grinned. 'And all thanks to you, someone tells me.'

'Russell?' Zoe was surprised to hear that.

'No, it was one of your sales team, they're all delighted with the result.'

She wasn't surprised at that. Russell wouldn't give her credit for anything now.

'You haven't told me why you broke up with Russell. I'd like to know why I've lost a lovely daughter-in-law.' He sat back in his comfortable leather chair.

She hadn't really planned this, and didn't actually know what she was going to say but decided that if she was to tell anyone outside her immediate circle then it should be Clive.

She explained what had happened on Christmas Eve.

'You mean to say Russell refused to marry you because your brother had been in prison?' Clive was astonished. 'Was it a very serious crime?'

'Yes.' She was reluctant to give the full detail.

'What is your brother's name?'

'Matthew …Matt.'

He jotted it down.

'I seem to recall the name from my law days. What year was the court case?'

'Two thousand and six.'

'Yes, that would be before I retired from the Bench. I remember his case. After Matthew had been sentenced, myself and my brother expressed a doubt that it had been a good result. Of course, he only had legal aid, but if he had people like us representing him there might have been a very different outcome, and perhaps he would have been cleared on the grounds of diminished responsibility.'

'We weren't allowed to follow the case, we were younger than Matt and my father kept us away from court and sent us to stay with an aunt. It was much later on when I looked it up online.'

'Understandable.'

'When it all blew up on Christmas Eve, Russell walked into the middle of it. It was a big shock for him to realise that I had a brother who had served a prison sentence. I had intended to tell him before we were married but somehow the opportunity never presented itself. It's my fault that the wedding is off and that you and Jean spent so much money on the house and having the garden re-designed.'

'We can pick up the tab for all that, so don't worry,' Clive reassured.

'I hope Jean will meet me soon.'

'I'm sure she will.'

'I wouldn't like to lose contact.'

'That won't happen, and you and I will see each other in the office.'

Zoe still found it difficult to deal with the bitter atmosphere between herself and Russell. Initially, when she had gone back to work after New Year, she had dreaded seeing him at all, and as for speaking to him face to face, that was even harder, as he treated her like someone who had stolen the cash out of the safe.

Zoe wondered if he would offer to buy out her shareholding in *RZ Gaming* so that he could get rid of her altogether but as yet there had been no mention of that. There were only three shareholders. In the beginning, Russell and Zoe had established the company. Russell invested ninety per cent, Zoe ten per cent. When they needed extra financial assistance in the earlier stages, his father, Clive, had stepped in and bought up some of Russell's shares.

Then a thought pushed itself into her mind. What if she sold her shares, left the company and set herself up in another business? But to start all over after such achievement in *RZ* would certainly be a cruel hardship when she thought about the plans they had for the future of the company.

Later that week, she received a call from Clive inviting her to Langton on Saturday for dinner. She was so glad that Jean was willing to forgive her for all the upset, and hoped that Russell wouldn't be there. She drove down early hoping she would have a chance to talk to her before anyone else arrived if it was a bigger gathering, but hoped it would just be the three of them. As she swung the car into the circular gravel driveway, her feelings of loss were somehow much more intense than she had expected, remembering that she would have been married in this beautiful place if everything had gone according to plan.

She climbed out of her car, and took a bouquet of flowers and a bottle of champagne from the back seat. She needed to make an entry at least. Clive appeared at the top of the steps and came down to meet her. 'Thanks for coming, it's lovely to see you. It's been so busy in the office there's been no time to chat.' He kissed her and took her by the hand into the hallway. 'Jean is in the sitting room, come on in.'

'How is she?' Zoe asked.

'She's doing much better than she was,' he said and ushered her through.

Zoe walked over and kissed Jean on the cheek. 'Jean, I'm so sorry about everything.' She handed the bouquet to her.

'How pretty,' she murmured vaguely, putting them on a side table close to her.

'And champagne too.' She handed the bottle to Clive.

'Thanks so much,' he smiled. 'Right, I'll put this on ice. In the meantime, what would you like to drink, Zoe?'

'I'm driving, so I'll have something soft. Anything at all.' She felt awkward after Jean's rather cool reception.

'I'll get you a glass of Kitty's apple juice, back in a minute.'

'Is there a vase for the flowers?' Zoe asked.

'Certainly, there will be one in the kitchen.' He picked up the bouquet.

Zoe sat opposite the older woman. 'How are you now, Jean, I hope you're feeling better?' she smiled, unsure how to approach her, considering what had happened.

'How do you think?' She turned her pale eyes on Zoe, anger in their depths.

'I'm sure it's all been very upsetting for you.'

'It's been a nightmare, you've no idea.'

'I'm very sorry such a thing happened, I deeply regret it,' Zoe said softly.

Jean sniffed.

'Did you enjoy your trip to California?'

'I did.'

'And your family are all well?'

She nodded.

'It must have been nice to see them.'

Clive came back with a jug of apple juice and glasses on a tray. He set them out on a low table. 'Jean, would you like another sherry or some juice?'

'Top up my sherry.'

'Right you are.' He picked up the bottle and poured. 'Say when?'

He handed Zoe a glass of juice. 'Thanks Clive,' she said.

She noticed he didn't receive either a smile or a *thank you* from Jean.

Kitty came in with the vase of flowers. 'Where will I put these?' she asked Jean.

'Over there …' she motioned in the direction of a small table in a corner practically out of sight behind the grand piano.

'Clive, I was saying to Jean that I very much regret what happened between Russell and I.'

'We all do, Zoe.'

'Particularly my friends and family, Zoe,' snapped Jean. 'It hurt me deeply to have to tell them that the wedding was off. They were so shocked. It was extremely embarrassing to say the least. I can't think of a word to describe the feeling. I had to have two sessions with a therapist before I went to California. Imagine that? I never needed therapy before and now I can't get through the day without medication.'

'Sylvia has been a great help,' Clive intervened.

'I couldn't have got through it without her, this Christmas has been the worst in my life.'

'She's coming tonight, it will be pleasant to talk to her,' Clive said.

Now Zoe felt like she was going to be up in court. Held to blame for this catastrophe and asked to explain why she had allowed it to happen.

The doorbell rang.

'That must be her.' Clive rose and went to answer it.

Zoe could hear voices chatting in the hall and then Sylvia floated in, glamorous as ever in a smart turquoise coat. Zoe stood up, but Sylvia went towards Jean immediately, kissed her and then handed her a small gift bag. 'How are you Jean?'

'Not much better really.'

'We'll cheer you up,' she said and turned to Zoe.

'Hello, Sylvia.' She held out her hand.

'You poor thing, how are you managing now?' She enveloped her in a warm embrace.

'I'm fine, thanks.'

'It must have been so hard on you.' She gave her another quick hug.

'Not as bad as it has been for us,' Jean muttered.

'I'll take your coat,' Clive said and helped her off with it, hurrying into the hall where he put it away in the cloakroom.

'The bride and the bridegroom are the hardest hit when something like this happens. I've had a number of cancelled marriages over the years and I can tell you it's extremely traumatic.'

'Surely it's just as bad for the parents?' Jean asked.

'They must be supportive of their children. That most of all.'

'No-one thinks of us, we're the ones who need support not the children who have caused it.'

'I'm sure you don't mean that now, Jean, you were never a selfish person.'

Jean said nothing.

'An aperitif, Sylvia?' Clive asked.

'Driving as usual, Clive. What a life it is. I can't go anywhere and have a drink.'

'Kitty's apple juice?'

'I would love some, thank you.'

'You should take a taxi?' Jean suggested.

'It's a bit of a distance, and a taxi would be too expensive.'

There was a discreet tap on the door and Kitty came in. 'Dinner is served.'

'Thank you, Kitty.' Clive was on his feet smartly and ushered Jean and the others through into the dining room.

Now Zoe was very glad Sylvia was there. Jean was in such a bad humour it was very difficult to make any conversation with her. But Sylvia kept the chat going, always a story to tell which had them in a state of continuous laughter.

The food was delicious. Salmon. Roast rack of lamb, vegetables, and plum tart for dessert.

'Kitty is a wonderful cook,' commented Zoe.

'She is indeed. We are lucky to have her,' Jean agreed with a wide smile as Kitty came in with a trolley.

'I could take a few lessons,' Sylvia groaned. 'How about that, Kitty?'

'Any time,' she smiled, obviously pleased.

Afterwards they sat in the conservatory and had coffee.

'I presume you still have your wedding dress, all the accessories and Gail's dress too?' Sylvia asked.

'Yes, although I haven't thought much about them. They will gather dust on top of the wardrobe no doubt.'

'If I had an offer for them, would you be interested?'

Zoe was surprised. 'Is it possible that a bride would buy someone else's dress?'

'There are a lot of people with different budgets and it's never been worn or Gail's either.'

'But what about the bad luck attached to it?' Jean didn't sound very enthusiastic.

'If a person finds a beautiful dress and it is reduced in price that's all they're interested in, and a bride won't worry about the fact that someone else owned it before her.'

'Thanks so much, Sylvia, I really appreciate it.'

'I'm shocked,' Jean burst out. 'My wedding dress and veil are still in layers of tissue paper in the attic. I wouldn't dream of selling them.'

'You can keep it for sentimental reasons. For Zoe it's different. She has had a great deal of expense and if she can sell it all the better. Anyway, she doesn't want to be reminded ...'

Zoe was very surprised. She would never have expected Sylvia to be so understanding.

Clive nodded.

'Leave it with me,' Sylvia smiled at Zoe, looking as if she was delighted to get one over on Jean.

'It seems very cheap, somehow,' Jean muttered. 'Like the way people sell their stuff on line.'

'If Zoe can sell the dresses through Sylvia then that's the best way to go,' Clive said. 'More coffee anyone?' he asked then, picking up the coffee pot.

The evening came to an end shortly after that. It had been surprisingly pleasant and even Jean seemed to be in better form when they said goodbye.

'We should have driven down together,' suggested Zoe, as they walked to their cars.

'I didn't know you'd be here,' Sylvia laughed.

'Or I you.'

'Let me know if you decide to sell your dresses, Zoe.'

'I'll think about it.' She had almost decided but didn't want to commit herself yet.

'We shouldn't lose contact either.'

'No, I'll be in touch.'

'See you soon.' Sylvia hugged her.

'Take care on the road.'

Zoe drove back feeling she had found a friend. There was something very genuine about Sylvia which had never struck her before. And she did intend to keep in touch if she could. It was always very difficult to see her friends because of work, and had been hard enough to sustain a relationship with Russell.

Now she wondered whether a marriage in the normal sense of the word would have ever been possible between them.

Chapter Twenty-two

It was the first scheduled Board Meeting this year and Zoe had just flown in from Madrid the night before where she had been discussing a deal with a Spanish client. There were just eight of them on the Board. Clive was Chairman, Russell, Chief Executive Officer, Zoe, Sales and Marketing Director, the IT, HR, and Accounts Directors and two directors from outside the company.

They discussed the accounts for the previous year and talked about the figures. One of the directors was resigning and they had to appoint another. They talked about the expansion of the company in Japan which had gone very well. The next stage was China and they were hopeful for success there too.

'I'll handle the Chinese expansion myself,' Russell said.

'But surely Zoe has all the experience with Japan, it's a very similar society,' the Accounts Director pointed out.

'Yes, I'd agree with that,' Clive said.

'I've been mostly dealing with the US,' Russell said. 'And I would like a further challenge.'

'Zoe has done very well in the Japanese market,' added Clive.

'What side are you on?' snapped Russell.

'I'm not on any particular side, I have the company's interest at heart. It's just that I feel Zoe is the most suitable person to carry the company further into the east,' Clive insisted.

'The Chinese won't be easy to deal with,' Russell warned.

'We all realise that.'

'It's a huge country and it mightn't succeed at all. Therefore, it's my responsibility,' he insisted.

'We'll take a vote on it,' Clive said.

Russell looked very put out.

The secretary put it to the Board.

They raised their hands and it was a unanimous vote for Zoe, with the exception of Russell.

They went on to *Any Other Business*, and the HR Director proposed an item.

'I'm sorry, Russell and Zoe, but from my point of view I do feel that your personal relationship is affecting the company negatively. This decision about China has been made because Russell wants to control Zoe.'

'That's ridiculous, I don't want to control Zoe,' Russell retorted.

'Your personal view of Zoe is influencing the way the company is run on a day to day basis and on into the future.'

'I don't think Russell is behaving in any particular way towards me, he has his own thoughts on the matter of China and he's entitled,' Zoe was astonished.

'You may not see it the same way as we do,' the Accounts Director insisted. 'And there is another matter …' she hesitated and looked down at her notes.

The rest of the members around the table listened attentively.

'Since the New Year a very unpleasant atmosphere has infected the company generally. You, Russell, are unapproachable a lot of the time, and while we have always had a very open policy among the directors and staff, now people feel they certainly don't have that with you, Russell. On many occasions people's heads have been practically bitten off by you when they call in to your office to discuss some subject or other.'

'That's certainly true,' the IT Director added.

Russell's face was flushed and he looked as if he was about to explode.

'For some strange reason, your rather unpleasant attitude has permeated down to lower management heads and staff are feeling under extreme pressure. This is a very serious situation.'

Zoe was astonished. As she was away quite a bit, she hadn't been aware of this situation, and none of the staff had mentioned it.

'Have there been many complaints about myself?' Zoe asked.

The Directors both answered in the negative.

'Are you sure?' Zoe insisted.

They shook their heads.

'This can't be ignored,' she said.

'How do we know it's true?' Russell demanded.

'It is true,' the Accounts Director said.

'Our one promise to ourselves and our staff when we set up the company was to make sure that anyone who wanted to talk could do so at any time, within reason obviously,' Zoe said firmly.

There was a rather tense silence.

'As there have been extenuating circumstances,' Clive said. 'Perhaps we should give time for this to resolve itself. I know Russell is my son but I hope that I would give anyone else the benefit of the doubt. I suggest that we have a EGM in four weeks' time during which we will gauge whether there has been an improvement in morale generally and that perhaps Russell may be better able to handle the job day-to-day and be more pleasant to the staff.'

'I'm the CEO,' Russell snapped. 'I don't need someone to give me extra time to resolve myself. An EGM is idiotic. The morale in this company has always been top notch. I don't believe a word of it.'

'We'll see how it pans out,' his father said smoothly. 'And there will have to be an improvement in your attitude to your work.'

'This is outrageous,' Russell growled.

'You must keep your personal life outside of the company, you're not entitled to such a luxury,' Clive added.

'The same applies to all of us too. I have to say that I have experienced a certain amount of upset myself but I hope that I haven't impinged on others,' Zoe said.

'I'm not going to put up with this. It's some sort of heave to get me off the Board. Is that what you're doing?' he flashed. 'Well, don't think you're going to succeed, let me tell you that, no way.' He grabbed his files and laptop and marched out of the room banging the door behind him.

There was silence.

'I think we've said everything.' Clive took out his phone and switched it on. 'How about April fifth, ten o'clock?'

The rest of the Board checked their diaries and agreed with the date.

'That's it then.'

Zoe sat at her desk catching up on some work. She couldn't believe what had happened. For Russell to be accused in that manner was amazing. If anyone had to be blamed for inconsistencies of some sort as a result of the breakdown of their marriage plans it surely would have been herself, she thought. But then she rationalised that because she had been away from the office so much she hadn't been aware of people's upset if they were at the butt of Russell's ill-humour. She knew how irrational he could be.

Her door burst open.

'What's all this about?' Russell had a look of venom on his face.

She didn't know quite what to say.

'Don't stare at me in that way as if you don't know what I'm on about. That little farce in there was well orchestrated to put me on the wrong foot. And my father in the middle of it as well, I can't believe it.'

'The Board have decided to have the EGM on April fifth.'

'So I've been given a month to behave myself? What a laugh and I'm the boss of the company. What I say goes, remember that. I'll organise things as I wish.'

'Russell,' she sighed. 'Don't go at it like that. Let's just keep our personal lives out of the office and then no-one has anything to complain about. I'm sure I haven't been perfect either.'

'You certainly haven't.'

'I could let fly any day as well as you. So let's both curb our emotions and things will go back to normal,' she said gently.

'Don't talk to me as if I was a child. You and your cronies can just fuck off.' He stomped out of the office.

She sat there, stupefied.

Now it was even more difficult. Russell treated her abominably when they met to discuss projects. He took no notice at all of her opinions and pushed through his own, forcing her to follow. This treatment made her feel as if she was a junior in the company and had no authority at all. She began to dread coming into work and was only able to operate normally when he happened to be away and she could communicate with him through email.

She began to bring work home in the evenings and avoided Russell. Spent more time with her friends and Gail and sometimes included Sylvia in their outings as she seemed to have few friends and was delighted to be asked along. Gail got tickets for shows of well-known artists and while Zoe would have liked to invite Matt, she knew that Gail wouldn't tolerate it.

The date of the EGM loomed closer and Zoe dreaded the result. Still, she could understand how staff might assume that Russell and she would get together again, and then it could be very awkward for both of them. She hoped that Russell might have realised that. But no-one said anything at all to her, or even indicated by their attitude that they were feeling unhappy.

She rang Matt regularly, and they continued to meet, getting to know each other better, filling in the gaps in their lives. She had been very impressed by the website he designed for the shelter, blown away by the expertise used in its construction. It had links to social media. And had gone through a funding scheme which had raised ten thousand euro. She would have loved to have him working at *RZ*. His talent could be used to the full, and even enhanced with training. Having him on board would add a lot to their business. But her relationship with Russell had deteriorated to such an extent she knew that it would never happen.

Chapter Twenty-three

Gail was glad to have Zoe home, although she was very unhappy that Zoe's engagement to Russell was over. It reminded her of Pierre, her ex-partner, and the time their relationship had collapsed because he was seeing another woman. It had been going on for a year or more apparently and she had been completely unaware of her existence. Looking back there had been signs of course. But she had deliberately ignored them. The phone calls which had been cut off abruptly when she came into the room. The hurried texting and the phone slipped back into his pocket with a look of guilt on his face. He also made some trips to Paris which had no explanation other than to say that he was going to see his brother. Earlier in their relationship she had been brought along too, but this last year he had stopped inviting her.

The final cut happened when she picked up his phone which he had left on the kitchen counter and read a text which had just come in, shocked to see a loving message from someone called Claresse. She had breakfast made by then and as they sat down she tackled him.

'Who is Claresse?' she asked, handing him a plate of warm buttered toast, and pouring his coffee.

'Just someone I know,' he said, biting into the crust.

'The text sounds very intimate.'

He shrugged, sipping his coffee.

'It's a French name isn't it?'

'Yes.' He was busy spreading more butter on his toast.

'Are you having a relationship with her?' She tried to control herself and ask basic questions instead of losing her head.

'No, not a relationship, *chérie.*'

'An affair?' she retorted.

'You could call it that,' he said slowly.

'What about us?'

'It doesn't affect us.'

'How is that?'

'I still love you.'

'You've a strange way of showing it.'

'*C'est la vie,*' he said lightly.

'Do you love her?'

'In some ways.'

'How can you love us both?'

'Why not?'

She was nonplussed. French men had a different approach to love and she was aware of that. They were together for six years, and had been very happy for all of that time.

'I don't want to be part of a threesome. Do you intend to go on with us both in the future?'

'Only if both of you want it.'

'Have you discussed me with her?' She was becoming more annoyed with him.

'On occasion.'

'Where does she live?' she snapped.

'Paris.'

'And you see her when you go over to visit your brother. Very convenient.'

'Sometimes.'

'What does she want?'

'She wants me all to herself of course.'

'And is waiting to jump into my shoes?'

'I don't want her to do that. I like things the way they are.'

'The best of both worlds?' she asked, with an edge of sarcasm in her voice.

'It suits me. She's not an easy person to live with. Anyway, she has a husband.'

'What?'

'I don't think she will ever leave him.'

'She sounds like a right bitch.' She almost spat at him.

'It's not unusual in France.'

'If she doesn't leave her husband and I leave you, what will you do then?'

'I'll be OK.' He shrugged.

So bloody French. She thought. 'You're not the person I thought you were.'

'Perhaps I'm not. People imagine a lot of things.'

'But I trusted you.'

'And I trust you.'

'But I'm not doing anything underhand.' She was furious, unable to believe that this was happening. It was all so bizarre.

'I must go, I have an appointment.' He stood up.

'Go then, get out of my sight.'

He said no more. Just went to get dressed and left.

Gail was distraught. He was so matter of fact about it. She sat sipping her coffee, thinking about her plan to take a cycle ride in the park and call to see a friend. But now she wondered if she even wanted to talk about it, and knew that she wouldn't be able to hide her upset. Her friend would be so sympathetic and that would probably be the worst thing. She stared out the window of the high apartment block and couldn't help bursting into tears. She was caught in the eternal triangle.

In the end, she decided she couldn't put up with it. Every time he went out the door she imagined that he was going to meet Claresse. The two of them together. What did she look like? Was she beautiful? Tall? Leggy? Sexy? She wanted Pierre to say that she wasn't any of those things, and that she was all in her imagination. But he seemed to think she should accept her.

Things became very dark between them as he wanted to continue with the weird threesome. It was too much for Gail. Her job contract was up for renewal soon and that gave her the opportunity to come back to Dublin. Although the company wasn't pleased to see her go, they did give her an open door to return at any point in the future and she was glad about that. Pierre had not changed in his attitude towards her, but she couldn't bear him to touch her and moved into the spare room. That made a definite line of division between them. So many times she wanted to put her arms around him and forget that this situation had ever happened, but she knew that he would respond as he always did. Telling her he loved her. To forget about Claresse. She didn't matter. But Gail couldn't live like that and so she slept in the spare room and lived like a nun. But that even became claustrophobic and she moved out to stay with a friend.

Living back in Dublin now, she would have preferred to have her own apartment and suggested again to Zoe that they might try to find somewhere to share.

'I'm not sure.'

'But I thought you were going to consider it?'

'I know.'

'I feel we don't have our own lives here. Can't bring a fellow back or anything.'

'My financial situation is not good, Gail,' Zoe explained. 'All my savings have gone on the wedding and it's so difficult with Russell. There are days I'd just up and leave, but I can't do that. So until I know exactly what's happening, I'm holding on here. I'm glad really, home is like a soft cushion of support.'

'I suppose Dad needs us here anyway,' Gail said.

'He still seems depressed.'

'Has he said anything about your breakup with Russell?'

'I told him we had split, and he was sympathetic.' Zoe handed her a piece of paper. 'Here, have a look at that.'

'What is it?'

'Another of those half letters.'

'I'm so sorry, I never meant to be so cruel towards you.' Gail read the words aloud.

'What do you think they mean?'

'I'm not sure.'

'Does it refer to the row on Christmas Eve?'

'Maybe.'

'It's surprising to think that he would apologize to Matt.'

'I can't forgive him. He destroyed our family and our home.' Gail wasn't sympathetic.

'It was a terrible time,' Zoe admitted. 'Although we were shielded to some extent being sent over to Auntie Peg.'

'We were lucky she was there for us. That's why I don't want to meet Matt again. I never want to revisit that time.'

'And Dad never talked about it. Not a word. And when I was older I wouldn't have minded talking about it with him but couldn't.'

Gail shook her head, and shuddered. 'No, me neither …'

Chapter Twenty-four

Meeting Zoe so often, Matt had become more positive about his life. His ambitions had soared until that last day when he met Zoe and Tom together, and Tom had asked her if there would be any sympathy in the family for Matt. When she had replied in the negative, his mood had crashed.

He was like all those others who live life on a day to day basis never sure where they will be in the next moment. Blackened fingers hung on to a cliff edge which began to crumble as their weight increased and threatened to collapse altogether and take them with it into another sphere. Flying down into a void. Wind rushing past their ears. Screaming. Screaming.

He sat up in his bed with a jerk and stared into the darkness. Relieved that he had woken up and wasn't still in that terrifying place, falling into nothing. But then he listened for the noise of intruders. What had disturbed him? He threw back the duvet and climbed out of the low narrow bed, pulled on his jeans and fleece and went outside. There were a couple of men lying on the floor in their sleeping bags, but they slept heavily, not a sound out of either.

His feet made no sound on the floor as he walked to the door. He pushed it open and stared out into the corridor. Then he decided to take a look around. It was something he often did. Never a good sleeper, it was an opportunity to keep an eye on the place. But he knew that Rex would have barked if there was an intruder but there was no sound from the dog.

He went into the kitchen, boiled the kettle and made himself a cup of coffee. As he sat there sipping it, he had a strong urge for a line of cocaine. This occasionally happened but tonight he managed to resist the urge, got down on the floor and began to do a few push ups. Starting slowly and then building up to a fast rhythm. His breathing was heavy. His blood pumped. Perspiration studded his skin. The exercise gave him that emotional surge which always made him feel better. He kept up the regime for as long as he could and then began to slow down until he finally lay on the floor again. After a while he pushed himself up. Knowing that he wouldn't sleep now he took a shower and went into the store room. He spent his time sorting clothes until the first of the volunteers came in, and the day began in earnest.

This was it. Each day the same. Each night the same. It was only now since Zoe had come back into his life that he realised how narrow it was. He wanted somewhere to live, but couldn't imagine it happening in the near future. Yet he still longed for his family. And for home.

Chapter Twenty-five

It was the day of the EGM. They met at ten o'clock in the Boardroom and everyone was already there when Zoe arrived. Clive immediately asked for reports from the various Heads of Department about the complaints against Russell.

'There have been less complaints,' the IT Director said. 'But when I followed up with the initial complainants, they didn't feel that Russell had gone out of his way to make them feel better. He was still rather distant.'

The Accounts Director reported a similar response.

'It seems you haven't learned anything, Russell,' Clive said.

'Was I being sent to school?' he snapped.

'We have to adhere to the policy of the company. We need to keep our staff and if we don't our work will suffer and the success of *RZ Gaming* will be at risk.'

'I am *RZ*,' Russell said bluntly.

'But you're not the only person in the company, and if you are the cause of problems then you have to make an effort to sort that out.'

Russell threw the bundle of files in front of him on the desk at his father. They tumbled across his chest and on to the table. There was a shocked silence. A sucking in of breath from the members of the Board. Zoe said nothing. She really couldn't take the chance of drawing Russell's aggression down on herself, it would make her own situation untenable.

The meeting closed and the members of the Board left the room.

'Will you come into my office, Russell and Zoe?' Clive asked.

'You want to give me more hassle?' Russell barked.

'No I don't. But I want to have a chat with you and as it won't be a formal Board Meeting, then it's better in my office.'

He and Zoe left the room, followed by Russell, who had picked up his files from the table and the floor.

Clive stood behind his desk. 'Russell, what is the matter with you,' he demanded.

'Are you playing the Chairman role or the father role?'

'Neither at the moment, I just want to know what is going on with you?'

'There are problems in my life as you both very well know,' he glared at Zoe.

'If you want to change the situation, then you're not going about it in a very sensible way.'

'I don't want to change anything, although I would like to get rid of her. To have to deal with her every day, discussing projects, and attending meetings, is just too much.' He took out his phone and checked it.

Zoe stared at him. She couldn't believe that he had spoken like that about her. That a man who professed to love her a few months ago could now say such things was utterly shocking, and she was deeply upset.

There was silence in the room. Clive said nothing and neither did Zoe.

'If you can think of some way to sort this out, Zoe, I'd appreciate hearing from you, otherwise I don't want to have any contact with you.' Russell left.

'My God,' Clive sighed. 'I didn't think he felt as bad as that. This is a major problem in the company and you must feel really awkward, Zoe.'

'I feel terrible, Clive.'

'The three of us have built up this company into what it is today. But at this rate it could collapse.'

'We have been doing really well and the prospects for the future are bright, but now …' She wiped the tears in her eyes.

'I don't know what I can do.' Clive sat down.

'Maybe I should resign and sell my shareholding?'

'It's been your life,' he said, sympathetic.

She nodded.

'You should do very well by selling your percentage of the shares.'

'But who will offer to buy them?'

'Perhaps Russell will do that himself?'

'Will he be able to raise the funds?' Zoe was uncertain.

'I think you should talk to him,' he said. 'You are being railroaded into selling, and I know you don't want that.'

She shook her head. 'I'll go in to see him when he cools down.'

'I'm sorry this has happened, but one word of advice. Take your time. Try to get into his head and find out what he really wants.'

'That's not going to be easy. I'm not sure if I ever did,' she grimaced.

'Russell always kept himself to himself, he's Jean's boy,' Clive admitted with a nod of his grey head.

Zoe walked along the corridor. Glass walled. All the staff visible to her as they sat at their desks working. She and Russell had planned it this way. The people gathered in hubs. The exception was Clive's office. He was one of the old school and hated the thought that everyone could see what he was doing. Personal areas used by the staff had normal privacy as well. The only rule was that a person should always knock on the door before entering. If the occupant waved you in, fine, if a hand was raised to stop, then you came back later. There were no secretaries as such. Everyone wrote their own emails, and dealt directly with the staff and clients. The system worked well and everyone liked it.

Zoe and Russell had spent a lot of time designing the company when they set it up originally. All jobs were carefully defined and they all understood their own role within the business. She came towards

Russell's office and could see him inside. She was just about to stop and knock when something made her change her mind and she continued on into her own office. At her desk she immediately began to type a report of the meeting. Short though it was, she was anxious to keep it fresh in her mind as it referred directly to herself and Russell. Although everything which had been discussed at the meeting had been recorded as usual, and was available to any of them, it was her immediate reaction she needed to note down and make sure nothing was forgotten.

She typed out her initial thoughts quickly. This wasn't for public viewing so she saved it in a personal file. Reading it back a short time later, she was again shocked that Russell could have behaved in such an appalling way towards her. She printed it out then and deleted the file on her laptop. As she pressed the key, she questioned her logic in doing this. Did she think someone would read her files? Why did she feel suspicious?

Zoe put the sheet of paper into her handbag, and then stared at the screen of the laptop. Trying to look as if she was in deep concentration. She thought again about her conversation with Clive and her own suggestion that she should perhaps leave the company. But that was a very drastic move and she had already begun to have doubts about it. What would she do if and when she left? What was the next move? With her experience, she would surely find another job, but perhaps it might not be at the same level of expertise, or at the same salary. Although she didn't mind so much about that. Maybe she might set up another company if she sold her shares in *RZ* which in itself would be a difficult move. Or could she stay on and put up with Russell's aggression every day? But that was very difficult to endure and she didn't know how long she could put up with it. What was she going to do?

She tried to avoid his presence, particularly at meetings, but he didn't want to have anything to do with her.

'He's being really vicious towards you,' Gail said later.

'I'm very surprised,' Zoe admitted. 'I expected more from him.'

'And the business about Matt, that's not your fault really.'

'But I never told him. That's his main complaint.'

'I suppose he has a point. If you're going to live together for the rest of your lives you must have honesty.'

Zoe nodded.

'It's a bit like Pierre. He actually felt I should accept Claresse and continue on.'

'A little threesome?'

'Exactly. While he still loved me he wanted his little bit on the French side as well.'

'Men,' Zoe sighed.

'But …' Gail hesitated.

Zoe looked at her.

'He's been texting me over the last couple of weeks, and there's been a few emails as well.'

'What's he saying?'

'Wants to talk.'

'And are you talking to him?'

'I've replied to some of the texts and emails, and not to others.'

'Do you think he wants to get together with you again?'

'Seems like that.'

'How do you feel?'

'Confused.' Gail ran a hand through her short red hair.

'Do you still love him?'

'I suppose.'

'It's difficult to cut someone out of your life completely when you've been together for so long and persuade yourself that the love you've always felt for him doesn't exist anymore.'

'He wants to come over next weekend.'

'What have you said?'

'Nothing yet.'

'Do you want to see him?' Zoe asked, smiling.

Gail looked at her, eyes moistening.

'I can understand exactly how you feel. If Russell rang or emailed wanting to see me again I'd be in exactly the same position as you. I've even imagined how it might be. And when the phone rings late at night I instantly stare at the screen to see if it's him and I'm always disappointed.'

'I'm surprised that Pierre made contact at all, I was sure he had hooked up with that French bitch by now.'

'Maybe she turned him down?'

'Then I'm not going to be second choice,' Gail retorted.

'None of us want to be in that position.'

'We'll find new men,' Gail said vehemently.

'Easier said than done,' Zoe reminded. 'It's a harsh world out there and the biggest problem is who to trust.'

'I haven't done well in the trust stakes. I'm not even sure how long Pierre's fling with Claresse was going on.'

'And I've fallen down at the first fence.'

'You're not the sort of person who would hurt Russell deliberately, why can't he see that?'

'I expect he wanted more.'

'Has he been absolutely honest with you?' Gail asked.

'What do you mean?'

'Well, how much do you know of his past life?'

'He had a relationship with another woman before we got together.'

'What happened to her?'

'Don't know. He's not the easiest person to live with, a workaholic, but as we were working at the same pace it wasn't that noticeable.'

'But you've already had doubts about marrying him, haven't you?'

'Yes,' Zoe admitted.

'Then your relationship ended suddenly?'

'And I had no choice in the matter. It was all his decision.'

'What a pair we are,' Gail said, laughing.

'At least we have each other.' Zoe hugged her sister.

Chapter Twenty-six

Feargal went back over his work. Re-reading the pages. Making small changes. Striking out words and inserting new. But then he tore out a complete page, crumpled it up in his hand and threw it towards the bin which was already full of paper. Then the notebook followed and flopped on to the floor. He stared at it for a few minutes, and then went to retrieve it and began to write again.

The front door opened and closed. He raised his head and listened.

'Dad?'

'In here, Zoe.' He continued writing.

'Hi?' She put her head around the door. Crossed the room and kissed his cheek. 'What are you up to?'

'I was cooking and there is a stew in the oven for you,' Feargal said. 'Mrs. Moran took me shopping and then she helped me to cook it.'

'Thank you so much, Dad.' Zoe was astonished. While her father could always cook, he hadn't made dinner for Gail and herself in a long time.

'I was keeping it warm for you.' He led the way into the kitchen. Opened the oven and with two oven gloves he lifted out the dish.

'It smells delicious.'

'I know you always liked a stew,' he smiled, seeming more like his old self.

'I'm looking forward to it.' She took out cutlery and glasses.

'What would you like to drink?' she asked.

'Water, thanks.'

'Me too.' She filled a jug.

They ate. Slowly. She was glad to share the meal with him. It meant a lot. 'This is really tasty, you were always a good cook, Dad. We'll keep some hot for Gail. She'll be in later.'

'I have had some practice,' he said, smiling.

'I'll try and come home earlier in future.'

'Sounds like that would be difficult.'

She shrugged.

'You work too hard. Both you and Gail.'

'It's the way it is. There's no choice. Everyone works hard.'

'How long do you think you'll stay at home?' he asked.

'I'll probably look for a place soon.'

'When?'

'I can't say, these days it's very hard to buy somewhere, or even rent.'

'How are you …without Russell?' he asked.

She didn't answer and concentrated on eating.

'Better off without him maybe.' He finished the last of the lamb on his plate, and wiped his mouth with a paper napkin.

'Probably.'

'Better off …' he repeated.

She put her knife and fork down on the plate and pushed it away from her.

'Maybe I shouldn't have mentioned it …' he hesitated. 'But I've been waiting for an opportunity when we were together.'

'Don't worry.'

'Gail made an apple pie for me, will you have a slice?' He pushed himself up from the table. 'And there's custard, you always used to like that.'

'You've a good memory,' she smiled, surprised.

'Some things stick in your mind.'

'I'm glad.'

'Since you've come home I'm remembering stuff, it's odd.'

She stood up, and lifted their plates. 'You seem in good form these days.' She put them in the washer.

'To have you both here is nice …my two girls. It's been a long time.' He wanted to let her know how much it meant to him. It felt like they were a family again. He cut two slices of pie and poured custard.

'Do you want to heat it?' she asked.

He shrugged. 'Not for me, I'm not fussed.'

'Me neither.'

'Gail would have insisted on everything being piping hot like your mother,' he said.

'Mum and Gail were a lot like each other,' she said slowly.

'Both beautiful.'

'And excitable.'

He touched a glass figurine of a dancer on the window sill. 'Rachel loved that,' he said. 'I keep it clean, just in case she can see me here.' He took his handkerchief from his pocket, lifted the figurine and rubbed it.

'I didn't think you believed in that sort of thing. What was it you used to say?'

'Stuff and nonsense,' he smiled wryly.

'Mum felt she could communicate with her mother and grandmother.'

'I couldn't imagine such a thing then, but now …'

'Now?'

'Sometimes I think she's still here with me.' He stared around the room, a haunted look on his thin features. 'Maybe there's something in it,' he murmured.

Chapter Twenty-seven

Sr. Teresa encouraged Matt to take some time out. 'I've said this to you before, but I'll say it again, you can't spend all your life here, you have to make your own way.'

'This place has been a haven for me,' he said. 'I'm so grateful. And I like looking after people. You've given me the chance to help others like myself.'

'But you can't give your life to them. Even I go home in the evenings. I have my own social life. I see my family. This is a job for me, even though I love every minute, it is still a job. Do you understand?' Her eyes looked into his with concern. 'Also, I've had some very good comments from people about the website you designed, and another one came in today. It's from a new homeless charity and they were wondering if you could help them with the design of their website?'

He nodded immediately.

'And there will be payment for doing the work,' she said.

'There's no need for that,' he protested.

'There are costs in running every charity, Matt. We can't run our organisations without incurring expenses. And as the design of our website has brought in a lot of donations, you deserve to be paid for your work. So it's money well spent. Not only that, you have us on Facebook and Twitter and other sites and that keeps our profile up there in people's minds.'

'I won't take anything from you, Sister, that was a gift for everything you've done for me. I don't know where I'd be if I hadn't found you.'

He didn't want to be paid. Sr. Teresa and everyone at the shelter had been so good to him he couldn't have taken a cent.

'Pierce Mullen is the man's name and this is his phone number.' She handed him a sheet of paper across the desk. 'He is away until Monday, and he said to call him then.'

'Thank you,' he said, relieved that the name wasn't familiar to him. One of his greatest fears was that he would meet someone who knew him from the past and still recognised him. That scenario was always played out in the nightmares which woke him up in the middle of the night. People shouting at him, intercut by the mournful wail of the foghorn which always took him back to his childhood, and was a recurrent sound in his dreams. A warning of danger. To sailors who fought the monstrous seas which swept them on to the rocks to gash holes in the hulls of ships. Water swirling, swamping, and sucking the breath of men. And warning him too.

'Have you met with other members of your family apart from your sister?'

He shook his head, immediately downcast.

'Your father?'

He found it difficult to talk about him knowing that he would probably never want him to come home.

'It's a pity. Do you think he'd be open to talking to a mediator?'

'I don't think so.'

'Now Matt, I want you to take the weekend off, Saturday and Sunday, I don't want to see you until Monday. You'll be relaxed by then and will feel an awful lot better.'

The thought of two days without anything to do yawned ahead of him, it was a terrifying prospect. 'I'd prefer to work, Sister. You need volunteers and I'll have nothing to do, nowhere to go. I hate the thought of doing nothing.'

There was a knock on the door.

'Come …' Sr. Teresa responded.

There's someone to see you …' A volunteer looked in.

'I'm sorry, Matt, we'll talk again.'

Saturday was a pleasant enough day, bright, sunlit. Matt walked in the city with Rex. Along the various streets. Always hugging the buildings. Avoiding the gaze of people. Fearful of open spaces. The *Luas* tram trundled along the tracks. Faces stared at him. He stopped and stood against the wall of a shop. One hand pressed against the cold concrete. After a couple of minutes, he continued on.

'Mister, have you …' A boy stared up him, his hand out.

Matt searched in his pocket and gave him a two-euro coin.

'Thanks mister.' The grimy hand closed on the coin and he was gone, mingling with people.

Matt looked after him but couldn't identify him in the crowd.

Poor kid, he thought, hoping he had a home and wouldn't come in through the door of the shelter one of these days looking for food.

He thought of the bucket collections done by Sr. Teresa. There was one coming up the following weekend and she had asked him would he be prepared to help. He had agreed immediately but now wondered could he stand exactly where he was now and face people. To shake the coins in a bucket and hope that they would be generous. He continued on around by the bus station, went into the terminal and sat down with the dog lying underneath the seat. It was warm. He watched passengers hurrying in and out. Some sat or stood as they waited on their buses. Bags clutched in hands or piled on the ground. There was an air of anxiety. Eyes watching the read-out of the times of departure and arrival of buses. Relief on their faces as they were issued their tickets, gathered their bags, and quickly walked out to the buses parked outside, the wheels on trolley bags rumbling as they dragged them behind.

He bought a copy of the Irish Times. Usually, he read the newspapers at the shelter, but it was a pleasure to open his own copy, pages crisp and untouched.

He stayed there for over an hour. But left then, self-conscious. He didn't want to be asked to leave. Hungry, he went to a small take-out place that sold oriental food. He liked it here. It was anonymous and no one took any notice of him. And it was cheap, six euro for a tub. Again, to pay for his own food made him feel independent. Like he was a normal person living a normal life.

He sat outside on a stool and took his time, eating slowly, and gave Rex a handful of dog food pellets as he watched the people passing by. People who had a sense of purpose about them. All going somewhere in particular. Or on their way to meet someone who was waiting for them. Or perhaps going home. That last thought caused an emotional twist in his gut. Home. If only.

Chapter Twenty-eight

Gail sipped her wine and looked at Pierre. He had arrived on an early evening flight from London and now they were having dinner at an Italian restaurant she liked. The food was delicious, and they chatted about generalities. What she had been doing, her new job, and his own life since they had parted.

She had been very nervous before meeting him, but the moment she looked into his dark eyes, she had to admit that she was still attracted to him. So French, gesticulating with his hands as he explained something in great detail. Always smiling, the warmth in his expression swept her along with him. It was as if they had never parted. She couldn't believe how easily they had slipped into their old ways, remembering particularly those first magical moments when he had looked into her eyes and she had fallen in love.

'Gail …' he reached across the table and covered her hand with his.

His skin was warm and soft and his touch was so intimate her eyes moistened. Immediately she wanted to move closer to him but something held her back. His hand clasp grew tighter.

'I've really missed you. I don't know what made me do such a foolish thing with Claresse.' His fingers moved softly over hers.

'Are you still with her?' She had been afraid to ask but once he had mentioned the woman's name the question on the tip of her tongue spun off without warning.

'I wasn't with her, as you say.'

'She's still in Paris?'

'She decided that she wasn't going to leave her husband after all.'

'Did you ask her?'

'She persuaded me that it was what she wanted, but when you had left me then suddenly I wasn't so attractive.'

Good enough for you, Gail thought, almost laughing.

'I was a fool, Gail, and I knew it soon enough. But I hadn't the courage to come to you and apologise for my stupidity.'

'I don't know what to say.' She was taken aback, and certainly had not expected this announcement. Of all the people she knew Pierre was the last who would ever say he was sorry about anything. It used to annoy her, but was something she had to live with. She could never make Pierre do anything he didn't want to do, and had rationalised that she had idiosyncrasies too which no doubt drove him insane from time to time.

'Come back to me, Gail, I can't bear life without you,' he begged.

'But what's going to change?'

'There will be no Claresse, and no one else either. You'll be the only one for me, Gail.'

'I don't know.' She was confused.

'I love you, believe me.'

'I'll have to think about it, I have a very good job here now and I don't want to give it up.'

'But surely you wouldn't let a job come between us?' He seemed astonished by that.

'It's my career, Pierre.'

'You can always get something in London in the event field, probably a better job than you have here, and with a bigger salary as well.'

'Perhaps, but I'm enjoying being home, Dublin is a hell of a place you know, lots of stuff going on.'

'You couldn't beat London surely?' he laughed out loud.

'Small is beautiful.'

'Well maybe, but think about your friends, they've all missed you.'

'You're obviously talking about your friends?'

'Our friends, Gail.'

'I haven't had any contact from them.' That had been so noticeable since she came back.

'When I mentioned I was coming over, they all sent their best wishes.'

'I'm sure they did.' She couldn't help the edge of sarcasm which crept into her voice.

'Will you come over to London soon, or I'll come over again? Whatever you like?'

'No Pierre, I'll need time.'

'But you will think about us?'

'Yes.' She had to agree.

'I'm so happy.' His hand cupped her cheek. 'Let me sit closer to you.' He moved across to the bench seat she was sitting on, and the next thing she knew he was kissing her. His lips soft on hers. But she found the pressure uncomfortable and felt self-conscious in the packed restaurant although the tables had a reasonable amount of space between them.

'Not here, Pierre,' she pushed him away.

He looked down at her, surprise etched on his face. 'What's wrong, chérie?'

'It's too soon.'

'Why?'

'I'm not ready.'

He put his arm around her shoulders and pulled her close to him again.

'We should go,' she said.

'But it's too early. Let's go on to a club.'

'It's crazy on a Saturday night, not my scene.' She lied.

'Then come back with me to the hotel,' he cajoled. 'I want to hold you, it's been so long.'

She reached for her handbag.

'I'll get the bill,' he said and waved to a waiter passing by.

He ushered her outside and hailed a taxi.

'Thanks for a lovely evening. It was really nice to see you again,' she said.

'But I'll be here tomorrow, my flight isn't until later in the day. Can't we meet?'

'I don't think there's any point, Pierre.'

'But I love you, weren't you listening to me?'

She shook her head.

'I want us to be together again.'

'It's too late now, Pierre.'

'What do you mean?'

'I don't love you in the same way any longer. You hurt me too much by having an affair with Claresse.'

'But she meant nothing to me.'

'I wonder will she be replaced by someone else?'

'Of course not, I realise how stupid I've been, you are the only one for me, Gail. Come back to my hotel, we can relax, have a drink and just talk, please ...' he begged. 'I've been longing for you.'

'I'm sorry, Pierre, but ...' she struggled to find an excuse as to why she didn't want to go with him. Earlier she had an urge to get closer to him, but now it was the opposite and she was almost afraid of him.

'Come on,' he coaxed with a broad smile, touching her cheek with his finger and holding it there.

'Pierre ...' She took a deep breath. 'It's finished between us.'

'I don't believe you, I saw your reaction when we met, you still love me, I could see it in your eyes.'

'You're very sure of yourself, Pierre.' She couldn't resist.

'When a woman loves me and I love her there is no doubt in my mind that we are meant to be together,' he said, smiling confidently.

'And you are too arrogant by half, Pierre,' Gail snapped as she climbed into the taxi and banged the door shut.

She stared out through the window and watched the traffic. She was glad she had managed to get the last word with Pierre, but was surprised that she felt so emotional. Perhaps it was knowing that she would never see him again which caused this response. Something had made her refuse him and she didn't know what that was. She could have taken him back. Fallen right into his arms again. His charisma had worked its allure on her like it always had. Maybe it was his accent. His Gallic ways. She never really knew what she loved in him. Just knew she had this desperate attraction which went beyond sense.

Chapter Twenty-nine

Zoe spent more time working from home. It meant that she didn't have to face Russell quite so frequently. His attitude towards her had hardened even more and it was making each day very difficult. While initially Zoe had had that impulse to do something really drastic and turn her back on *RZ Gaming*, she had hardened her mind set and decided that she wasn't going to be forced out of the company by Russell. She engineered their meetings to include other members of the firm, and used emails if it was necessary to discuss something in particular.

She made a cup of coffee for herself in the kitchen and glanced at yesterday's newspaper which lay on the table. Underneath was one of her father's notebooks. The blue cover unmistakeable. Her hand stretched out towards it, and she was about to pick it up but hesitated as a sense of guilt swept through her. I shouldn't do this, she reminded herself. But something made her ignore the misgivings and she flicked open the first page on which there was a drawing of a lighthouse in her father's hand.

She turned the pages quickly, unsure of what she was looking for. The notes which had references to Matt had been short. Just a few words scribbled in pages which had been torn out of notebooks like this. She scanned the handwriting which described her father's job as a lighthouse keeper. It was neat and ordered as was his day-to-day life with the other men. They were like men in the navy, and followed a strict regime.

Then more erratic handwriting gave colourful accounts of wild storms which lashed the coast, and the unstable nature of the events he was trying to capture in his writing. She flipped the last few pages at the back of the notebook, and a loose page curled out. The handwriting here was in his usual measured hand. And this time, instead of the rough phrases she had seen before there was a number of lines addressed to Matt. Carefully scribed.

'Matt, I'm sorry. I couldn't say it before now. But it has been on my mind for a long time. I'm getting older and my health is not good. Each day I think of you in that terrible place and my guilt knows no bounds. I let you linger year after year because I couldn't face the truth. I am a miserable coward. I do not expect you to forgive me as I have kept a secret in my heart for all this time and I am still haunted by it. If I had the courage to let it be known then you would be free, but I am such a wretched creature I know it will never happen until I die and someone reads this.

Your father, Feargal Sutherland. 6th April, 2012.'

Chapter Thirty

Matt and Rex went back to the shelter. He couldn't have stayed around the city any longer, having time on his hands and nothing to do. He returned to help the men who came in. And he did the same on Sunday, in spite of Sr. Teresa's advice that he should take time off.

'Sorry, I find it hard to hang about,' he explained.

'I understand …'

'But I'll get on to that guy who wanted to talk about a website tomorrow.'

'Do that, and go straight over to see him.'

On the dot of nine o'clock he called Pierce Mullen. Delighted when he found that he was more than keen to meet him as soon as possible. They arranged an appointment for two o'clock, and he made his way through the city to the hostel.

'I really like the website you designed for Sr. Teresa, Matt, and we were keen to see what you might do for us.'

'What have you in mind?'

'A web design which might encourage people to donate money basically,' he said, with a broad grin.

'We've done well, Sr. Teresa was pleased.'

'She was telling me.'

'Have you any idea of what you want?' Matt asked, hoping that Pierce might give him some direction.

'We're completely open and are looking for ideas from you.'

'I'll think about it, I hope I can come up with something.'

'I'm looking forward to seeing whatever you create.'

'Thanks for giving me the opportunity, I appreciate it.'

Pierce stood up and reached to take Matt's hand. 'Let me know how much it will cost. We do have a budget.'

'It won't be astronomical,' Matt smiled.

'Thank you.'

He left the meeting on a high and felt better than he had done for some time, delighted that there was a chance of work. As he arrived back at St. Teresa's his phone rang and he pulled it out of his pocket.

'Zoe?'

'Matt, how are you?'

'I'm fine thanks.'

'Could we meet?'

'Sure.'

'How about tomorrow morning? At the main entrance to St. Stephen's Green? About eleven?'

Chapter Thirty-one

'Gail?' Zoe hurried into the hall as soon as she heard her sister's key in the front door.

'Yes?' Gail closed the door behind her.

'I've something to show you,' she whispered.

'What is it?' She took off her jacket. 'I'm shattered, I've an early start in the morning, will it take long?' she asked.

'You remember we talked about the notes Dad had written to Matt?' She kept her voice low.

'I don't want to talk about him,' Gail retorted.

'I had a look at one of Dad's notebooks and at the back I saw a full letter.'

'What do you mean?' Gail asked sharply.

'It was addressed to Matt.'

'What did it say?'

'I'll show you.' Zoe picked up her phone and took a moment to find the photo. She handed the phone to Gail.

'I don't think I want to.'

'I think you should.'

'You know how I feel about him.'

'This might change your mind,' Zoe said gently.

'Nothing will change my mind,' she snapped angrily.

'Read it,' she insisted. 'Please?'

Gail scanned down through the lines. And then she looked at her sister, puzzled.

'Do you understand what is written there?' Zoe asked.

'Dad feels guilty because he shouted at Matt at Christmas.'

'There's more to it than that,' insisted Zoe.

'I don't see how.'

'Dad wrote this letter in two thousand and twelve which is years ago, and so it doesn't relate to Christmas. What if he knew something and didn't admit it at the time of Matt's trial?'

'What do you mean?'

'He's admitting guilt. Of something. Withholding evidence perhaps?'

'It was an open and shut case. And Matt confessed,' Gail flashed, handing her back the phone.

Zoe nodded.

'There's no point in going off on some tangent, won't do any good now anyway. It's just the ramblings of an old man,' Gail added.

'Think about it,' Zoe urged.

'No.'

She didn't say anything for a moment, reluctant to let her sister's anger come between them.

'You're letting Matt get to you. He's like that. Always was. Manipulative.' Gail walked up a couple of steps. Turned back then and kissed her. 'Night.'

Zoe looked at the photo of the letter again. Reading down through the lines trying to find something in it which would explain what was going on in her father's head.

Matt was already standing at the gates when she hurried up. There was a broad smile on his face when he saw her.

She hugged him. Watching him with even more attention than she had before. This man was her brother. He was definitely part of her family. She had to stand by him. Someone had to do it.

They began to stroll slowly along.

'I've got a job,' he said, with a pleased grin.

'Congratulations.' She was thrilled for him. 'Tell me about it.'

'I was asked to design another website.'

'That's great.'

'And I'll get paid for it too,' he laughed.

'Where is it?'

'Another homeless shelter. We've done well with our website, and raised a lot of money. So they're keen to do the same.'

'Can I see the one you've designed?' She looked at her phone.

'If you like.'

She googled and it came up. She looked at the various pages. 'This is fantastic Matt. It's really good.'

'Thanks.' He seemed shy and awkward.

'I love it.'

'I'm hoping to produce something different for these other people.'

'You will,' she smiled at him. 'I'm sure.'

'It's what I enjoy.'

'Have you done any game work?'

He shook his head.

'Would you like to give it a go?'

'Love to.'

'You can go online. There are animation websites and forums as well.'

'I completed a module on animation when I was doing my degree. But I don't have a laptop which has a high enough spec.'

'I might be able to help there.'

His eyes widened. 'Thank you, that would be great.'

'I'll get you a computer with the software for animation and you'll be able to work.'

He smiled broadly. 'I can't believe it, a new computer, how wonderful. My own one is old …' Looking at him, she could see that he was very emotional. How often did anyone give him a present, she wondered. This seemed to mean a great deal to him.

'I don't mind if it isn't brand new, that doesn't matter, you're just so generous …but I want to pay for it, although that could take a bit of time.'

'Don't worry, there's no need for that. I'll call you as soon as I have it and then you'll be able to work on the website. Now I must get back,' she stood up. 'But before I go there is something I want to show you.'

He looked at her quizzically.

'Let's sit.' They moved over to a bench, and she took her phone from her handbag. She scrolled through it searching for the photograph, and handed it to him.

Chapter Thirty-two

'I showed it to him,' Zoe said.

'And?' Gail snapped.

'He read it, and handed the phone back to me. Then we just continued on out of the Green and said goodbye as if it had never happened.'

'What did you expect him to do?'

'I don't know,' Zoe said slowly.

'Why should he even react to something which was just an apology for God knows what. Maybe Dad remembered some row they had. And there were many of those.'

'But those lines about Matt being free have a relevance surely?' Zoe insisted. 'It's like Dad knows something which could have helped Matt's case and didn't say anything.'

'What could he know? Matt confessed.'

'I'm disturbed by it.'

'Are you going to talk to Dad?'

'I'm going to look for more letters.'

'There's enough stuff around anyway.'

After that Zoe took every opportunity she had to search through the notebooks. She had to admit what she read was fascinating and there was easily enough written for a couple of books. What a memoir. He would get a publication deal without any trouble, she thought, and make some money into the bargain. Still, to persuade him to share his life history would be a difficult task she thought, but hoped that some day his story would be told.

But how would she ever manage to talk to her father about Matt? Feargal's reaction to even seeing his son at Christmas had been extremely aggressive to say the least.

She re-read the letter so often the words were imprinted on her brain, particularly the lines about Matt being free and the mention of a secret which her father couldn't divulge and would never be known until after his death. She became obsessed, and couldn't put it out of her head. She was caught in a spider's web of intrigue and didn't know how to escape.

This was something between herself and Matt and her father. The knowledge slid through her. She couldn't differentiate between them. An older man. A younger man. A father. A son. She tried to fit herself into the triangle. A member of a family. A daughter. A sister. To know once again the closeness between them.

But the edges of her mind were blurred. She couldn't grasp the differences. But she had to try. It was imperative. Something forced her. Matt needed help. And she was the only one who even understood.

Zoe wanted to talk to her father. But hesitated each time she even considered the possibility. How would he react if she mentioned Matt? If she referred to the letter would he explain why he had written it? Explain each word. Literally. Admit what was behind the meaning of his words. And as Gail didn't support her in this, it was something she would have to do on her own.

But now she had to force herself to concentrate on work. Tomorrow, she would fly to London and it was necessary to prepare for it. By the end of the evening she was tired. She wasn't sleeping well. Dreams swept her back to those days when Matt had run their home in Ballystrand. He was the instigator of trouble. The rows which exploded between Matt and his father, and swept up in the explosive air of tension which dominated their home life were Rachel, Zoe and Gail, who were helpless victims.

It was as Matt grew into his teenage years that life became more and more difficult. He became indifferent to everyone at home except his mother. Was extremely aggressive and hung around with a gang of older boys who had no interest in study, and spent his time with them drinking and taking drugs. But he was careful to avoid expulsion from school and did the minimum amount of work to escape the headmaster's wrath.

At home the family's lives were encircled by questions. Why was Matt the way he was? Why? What was wrong with him? No-one had any answers.

Chapter Thirty-three

Feargal lay in bed. Three pillows were propped up against the mahogany headboard. White cotton crumpled against shining wood. He picked up a book from the uneven pile on the bedside table and it unbalanced the others. Books fell on to the floor with a series of thumps, pages fanned out from spines, the whole lot eventually settling in a lopsided heap.

He stared down. Disinclined to get out of bed and pick them up. He opened the book which lay on his thin bony knees and turned a page, its position marked by a bookmark. A worn cardboard strip from some shop or other which he had picked up years before. The lamp shone a soft golden light on to the page and he shifted a little and found a more comfortable position, looking forward to reading this chapter. It would take him further on in the story. To eat up more words. To soak himself in the history of the lighthouse. It was the end of the day. The time when he most enjoyed to read. It got him to sleep. To drift off and dream on some long-remembered storm.

There was a sudden rumble. Was it a banging door? Or footsteps on the roof? He wasn't sure what it was. He stared up at the ceiling. It was just the wind he decided. Just the wind. His eyes went back to the text. Caught up in the descriptive lines. The curtains moved slightly. Caught his eye and drew his attention over to the other side of the room. A vague shadow crossed his eyes. He stiffened.

'Feargal?'

A voice whispered his name.

His heart thumped.

'Feargal?'

He closed the pages on his fingers with a snap.

'Don't blame him.'

He shivered, frightened now.

'You must take responsibility.'

He shook his head. 'Fuck off.'

'Why do you have to use bad language?' the voice reproached sharply.

He stared around him. His lips quivered.

'You'll never change. Always the same.'

He pulled the duvet over his head and snuggled down underneath. Terror swept through him. He couldn't bear to hear this voice speaking to him. He wasn't going to listen. It was crazy. It was coming out of nowhere. Terrorising him. 'Fuck off. I'm going to sleep,' he shouted.

He turned in the bed. Closed his eyes and tried to push the sound of the voice away. 'I'm not listening,' he said to himself. 'Not listening.'

The whispers continued. But the voice grew softer, almost inaudible, but yet still insistent.

'Tell him.'

'No ...get away from me.'

'Tell him.'

Chapter Thirty-four

Matt was shaken when he read the letter on Zoe's phone. But he wasn't sure what it meant. His father was apologising. For what? The more he thought about it, the more it drifted away from him. He tried to retain the words but his memory played tricks and he couldn't remember the meaning behind them. Zoe had seemed to think that it was very relevant but she had simply handed him her phone and in that moment he had to try to cling on to the meaning of the writing on the screen. But it became all the more nebulous like a drifting mist in the air and his grip on its reality grew even weaker.

His father had written the letter in two thousand and twelve. He pondered that. Was the date important? Before seeing his father on Christmas Eve, he hadn't seen him since that day in court when the judge had handed down his sentence. His mind took him back to those years. He could see the courtroom. Wooden panelled. Clerks, solicitors, barristers, the public gallery packed with curious onlookers. His father sat looking at him. His eyes bored into him when he appeared handcuffed to a prison guard. Matt had looked at his father for just a few seconds until the anger in those eyes forced him to lower his own. And he stood there like that. He never raised his head again during the whole of the proceedings in that court room. Now Matt decided that he would ask Zoe to print out the letter from his father and bring it next time he would see her. So that he could read it. Each word. One after another. And understand their exact meaning.

They met in the usual coffee bar. The staff knew him now by sight and today smiled and nodded when he arrived. It felt good. He was so glad she was coming to see him. Just to talk to her meant so much, the only member of his family who wanted to have anything to do with him. He longed for Gail and his father to forgive him and a terrible need to know them again swept through him. Now all he wanted was to open a door between them into a timeless place where only love existed.

Zoe rushed in a moment later, smiling. 'Sorry to be late, but I had a meeting with a client and couldn't leave. I'm always the same, so much going on, forgive me.'

'Don't worry. I'm not here that long.' He waved to the waitress. 'Coffee?'

'The usual, thanks.' She put a black computer case up on the table.

He ordered.

She unzipped the case.

'Thank you so much.' He was very grateful and couldn't quite explain how much he appreciated Zoe's generosity.

'This laptop has game softwear installed, and I've included broadband as well. You will need to be online.'

'I hadn't really thought about that.'

'I'm sure you'll come up with something really interesting.' She took out the laptop.

'A *Mac*? how amazing.' He opened it, and smiled broadly. He stood up, leaned across the table and kissed her on the cheek.

'We use various PCs and laptops but I like the *Mac* myself, and some of the games we've created are on it, you might be interested in having a look. I'm sure that you'll come up with something really interesting. I can't wait.'

'I hope so …' Immediately he wondered whether he would be able to do what she wanted. He had a feeling of dread about his ability to design games, he didn't know much about that skill.

'You will, I'm certain.'

He ran his fingers across the keyboard with a loving gesture. A sense of possession. Wanting to do this for her above everything. Because she felt he could do it. She had faith in him. That knowledge slid through him. He was a young untried youth when he had been convicted. And now he felt like a grown man for the first time in his life.

'I brought a copy of the letter.' She handed him an envelope.

'Thanks for that. I couldn't remember the exact words.' He gripped it. Fingering the crisp silky surface of the paper. Where was this letter going to take him? Suddenly he was full of anticipation. But that excitement was mixed with foreboding. He couldn't look at Zoe, and placed the envelope on the table beside the almost empty cup. Dregs of the coffee gathered at the end. He stared at it. Imagining that there was some message in the roughly formed grains. What if he could understand them? Like his grandmother could tell the future from the tea leaves.

'I don't know what it's all about or why Dad should want to apologise to you,' Zoe said.

'I don't know either,' he had to admit.

'The letter was written about half way through your prison sentence. I wondered about that. Did he make contact with you at that time?'

He shook his head.

'When I read the letter it seemed to me that he felt he should have done something which would have affected the length of your sentence.'

'It was all my own fault,' Matt muttered. 'I made life hell for everyone.'

She managed a smile, but then hesitated for a few seconds, before leaning across the table towards him. 'What happened on that night, Matt?' she whispered.

'I …have no memory of it.' He was ashamed.

'No recollection at all?'

'It's as if I was in a fog.' He tried to drag his mind back to that time.

'But you admitted it? How could you do that if you didn't recall the circumstances?'

He had no answer for her.

Chapter Thirty-five

Zoe had to go into the office. Something she disliked intensely these days. But a Board Meeting was scheduled and there was no choice. As she and Russell had agreed to keep each other informed of their travel plans, she always went in whenever he was away, but wasn't looking forward to the meeting today.

'Zoe?

Walking through the automatic swing doors, she met Clive.

'It seems every time I'm here you're working at home or travelling.' He hugged her.

'I work better at home, and I do get a lot more done. You know how it is, so much needing attention, and people sticking their heads into my office with queries which could be emailed. At home, I can handle items in a much more ordered fashion.' She put her arm through his. 'How is Jean?'

'She still hasn't got over the fact that you're not going to be part of our family.'

'She should be relieved,' Zoe laughed.

'Not at all. I wanted you to be Russell's wife and I feel that he has made a very bad decision.'

'Does Jean know the reason?'

'No, I didn't tell her.'

'I'm glad of that. Thanks.'

'Does your brother realise that Russell decided to back out of the wedding because of him?'

'No,' she replied sharply.

'I'm sorry,' he immediately apologised.

'I couldn't possibly tell him that. He's very sensitive. I've met him a few times recently, and he finds the fact that the family don't want to see him very tough.'

'Where is he living?' Clive asked.

'In a shelter.'

'My God.' He was surprised.

'He works there so he's happy enough.'

'Works?'

'Helps out. Designed their website. And is working on another one for someone else.'

'Maybe we should have him working here.' They arrived at his office door.

'There's no way Russell would agree to that.' Zoe was very sure.

'Probably not.'

She could be honest with Clive and know that what she said would never be repeated.

'Fancy having lunch after the meeting?' he asked.

'I shouldn't really, but we'll just have something quick. I have to get back. I've a lot to do.'

'Suits me, I only want to have a chat with you. A bit of privacy in a corner of a pub somewhere, how about that place around the corner?'

'Let's do that,' she smiled.

'We'll catch up.' He ushered her inside.

She sat down, feeling nervous as she waited for Russell to appear.

The meeting went smoothly for a change. The items on the agenda were dealt with fairly rapidly. The previous quarter accounts were shown on a large video screen, and they discussed where they were at this point in the year. There was some discussion and then their plans for the rest of the year were detailed. To her surprise, she found Russell unusually quiet and was glad of that.

'The company is going well,' Clive commented as they ate lunch. 'Particularly in Japan.'

'You must be pleased.'

'I am, but it's tinged with regret. Russell and I had such hopes for the company and now we don't even share the successes, big or small. And he doesn't even speak to me unless it's absolutely necessary. You saw him at the meeting today.' Zoe missed the excitement of winning contracts and developing new games, hoping that they would hit the big time.

'I can understand.' Clive nodded sympathetically. 'But I'm glad you didn't decide to leave.'

'I was going to, but something made me change my mind.'

'I'd like to meet your brother.' Finished, he put his knife and fork neatly in the centre of the plate.

Zoe was taken aback, and stared at him. She couldn't believe what she was hearing and didn't say anything at first.

'Why?' she managed eventually, sipping a glass of water.

'No particular reason.'

'I'm surprised.' She had to admit.

'Why is that?' Clive seemed puzzled.

'He's an ex-prisoner and has spent many years in jail for a serious crime.'

'And he has done his time,' Clive said gently.

'Yes …that's true.'

'Then he needs friends.'

'He has none as far as I know, and I'm the only one who sees him. Gail and Dad won't.'

'How sad.'

'I don't blame them, but I feel he can't be deserted altogether.'

'That's what I feel. Will you ask him to meet me? With my background in the law I feel I might be able to understand more clearly how he ended up in prison.'

Chapter Thirty-six

Gail stared at her phone. It was Pierre again. He texted and phoned constantly now. Her heart raced. Excitement swept through her. It was very difficult to resist his persuasion. Even though her head told her that her relationship with him was over, her heart tried to contradict that. This time her heart won and instead of ignoring the call she took it.

'Gail?' His voice was soft. 'I'll be in Dublin this weekend, could I see you?'

She felt herself drifting. Longing for his touch. His voice electrifying. 'If I thought I could trust you.'

'Of course you can, I told you Claresse is history.'

'I don't know …'

'Please, give me another chance, Gail. Can't you do that? You know how much I love you.'

'Well …' she wavered.

'We could have dinner at the same place as last time?'

'Eh …' She couldn't make up her mind and hated herself.

'It was good, lots of atmosphere,' he sounded upbeat.

'No Pierre, I don't want to.' She suddenly reached a decision.

He was silent for a moment. 'Have you met another man?' he asked then, a note of suspicion in his voice.

'I haven't.'

'I don't believe that. You're a party girl, *chérie*.'

'You can believe it. Work is priority at the moment.'

'But you've plenty of male friends I'm sure?'

'Look, I'm not involved with anyone, but I don't want to be with you either. So you'll have to accept it.' She was losing patience with him.

'I'll call you as soon as I land, it should be about three. You might meet me in the city and we can have a wander around?'

'Didn't you hear me, Pierre?'

'I want to see you, I know I can persuade you to come back to me,' he insisted.

'You'll be wasting your time.' She found it very difficult to continue to argue with him and was afraid that she would give in.

'I'm looking forward to seeing you.'

'I told you not to come,' she snapped.

'You'll change your mind, Gail.'

She grew angry with him. He was so sure of himself. 'You do what you want, but I'm busy at the weekend.'

'He doesn't even listen,' Gail said to Zoe. 'I can't get through to him. I'm saying I don't want to see him, and I might have been saying the opposite.'

'That must be hard if you still have feelings for him.'

'That's the trouble, I can't turn it off like a light switch.'

'I know,' Zoe hugged her sister.

'How do you feel about Russell?'

'Well, I did have doubts before the final break up so for me it's different. I'm glad I got out before I tied myself up for life.'

'But you must really miss his company?'

'I do, I suppose, but I'm getting used to it.'

'I feel as if I've lost my other half. I'm going around searching for him. Seeing him on the street. Any man of his height with dark hair and a foreign accent has to be him. It's a mystery to me how I managed to refuse him on Saturday.'

'I know exactly what you mean,' Zoe sympathised.

'I just didn't want to throw myself into his arms when he made his move. It wasn't easy, I can tell you.'

'Now that you're unavailable to him you will be much more enticing. See how anxious he is to see you. Flying over no matter what you say.'

Gail leaned back in the armchair, and stared pensively at nothing.

'Man always chases woman who runs away,' Zoe laughed.

'Imagine a cave man waving his club.' She joined in her laughter.

'I hope you won't be hurt again.'

'If I meet someone new there's always the chance that could happen. There's no protection against it. Put your heart on your sleeve and you leave yourself out there for the wolves.'

'I know what to expect then,' Zoe grinned.

'If you ever start looking for a man again.'

'There's plenty of time.'

'Go online, we'll have some fun together.'

Zoe shook her head. 'Give me a few years.'

'You can't leave it that long, it takes time you know. And you have to think about having a family too.'

'That's enough, don't push me.'

'Is there anyone you've met that you fancy?' Gail asked.

'Well …' Zoe looked coy.

'Come on, what's this?' Gail was immediately curious.

'I met a man very briefly and …he was nice.'

'Tell us more.'

'There's nothing …'

'I want to know who he is.'

'I'm not going to tell you.'

'Go on. Please?'

'Can't,' she said flatly.

'Hey we're sisters.'

'I know, but I've only just met him.'

'I still want to know who he is,' she insisted.

'Don't push it, Gail. When I know, then you'll know.' She hugged her.

'You've made me so curious, you know I hate to be the last to find out anything.'

'You're just going to have to be patient, there may be nothing to tell at all which is much more likely,' Zoe said with a laugh.

It was late. Dark. Gail awoke suddenly, her sleep disturbed. She sat up and listened, but couldn't hear anything at first. But still she climbed out of bed and opened the door which led on to the landing. Walking along, she passed her father's door and it was only then she heard a sound from inside. It was a cry. A strange strangled whimper. She immediately stopped. Put her hand on the brass handle, pressed it down and pushed open the door. 'Dad?'

The room was in shadow, the only light a diffuse glow from a lamp on the bedside cabinet. Her father was on the far side of the room, cowering in a corner.

'What's wrong?'

'Go away.' He waved his hands at her.

She knelt down beside him. 'Dad, can I get you anything?' she asked gently.

'She was here, telling me …'

'Who was here?'

'She was …' His lips trembled.

'She?' Gail couldn't understand what he was on about.

'All the time saying I should tell him …'

'Tell who?'

His body shuddered.

'Can I help you up?'

He shrank further into the corner.

'You should go back to bed.' She stood up.

He shook his head. 'I'm afraid. I can't do it.' There were tears on his cheeks.

'I'll sit with you.' She did that, and put her arms around him trying to give him some comfort.

'Did you have a bad dream?'

He shook his head.

Gail wanted to call Zoe but thought her sister wouldn't be able to hear her, so she just hugged him hoping that he would calm down soon. He leaned against her, his head on her shoulder, until gradually he became less agitated and she managed to persuade him to get back into bed. She stayed with him until finally he slept.

Chapter Thirty-seven

That night Matt sat on the edge of his bed. Then he took the envelope from his inside pocket, put his thumb under the flap and slowly raised it, trying not to tear it too much. He pulled out the letter, his fingers shaking. He hesitated for a moment before he unfolded it. Then he took a deep breath.

To see his father's handwriting so clearly was a shock, and he found it hard to contain the emotion which flooded through him. He read every line, trying to understand each word. What did his father mean? The suggestion that there was something he knew that wasn't admitted sent a shiver down his spine. How was that possible? Every aspect of the case had been brought forward in the court until they produced the photographs. He squeezed his eyes shut. Trying not to see them. But that didn't work for him. The body was lying on the floor. The arms and legs were crooked. The head turned to one side in a dark pool of blood.

Up to that point he had refused to speak. But then he changed his mind. His guilt was there in front of him. He couldn't escape it.

'I did it,' he said. Still keeping his head down.

There was a stunned silence.

'I'm guilty.'

The barristers stared at him and then at each other. There was an unexpected mood of tension in the court room. And then a rush by both prosecution and defending barristers up to the judge, who called a recess.

Matt was taken down to the cells. He sat there until he was brought up again. Everything went very fast after that. He couldn't even keep up with it. But he knew he was going to prison for a long time.

At Sr. Teresa's behest, he took another day off and found himself drawn back to Ballystrand. Reluctantly, he had to leave the dog behind as he couldn't bring him on the bus and missed his company.

He wandered along the coast to the old lighthouse. Climbing across rocks, and running along narrow stretches of sand, splashed by the waves. The lighthouse stood on the point. Painted white with red stripes. He sat on the rocks and stared out to sea. Enjoying the sounds of the seabirds as they whirled around and the crash of the breakers.

Now memories invaded Matt's mind. Images flickered, like flash photographs of events in his life. Always a subliminal line of division. Before. After. Heaven. Hell. He was held captive by those events. The sound of the foghorn reminding.

And then the days associated with his mother. Bright days. Sun splashed. All so real. He remembered her bringing him to the village school on that first day. Her soft hand holding his small one. Wiping his tears with her handkerchief, and hugging him close until eventually he was forced to say goodbye by the teacher.

Her birthday. His birthday. Her screams of excitement as she stood on the side-line at school hurling matches. As he struggled with homework, she sat beside him at the big kitchen table and helped him work through the problems set by the teacher. Never a word of criticism even if he made a mistake. He was the eldest child. The one who was given everything. His parents only wanted the best for their children. But he clung to his mother, their relationship always so special. He visited the cemetery again, said a prayer for his mother and grandparents and put a bouquet of white roses on the grave.

The sky darkened and there was the threat of rain so Matt made his way back. As he waited for the bus in the village, he saw a sign for the monastery and remembered then the man who had given him a lift in his car that first time he had come back here. Again, he was reminded of the past. He would have liked to go up, but as it was growing late now, he decided to leave that for another day.

Chapter Thirty-eight

Zoe called Tom Sheridan, Matt's Probation Officer, leaving a message on his voicemail. She wasn't sure whether she was going behind Matt's back, but wanted to talk with Tom about the letter. When he returned her call, she didn't go into much detail but asked him to meet her. He immediately agreed and they met in the café on Grafton Street.

'I'm sure you're wondering why I asked you to meet me,' she said, smiling.

'I assume it's about Matt.'

'Yes, of course.'

'How is he?'

'He seems fine.'

'I'll be meeting him next week.'

There was a pause in their conversation as the coffees arrived, and then she continued.

'I found a letter ...'

He seemed interested.

'I'll just show it to you.' She opened her briefcase.

'Who is it from?'

She pulled out a file, took a copy of the letter and handed it to Tom. He read it slowly. 'It's from your father, is that right?'

She nodded, feeling awkward now and wondering had she been foolish to bring it to his attention.

'It's only a photocopy, do you have the original?' he asked.

'No. I had to take a photo on my phone.'

'Did your father give it to you?'

'No, I found it among his things, he writes about his life as a lighthouse keeper, lots of notebooks filled with information. There were other bits of paper with notes written on them as well, but this was the only full letter I found. I just wondered if it would have any relevance to Matt, and the fact that it seems to suggest that there might have been other evidence which would have made a difference to his conviction back then.'

'It does that certainly, but why would you bring it up now? Matt has completed his sentence.'

'I just felt an appeal with new evidence might clear his name.'

'It would be a very long and difficult process.'

'I understand that.'

'Would your father support it?'

'To be honest, I hadn't thought it through as far as that. I just wanted your opinion.' She sipped the last of her coffee. 'I hope you don't mind.'

'Of course I don't,' he smiled. 'But I have to say if your father had information and didn't disclose it then he could be charged himself.'

Her eyes met his.

'Defendants have a right to appeal to a higher court but the decision of the original judge may not always be overturned.'

'I understand.'

'There has to be very strong evidence that the conviction was unsafe.'

'What if vital evidence wasn't admitted to the court?'

'Matt pleaded guilty.'

'I know.'

'I'm not a barrister, I can only guess at things. If all the facts are not already in the court record then he would have to bring a writ, but it could be time barred, although I'm not sure of that.'

'It seems complicated.'

'Your father sounds as if he wants to make a confession.'

'That's in his head. It doesn't mean he's going to do it.'

'What was his reaction to hearing Matt was released?'

'He called to see us on Christmas Eve and Dad lost his cool with him, shouted at him and told him to get out.' Zoe remembered the night. The row with Russell. The end of it all.

'What did Matt say?'

'Nothing, he just left.'

'That was difficult.'

'For Matt.'

'For you too.'

She nodded. 'Do you think I'm crazy to think of opening up this whole thing again?' She pressed her hand on the copy of the letter.

'I can understand that you want to help Matt.'

'I want to find out the truth, that's all.' She was passionate.

'Talk to Matt.'

'You think he won't want me to do this?' she demanded.

'I don't know whether he would or not.'

'Since I read the letter, I want to clear his name. Why should a young man have to live under such a cloud. It's not fair.' She was incensed.

'I agree it's not fair. But sometimes uncovering the truth is very complex and it can cause rifts which are never healed.'

'But my father is old, surely they wouldn't condemn him?'

'If he confesses, then he'll probably do time. How old is he?'

'Seventy-two.'

'He's not that old.'

'I suppose not ...' She hesitated. 'But I want to thank for listening,' she said softly. 'You've been a big help.'

'My pleasure.' His eyes searched hers. There was a long moment between them. He covered her hand with his. The letter lay underneath.

Chapter Thirty-nine

'It's good to meet you, Matt.' Clive took a gulp of his beer. 'What would you like to drink?'

'I don't drink these days,' Matt admitted. 'I'll have an orange juice, thanks.'

Clive ordered it.

'Maybe you're just as well to stay off alcohol. I try not to drink too much during the week.'

'I've had more than one addiction.'

'But you've dealt with them. That's admirable, and not easy.'

The juice arrived.

'Why did you want to meet me?' asked Matt, curious.

'Zoe told me about you, I'm very fond of her.'

'You're the Chairman of the company?'

'Yes. And I want to help. Life must be difficult for you although Zoe tells me you've got a job designing a website?'

He nodded.

'And she's asked you to see what you can do for us on the gaming front.'

'It's really good of her, although I don't know if I can do what she wants. Your work is amazing.'

'We're always looking for new stories. You might well have a different angle.'

'Unlikely,' Matt said, belittling his own ability.

'Give it some thought anyway,' encouraged Clive.

'So far I haven't had any brainwaves,' he said with a smile.

'It's all about levels, persuading people to want to reach ever higher and win, there's a huge market out there.'

'I've been checking it up and there certainly is.'

'Are you a gamer?'

'No.'

'Let's hope you're on the way to becoming one. A bit of imagination is all that's needed. Don't forget fantasy. Science Fiction. Mythology.'

'Legends of the past.'

'How has it been since you were released?' Clive asked, a kindly expression on his face.

'I'm working through it,' Matt murmured slowly.

'Good days? Bad days?' Clive lifted his glass and sipped his beer.

'Sometimes I think of the life I might have had if I wasn't such a ...'

'You were young ...'

'That's no excuse. I just didn't want to do what I was told. Either at home or at school. I resented being pushed into a pigeonhole. You're going to be this or that. And my father had high hopes for me. College. A degree. A successful career.'

'That scenario is normal.'

'Have you a family?' Matt asked.

'We have one son, Russell.'

'Of course, he works with Zoe in *RZ Gaming*?'

'Yes, we're in the same business.' Clive was sorry that Russell had come into the conversation.

'And he's very successful obviously,' Matt said. 'I was a shit. I didn't care about anyone. Selfish bastard. You've no idea.' His hand gripping the glass began to tremble.

Clive noticed. 'I've known young people who had problems growing up. You're not unique.'

'I meet a lot of men and women who have become separated from their families and haven't seen them in years.'

'That's so hard for them.'

'They live on the streets. It's a hell of a life.'

'I don't know much about you, but from what Zoe told me I felt I wanted to meet you. It's not easy to be in your position and I had a mad idea that I might be able to help in some way. Although perhaps that's a bit arrogant …' Clive felt that he might have overstepped the line between the young man in front of him and himself, an old guy approaching seventy. 'I'm a barrister although I'm not practising at the Bar any longer but my brother still practises and I have a lot of friends in the courts.' He took a deep breath. 'Have you thought …?'

Matt took a gulp of juice. 'How much has Zoe told you?'

His voice was low. Almost suspicious, thought Clive.

'She just mentioned that you had been in prison.'

'Did she mention why?'

'A serious crime.'

Matt didn't reply. Just stared beyond Clive.

'I'm very fond of Zoe, she was about to become my daughter-in-law and I was disappointed that it all fell apart.'

'She didn't tell me that.'

'Russell was engaged to Zoe and they were planning to marry at the end of last year, then …'

'Then?'

'Something happened, I don't know what, and they broke up.'

'Perhaps they decided they didn't want to be married after all.'

'Probably.' Clive didn't want to mention to Matt that it was because Russell found out about him. It would be too much for him to handle at this point in time, he guessed.

'Did he know about me?' Matt asked hesitantly.

'I don't know.'

'I think I met him at Christmas, it must have been him.'

Clive didn't say anything.

'Perhaps I was the reason they split?' Matt stared at him.

'I don't think so.'

'Are you sure?' His eyes were wide and questioning.

'I'm certain.'

'I don't think I could bear that.' He ran his hand through his short hair with an air of frustration.

'Don't worry, I'm sure there was no connection with you.' He tried to reassure Matt and regretted that he had suddenly got hold of the idea that the break up between Zoe and Russell had anything to do with him. 'Neither of them told me the reason for their break up. Why should they?'

'God forbid it had anything to do with me.'

Chapter Forty

Feargal wrote feverishly. A thought which had developed into a phrase. And then into a sentence. And so on until he could see a page begin to develop in his neat handwriting. He was on the balcony of the lighthouse. Watching through his binoculars. Searching for ships caught in the troughs. He had this terrible need to save those souls who battled the elements. Could actually hear the voices screaming for help. The wind howling. People hanging on to the rails as the ship dived into the surges, the waves sweeping across the bow, and back again, dragging passengers out to sea as they flailed helplessly in their efforts to grab any handhold which would save them from the dark green depths.

'Have you seen Matt?' The whispering voice encircled him.

Feargal shook his head and put down his pen. He had got used to hearing her voice and had convinced himself that it was purely in his imagination. He had wanted her. Loved her. Yearned for her. All those years since she died. Until slowly he had brought her back to him. She was like someone who had been reborn. That beautiful gentle woman who had loved him then.

He dragged his mind back to the storm which raged in his mind. Above him the light slowly swirled. Casting its bright beam across the sea, the shaft cutting a glimmer through the wild rollers. He stopped for a few seconds and stared into the distance of the darkened room. A terrible sense of hurt swept through him.

These days were a penance for him. He wasn't sure who he was any more. He had no identity. Even his writing was proving less and less of a therapy. His memories were uneven. Images of places and people in his head were unclear, and although he fought to keep them with him all the time they eluded him just when he needed to see them. To reassure himself that they existed. They were true. Real.

He searched through the shelves which were crowded with books interspersed with his notebooks. He was looking for something. He didn't know what. His fingers gripped the spine of a book and he pulled it out from its jumbled companions. But a glance at the title made him throw it down on the floor and he continued staring at the shelves. He pulled out a notebook and flicked through the pages but it wasn't the one he wanted either and went on the floor as well. He grabbed another and began to read through it. Tore out some of the pages and crumpled them up. Then he sat down on the chair and rested his head on his hands, a blackness in his heart.

'Tell him that I want him,' she insisted.

'Why do you want him? What crazy notion is filling your head?' he snapped. 'You're not real, just a ghost in my imagination.' He looked around the room as if to convince himself of that. 'If you are real, then where are you? I can't see you.'

'He's my child.'

'Not any more. You've gone from him, me, all of us.'

'He'll always be mine.'

'How can you say that?'

'Because it's the truth.'

He covered his ears determined to shut out the insistent tone.

'I bore him. Inside me. I'm closer to him that you ever were.'

'He tore us apart.' He couldn't be tender with her. He had to wound her.

Chapter Forty-one

Tom moved his hand away seconds after he put it on hers as if he had been burned. A look of guilt flashed across his face. 'I'm sorry, please forgive me for being so forward. I don't know what made me do that.'

Zoe shook her head and smiled. 'Don't worry.'

He gripped his hands together, and lowered them under the table top. The letter lay between them. 'I'll talk to someone I know, maybe I can get an opinion.'

'Would you?' Zoe asked excitedly.

'Of course I will.'

'I'm very grateful to you.'

He smiled.

He had a nice smile, she thought. It lit up his face.

'I'd better go,' she said, suddenly aware of the time. But yet she didn't want to leave and would have liked to stay and talk some more.

He put a ten euro note down on the table, and stood up.

'Let me get it …' she insisted.

'Not at all,' he smiled and ushered her ahead of him. Outside they stood together. She turned to him. 'Thanks again, if you find out anything maybe you'd call me?' She searched for a card in her bag and handed it to him.

'I will, but …' he hesitated. 'I wonder …would you have dinner with me sometime?'

She looked at him, silent.

'It would be nice to relax one evening, have a chat ...'

There was a moment of doubt in her mind. Scared that a man had made even the mildest of approaches. Or was it mild? She didn't know, but decided to take a chance regardless. 'I'd like that,' she murmured.

'Have you any particular taste in food?'

They walked along for a bit among crowds of people hurrying around them. But she was oblivious to their chattering voices.

'Anything at all, I love my food.'

'Indian, Chinese?'

'I love Indian.'

'Now I know something else about you,' he smiled. 'But I'd like to know more.'

They reached the corner.

'There's not much to know,' she said, suddenly shy.

'I look forward to seeing you soon, and if I have any information about Matt's case I'll let you know.'

'Thanks, I appreciate that. Now, I must …' she said, suddenly feeling awkward, and gave him a quick wave as she hurried away. Suddenly she felt like a young girl who had been chatted up by a boy at school, and now was imbued with excitement at the prospect of seeing him again.

Sitting into the car, and starting the engine, she was unable to prevent herself smiling broadly. What was it about Tom? She couldn't put her finger on it, but there was something she really liked. Then her cautious side kicked in. She didn't know much about him. Was he married? Living with a partner? Had he a family? Was he into having affairs with other women. Perhaps that was what he wanted. A sense of dread raced through her.

Chapter Forty-two

Matt couldn't get the conversation with Clive out of his head. And the possibility that he had been the cause of the breakup of Zoe's engagement lay heavily.

He went back to the shelter. His mind a ferment. For the first time since he had come to live there he felt his control over his life was slipping away from him. The structure which he had managed to stretch above him was like a spider's web and it had begun to disintegrate. And he couldn't deal with that.

There was a long line of men and women waiting for food, clothes and sleeping bags. Matt managed to stay composed until the last of them had gone off with a bundle under their arms. Most of them were on the phone as they rang the various hostels to get a bed for the night. He tidied up the storage area. If the bell rang after that, Peter would open up and let whoever it was lie on the floor for the night. Sr. Teresa's policy meant that if at all possible no one was ever refused shelter, although there wasn't always space to accommodate the number of people who needed a bed and some inevitably had to be refused.

He took a shower, pulled the curtain around the bed, and lay there staring up into the ceiling above him. It was dark, and his eyes suddenly filled with tears, and sweat broke out on his body. His nerves were stretched and he felt dehumanised. He wondered did that make him less of a man too? He turned over and buried his head in the pillow trying to sleep, but had no success.

That night was a ghastly dark place. He drifted into manic nightmares which terrified him. Waking. Dozing. Waking again with fright. Shivering. Cold. Hot.

Was he always going to bring sorrow to those he loved? He cringed as he remembered what he was like when he was young. A dark entity who lacerated his parents and sisters over and over again. Was it always going to be that way? Now he had done it again. He had hurt Zoe, the only person who cared for him. His heart beat with shame. And he couldn't bear what he had become.

A craving raced through him and he wanted something which would help him fight the situation in which he was in. He castigated himself. He was weak. Useless. And hated that he was once again on a downward curve into drug usage which would take him into no-man's land where he would be lost forever.

He struggled against its inevitable lure but he was falling, spinning, twisting, helpless, as if drawn by a magnet which he couldn't resist.

The morning brought the normal daily activities. He took Rex out for a run and on his return, Danielle, one of the volunteers, passed him by, but then stopped to look at him. 'You look tired, did you sleep well?'

'Not great.'

'Something on your mind?' she asked, obviously concerned.

'I suppose there's always something on my mind,' he managed a rather lopsided grin.

'Why don't you talk to Donal?'

He shook his head. Donal was a priest in the local parish who called in to the shelter occasionally. If anyone wanted to talk he was there for them. But Matt felt he couldn't unburden himself. The day was tough. But he plodded on. Looking at the men and women who came through, he wondered did their demons drive them to the very end of their tether.

Some of them did tell him their own stories and they were heart breaking. People who had fallen victim to drugs or drink. Men who had been thrown out of their own homes. Women who had had to leave in a hurry with their children, ending up living rough, or in hostels. Women who had lost their children because of their own drug addiction. Families who became homeless because they were unable to keep up with mortgage repayments due to the loss of jobs. All the world was here. He was glad to be able to help, but would have given anything to tell them his story and receive no censure. But that would never happen and he knew it. His story would have to be kept close to his heart. A dark secret.

Most nights he joined the group who went into O'Connell Street and helped the other volunteers give out food to the homeless. They always brought a number of sleeping bags, ground sheets, tents, and a selection of clothes too. As usual, there were a lot of people who came around to have something to eat, and many didn't have anything to wrap themselves in for the night if they couldn't get a hostel bed. And there were those who preferred to spend the night on the street anyway.

It was almost one in the morning before he was back, and he lay in bed trying to sleep. But like the night before he tossed and turned as the hours crawled by. Tears drifted down his face, and he couldn't understand why he felt this way. A terrible helplessness permeated his mind. And along with that there was a huge sense of guilt in his heart. Why was it that he always hurt people? Flashbacks of his past floated in and out of his head. And now this, Zoe's marriage plans ruined because of him …it had to be his fault …had to be.

Chapter Forty-three

Zoe put down her briefcase in the hall. The house was silent, and she wondered why there was no sound of the television which would normally be the case, and that there were no lights on either. She hurried through into the sitting room, switching lights as she went. Then into her father's study. She stood in the doorway shocked to see him sitting in his chair, head down.

'Dad?' She rushed across the room. 'What's wrong? Talk to me?' She cupped his face, but he didn't reply, although he opened his eyes and stared up at her.

'Are you all right?' She clasped his hands. 'You're so cold. Let me get something to warm you up.' She went to get a throw from the couch and draped it around him. 'I'll make tea.' In the kitchen she clicked on the kettle and when it boiled, put a teabag in the mug, poured water, added milk and sugar, and brought it into him.

'Feeling any better?'

'A bit,' he mumbled.

'I'll get you a scone.' She went back to the kitchen.

He ate half the scone, but finished the full cup of tea.

She sat beside him.

'Thanks,' he said.

'What happened to you?'

'I don't know.'

'Did you feel ill?'

'I was confused.'

'About what?'

'This …' he waved his hands around him at the torn pages, writing pads and books which lay on the floor.

She picked up a few pages but none of them were letters to Matt. Then she looked at one of the notebooks, and on a page there was a couple of lines written. But still she asked. 'Do you mind if I …?'

He nodded.

'Why are you writing to Matt,' she asked gently. She was very anxious to know, but was aware that she had to tread carefully or her father might react badly, like he had on Christmas Eve. But she continued on. 'Why don't you talk to him. Surely it would be better than writing. You could explain how you feel.' She took his hand.

He stared at her, a horrified look on his features. 'I couldn't, he would never forgive me.'

Zoe was silent for a moment. Staring down at his hand in hers, the skin mottled and wrinkled.

'I shouldn't have …it's only now I …since that night …' He stumbled over his words.

'I'm sure he will forgive you,' she said gently.

'No.' He shook his head.

'If you ask him?'

'How could I expect that? You don't know what I did.' He glared at her.

She was shocked. What was he referring to? When had it happened? Memories of their childhood swept through her mind. Her father had a very short fuse where Matt was concerned. 'There has to be forgiveness between a father and a son,' she said gently. 'You can't keep up such hatred over so many years. Why not meet him, just once?'

'I don't hate him,' he muttered.

'He doesn't hate you either.'

'He must,' Feargal insisted.

'I know that he would like to meet you.'

'Have you seen him?'

'Yes, we've met a few times.'

He stared at her. 'Where is he now?'

'He's living in Dublin.'

'How is he?'

'He's quite well. I'll tell him you were asking for him.'

'No, don't,' he flashed immediately.

'Dad,' she coaxed. 'Tell him what happened. It might help. And if you say that you don't hate him any longer that would mean a great deal to him. He's a very lonely person these days. His only friend is a dog.'

He seemed surprised.

'Think about it, please. It would mean a lot to me too.'

He shook his head.

Chapter Forty-four

It was Sunday evening. Feet up, Gail watched a late film on the television. Zoe unfolded a white blouse and set it on the ironing board. Tested the heat of the iron and began to press the back section carefully. She loved ironing. It was so relaxing. Preparing her clothes for the following week gave her that time to mull over what was going on in her life. She would have her organiser to one side and as she worked would go through the items in the diary and think out each one, planning her strategy. While it might only be an hour, it had to be done, and she relied on the opportunity which usually happened at the weekend. When she was living with Russell she would rise very early, get through what needed doing at leisure, and then cook breakfast and bring it up to Russell and climb back into bed with him. A sense of regret and loneliness too swept through her then for those lazy mornings.

'Did you hear any more from Pierre?' she asked gently.

Gail shook her head.

'I don't know how you managed to resist meeting him when he came over to see you. It must have been very hard to say *no* to someone you love.'

'I felt very guilty, I wanted to find some excuse to get away from that concert and rush over to see him, but I didn't. All I could see in my mind was him sitting in the restaurant on his own, at the very same table, probably sipping a glass of wine and watching the door every time it opened. Was I a real bitch to do that?'

'He didn't treat you very well going back and forth to Paris.'

'I kept imagining him with Claresse, and every time I did that it strengthened my resolve.'

'If you went back to him you wouldn't trust him at all and every time he took a phone call or text or went out the door you'd be suspicious of him. You couldn't live like that.'

'You're right.'

'And you will probably never hear from him again.'

'I hope so, but it's hard to resist his persuasion particularly when I still …love him.'

'I know how you feel,' Zoe murmured sympathetically.

'We're in the same boat. Odd that, isn't it?'

Zoe nodded.

'I know I've asked you before, but how about you and Russell getting together again? Is there any chance of that?' Gail asked.

Zoe shook her head.

'Maybe it was all the fuss of the wedding?'

'I won't go through that again for anyone.'

'I enjoyed it.'

'You would, it's your thing, all that bling.'

'All those fabulous dresses at the bridal salon. I've never seen anything like them, have you?'

'No, I'm not in the habit of drifting in and out of bridal showrooms,' Zoe said smartly, hanging up another blouse on a hanger. 'I didn't tell you, Sylvia called and said she has a buyer for the dresses and the accessories.'

'How much?'

'Half price.'

'That's all right, nearly three thousand.'

'Anyway, I accepted it. I'll be glad to get them out of my sight.'

'And forget about it …if you can,' advised Gail.

'If there's ever a next time it will be a very simple affair.'

'There's bound to be a next time.'

Zoe laughed.

'Remember when we were young and tried to imagine what it would be like to be married and we used to dress up in Mum's wedding dress and veil and pose in front of the mirror,' she giggled.

'I miss her so much, she would have loved to be involved in the whole thing.' Zoe took another garment from the folded pile, and arranged it on the board.

Gail sighed. 'Although she wouldn't have been too happy about the break-up.'

'I know, but I'd love to talk to her. She was always so wise, and could sort out all our problems.'

'We were only kids then really.'

'And didn't know her very well.'

'I wish she was around now too.'

'Imagine being able to have a girly day out. Shop. Have lunch. Cocktails in the evening. It would be great.'

The door burst open suddenly.

'Where is she?' Their father appeared, dressed in his pyjamas.

They looked at him, astonished.

'What are you doing out of bed, Dad?' Zoe asked.

'And no slippers on, you'll get cold.' Gail went over to him.

'She said she'd be back. Have you seen her?' He wandered across the kitchen, opened the press doors and peered inside.

'Who is she?'

'Your mother.'

They were silenced.

'She told me to talk to him but he's not here.'

'Who are you talking about?' Zoe asked, taking him over to an armchair and sitting him in it.

'I'll get your slippers,' Gail went outside.

'Matt …' he muttered.

'What about him?' Zoe sat down on the arm of the chair.

'How will I ever say I'm sorry?'

'You don't have to,' reassured Zoe.

'She knew what happened.'

Gail came back with the slippers which she put on his feet. 'I don't know what's wrong with you these days, Dad,' she snapped.

There was a look of helplessness on his face.

'Why don't you come back to bed.' Zoe helped him up.

'He's driving me around the twist,' Gail exploded as soon as Zoe came back downstairs. 'I think he's losing it.'

'No, he isn't, he's just preoccupied with something,' Zoe said.

'It's dementia.'

'I don't think so.'

'What's all this stuff about Mum? He's gone back in time. The other night I found him in the bedroom in a state. It was the same thing. Going on and on, and saying that he sees her and she's talking to him. That's the way dementia is.'

'I don't agree with you.'

'Well, maybe I'm exaggerating ...but what if he gets worse, how will we manage?'

'It will be all right, don't worry.'

'What a family,' Gail sighed. 'Since I've come home it has all come back to me. I didn't expect that you know. I had pushed it to the back of my mind and thought it would stay there.'

'You're not thinking of going back to London because of it, are you?' Zoe asked, very concerned.

'I might. I was able to leave it all behind when I went over.'

'You might meet Pierre again, that could be awkward.'

'London is a big place,' Gail said, defiant. 'Look, why don't we go for a weekend break. I could do with it. You could do with it. We work hard. And I want to catch up with my friends and have a night out.'

'I will, I promise, but when is the question.'

'Have a look at your diary and I'll do the same. It would be great if both of us can get a weekend off together. We'll stay in a really nice hotel, enjoy some retail therapy, maybe take in a show, and just have a good time,' Gail giggled.

'What about Dad?'

'I'm sure Mrs. Moran would look after him.'

Zoe nodded, unconvinced.

Chapter Forty-five

Matt couldn't get up the following morning. Something held him in a grip. His body in spasm. While he opened his eyes, his vision was blurred with tears. He pulled the sleeping bag up over his head and cowered underneath. He had a crazy idea that by hiding no one would see him, point or make remarks. What a *waster,* he accused himself.

He could hear voices close by and realised that volunteers had begun to arrive. He tried to push himself up but couldn't manage that, falling back down on the pillow.

'Check the door …' someone said.

'How many have we?'

'One hundred and ten so far.'

'Order more milk, we mightn't have enough.'

'Where's Matt?'

That last question brought him to his senses. He listened to what was going on outside.

'Matt? I haven't seen him.'

'He's usually in here at this time of the morning.'

He didn't recognise the voices. Unsure who was actually speaking. A fog surrounded him. He shook his head. Aware of sounds in his head. A high-pitched wailing. Like Tinnitus. He pressed his hands against his ears in an effort to block it out. But that didn't work. He could still hear the repetitive noise which was driving him crazy. It was like a phone ringing or an alarm, or something like that. On and on. Without relief.

Someone pushed the curtain back. 'Matt? Are you all right?'

He couldn't understand who was speaking at first.

'Matt?' She shook his shoulder.

He recognised her voice. It was Mary. But he stayed hidden under the sleeping bag.

'Come on, man, it's time to get up.' She pulled the bag from around his head. He held on to it tightly. Refusing to let go.

She sat beside him. 'What's wrong?'

He couldn't answer. Still cowering.

'OK,' she said softly, patted his shoulder and pulled over the curtain behind her.

He was so glad she had gone. Mortified that he had been found like this.

But she was back in a few minutes with Sr. Teresa.

'Matt?' Sister bent over him. 'Are you feeling ill?' Her gentle voice was insistent.

Underneath, he shook his head. 'Go away,' he whispered to himself. 'Go away.'

He could feel their presence there for a while, murmuring quietly to each other, but then they left.

He didn't get up at all that day, except to go to the toilet, glad he met no one. Mary had brought food in to him that morning, and one of the other volunteers came in later. But he couldn't eat or drink. Lying in a foetus position in the sleeping bag, his knees up, his arms clinging to his body. Protecting himself. From what he didn't know. A terrible fear dominated him and in his head it was dark, very dark.

Chapter Forty-six

Zoe walked along the corridor in the office, nodding and smiling to various people as she passed. As usual, she wore a dark suit, a white shirt with a coloured trim, and comfortable shoes with wedge heels. But there was a sense of dread in the pit of her stomach. She always felt this way when she had to meet Russell face to face although trying to avoid direct meetings with him was difficult. But they were extremely busy at *RZ* with new contracts and that entailed having to make a lot of decisions so she couldn't work at home for the moment.

She swung into her office, put her briefcase on the desk and sat at her computer. She brought up the agenda for the meeting today, and perused it carefully. The games they had designed for the Japanese market had been received very well and already further orders had been placed by the company. She glanced at her phone, picked up her laptop and went into the Board Room. She was warmly welcomed by the people from the Design Department who were setting up the screen.

'This is exciting, I'm looking forward to seeing these new designs,' she said, smiling.

'Hope you like them,' the Manager said and grinned at the others there.

'Hope I like them.' Was a curt comment from Russell who had just come in.

Suddenly, there was a distinctly frosty atmosphere in the room as he didn't acknowledge anyone's presence. People looked at each other but no one said anything.

Zoe wasn't surprised, she didn't expect much from Russell these days, but thought his attitude to the rest of the staff still left a lot to be desired.

'Right, let's get on with it.' Russell sat at the head of the table.

The Design Manager said no more, and brought up the first game on the screen.

They sat watching silently.

After a few minutes Zoe was immediately captivated by the sound track which had a definite oriental flavour. The theme of this first one used the ninja, experts in the dark arts of espionage and silent killing. Tales of ninja and samurai were popular with gamers but this one had an interesting twist as the story had a science fiction theme.

'I like it.' Zoe was enthusiastic. 'The setting takes us into an alien world, and the characters are really weird. That should go down well with the Japanese.'

'I'm not so sure, I was hoping for something which had a more western slant,' Russell said slowly, his expression showing his dissatisfaction.

'But surely the Japanese wouldn't want that?' Zoe responded immediately, quickly scrolling down her screen looking through some of the correspondence with the Japanese company.

'We have two more which have a different angle. All could be used in various markets,' the Design Manager added.

'Let's see them.' Russell tapped his pen on the table and the sharp rapid noise echoed harshly.

Zoe tried not to listen, she found that sort of incessant sound extremely irritating.

'What we need is another success like our own *World of Thora*,' he snapped.

'We've been playing around with a sequel,' the Manager said.

'That's more like it,' Russell responded positively for the first time.

'But we still need new games, virtual reality especially, with multi-player components which will mean that there can be a competitive element there. Gamers are particularly keen on that,' Zoe added. 'Groups play together and families too, it seems to really appeal to them.'

'The sequel fits all angles,' the Manager explained.

'But new fresh ideas are vital,' Zoe was insistent.

'Where is the sequel to *World of Thora* ...' Russell asked.

The game came up on the screen.

'This is set in the same mythical world of dragons and griffins who fight to the death and take over the remnants of ancient cities in which they have their lairs. We have introduced the multi-player element this time so it's much more competitive and should have immediate appeal. There are different mythical animals in it this time which should add colour to the individual groupings,' the Manager explained.

'Have you got someone working on the sound-track, I'd like to hear that as soon as you have it. It gives us a better idea of the overall action of the game.' Zoe made notes.

'Yes, the Music Department are working on it at the moment and have promised to let us hear it later on in the week so hopefully it will be good.'

They continued on. Once a month they had a meeting with the Design Department, and Zoe was always very keen to see what new ideas they produced.

She didn't meet Russell's gaze and found today that she regretted how things had developed. Why they couldn't have been more pleasant towards each other she simply didn't know, but he had been the one who had frozen her out and now she couldn't break down that wall which had risen up between them. Even if their personal relationship was gone, they could at least have spoken to each other about business. It was such a pity. She was disappointed in him. How was it that she didn't seem to know him at all even though they had spent so many years working together.

As she sat there watching the various games, she was reminded of something which she had picked up in the news lately. There was a huge addiction problem with the Japanese gaming youth. It was the same in the west too but in the east it was particularly severe. Suddenly, she wondered if she had children herself would she want them to be playing these games?

'We insert these repetitive aspects into the games so people want to play them again and again. And there is that competitive element too between groups who play together and want to climb up through the levels, building points as they go until finally a winner emerges.'

As the Design Manager spoke, Zoe had an image of a group of people placing bets in the bookmakers. The tension as they waited for the race to begin and then the excitement of the start, everyone's eyes glued to the screen praying that their horse would win. If they were winners they went over to the window to collect their money, while the losers, which were in the majority, crumpled up their tickets and threw them away with an air of disgust. But then they were placing another bet on the next race, and they were off again, the losses forgotten, caught up in their addiction.

A sense of disquiet crept over Zoe. What happened to people who were addicted? Their lives had to be severely affected. And did that include the youth and adults who bought and played the games that *RZ* sold worldwide?

She and Russell were like drug dealers. The thought of that was horrific. How was it she had been so unaware of their role in this trend before now?

Chapter Forty-seven

Matt couldn't get up out of bed the following day or the day after that either. Everyone seemed very concerned about him, particularly Sr. Teresa.

'Matt, how are you?'

He couldn't reply. Still feeling emotional.

'I'll ask Dr. O'Neill to come in and see you this evening. Just tell him how you feel, that's all. I'll get a hot breakfast for you, and I want you to eat something, or at least drink a cup of tea. It will do you good.'

He felt a sense of panic. He didn't want to talk to the doctor. He knew him from coming in to see the men and women, but couldn't have explained exactly how he felt. It would be impossible.

The young doctor came in later with Sr. Teresa.

'Matt?' he pulled over the wooden chair which stood near the bed, and sat down.

Matt didn't answer.

'Come on now, we know each other well enough by now, you can tell me what's wrong,' he coaxed.

'I can't.' It was the first response he made to anyone who had talked to him.

'Do you feel depressed? Are you particularly worried?'

He didn't answer.

'What exactly are you concerned about? Tell me?'

'Everything,' he whispered.

'I could prescribe some medication which might help.'

'No.'

'Maybe you could take it just for a few weeks?'

He shook his head.

'You'll have to take something, otherwise I might have to send you into hospital. You will become dehydrated and very ill.'

'I'm not going.'

'You can't lie here day after day.'

Matt curled deeper into the sleeping bag.

'I'll come back in to you before I leave,' the doctor said.

And he did. 'Matt, I'll have to insist on checking you out, it's my responsibility and I can't leave you lie there, particularly as you haven't been eating or drinking.'

Matt turned in the bag, facing the wall now.

'Stretch out your arm and let me check your blood pressure.' He took out the cuff, and his stethoscope.

Matt didn't respond.

The doctor stood, reached into the sleeping bag and pulled out his arm.

'Come on now, don't go against me.' He wrapped the cuff around his upper arm and tightened it. Then gave it the required amount of time and undid it silently. After that he took his temperature, and checked his pulse.

'Blood pressure up, temperature and pulse too high as well, that's not a good sign.'

For the first time, Matt turned towards him and his eyes met those of the doctor.

'You'll have to drink water, Matt. You'll cause Sr. Teresa a big problem if you're ill. You can't put that burden on her. If you begin to eat and drink again, then hopefully you'll be all right, otherwise you could have permanent affects.

Matt stared at him.

'I know you're feeling bad, but you will have to do as I say.'

His mention of Sr. Teresa had an immediate effect on Matt. In his misery he had not even thought about how she might be feeling about him. Or any of the volunteers either. And the more he thought about going into hospital the less he wanted to be in such a regimented place. It reminded him of being in prison.

'Ok,' he murmured.

'Right, I'll arrange to get you something to eat. And when I say drink water, I mean that, and it is litres, not sips,' he emphasised. 'And there is something else, Sr. Teresa tells me you must attend at the Garda station on Monday. You'll have to make an effort between now and then so that you'll be fit enough to sign on.'

He nodded.

Matt drank as much water as he could. As for the meal which was made for him, he couldn't eat all of it but managed a little.

Sr. Teresa came in. 'How was that for you?' she asked.

'Sorry, I didn't finish ...' He handed her the plate, feeling ashamed.

'Not to worry, you haven't eaten for a few days so you'll have to take it gradually. But keep drinking, that's vital.'

'I will.'

'You should talk to someone about how you feel, Matt, maybe the doctor?'

Once he began to eat and drink again, he felt much better, but there was still a huge hole inside which reminded him of how useless he was. But as he lay there hot and sticky, he realised that he hadn't had a shower in days and immediately crawled out of the bag and went to the bathroom. As was his habit, he began with cold water and stood there, released. The shower so invigorating he was transformed, and suddenly felt more like his old self, as every nerve ending screamed reality. That night he didn't sleep well either but lying there in the darkness he was somehow able to gather his thoughts and think more logically.

Do you want to live with your misery for ever?

Do you want to carry the responsibility for the breakdown of Zoe's relationship?

Talk to her.

And then move on.

Don't grieve for those lost years.

Leave them behind.

Your youth.

Your imprisonment.

All of it.

Now is the time to live.

This is just the beginning.

You've been reborn.

It's all ahead of you.

But …and it was a big *but* …he was reminded of his life before prison. What happened then was the reason he was feeling so bad now. It wasn't what he lost in the last twelve years it was what happened before that he was paying for. The hurt he inflicted on his family. And was still doing that by hurting Zoe.

His very existence seemed to bring bad luck to everyone.

Chapter Forty-eight

Clive knocked on the door of Zoe's office. 'Got a minute?'

'Come on in.' She was glad to see him.

'I've been talking to my brother about Matt.'

She was immediately interested.

'And we both feel there is a case to be made if we can substantiate the evidence of the letter.'

'That might be difficult. I don't know how I could persuade my father to admit that he had held back crucial information from the Gardai. What about the time element?'

'My brother thinks he will be able to overcome that,' said Clive. 'He was the one who felt that it was a travesty in the first place.'

'I can't believe that. It's incredible. If I'd only found that letter when it was written originally,' Zoe said.

'Should I say anything to Matt if I see him again?' Clive asked.

'I don't know if we should raise his hopes, although he hasn't mentioned the letter to me at all since I gave him the copy.'

'Then I'll leave it to you.'

'There's something I wanted to say to you, Clive,' Zoe said hesitantly. She felt awkward. It was a delicate subject. 'You remember when Russell and I had a difficult time at the Board Meeting earlier this year, and I said I might consider selling my shares in the company and resign?'

He nodded.

'Initially, I decided against that, feeling that I wasn't going to be

217

'pushed which was what Russell wanted.'

'I've noticed things seem to have improved with him, he's not as volatile as he was.'

'That's because you and the other directors have talked to him about his general attitude, otherwise I don't think there would be any change.'

'True.' He nodded.

'Anyway, I've been giving it a lot of thought lately, and I am now considering selling my shares. Sorry, I hope that's not too much of a shock for you.' She had been worried about telling him.

'Don't be concerned, I'm not really surprised and when you first mentioned it, I thought perhaps myself and Russell could divide the equity between us.'

'That would be great if you wanted to do that.'

'But the company needs you, Zoe,' Clive insisted.

'I've become disillusioned because of Russell but there's another angle which has begun to bother me.'

'And what is that?' Clive asked.

'I've been thinking of what exactly we do. How we make our livelihood.'

'We sell games,' Clive laughed.

'But there is a huge addiction to computer games, particularly in Japan where we recently signed a lucrative contract.'

'That's the way it is in the world now.'

'I know, but I've been asking myself a question. Do I want to be selling a product which is causing such social problems? And gaming addiction has now been officially designated a *disease*.'

'By the World Health Organisation,' he said. 'I heard that.'

'And it's becoming more and more widespread,' she insisted.

'It's a business, Zoe.'

'I know, but it's like drug dealing.'

'What?' he laughed out loud.

'I've come to realise that and I don't think I want to be involved in it any longer.'

'But it's your whole life. You've given everything to the business over the last few years.'

'It's immoral,' she said vehemently.

'At the moment we're a small but very successful concern and the way things are going we could expand in the future and possibly become one of the biggest companies in this field in the world.'

'I know, but I'm still getting out.' Even as she said the words she knew in her heart of hearts that it was what she wanted to do.

'I'm so sorry, Zoe, I don't know how we're going to get on without you.'

'You'll manage. And I know that Russell will be delighted.'

'Have you mentioned this to him?'

'No, not yet. I wanted to talk with you first.' She knew Clive would always give her an honest answer.

'I have to say it hasn't been easy for you since you broke up with Russell, and your moral standpoint is admirable but I can't say I agree with it.'

'You think I'm crazy?'

'In some ways, but then you've always been your own person and I hope that whatever you decide to do after this will make you happy. Any ideas?'

She shook her head. 'There are ideas shooting through my mind all the time. All sorts of things, but nothing has grabbed me yet.'

'Give it time,' he advised with a warm smile. 'You'll soon find a challenge.'

'Thanks, I'd appreciate your help.'

'If anything occurs to me I'll let you know.'

'But first you must decide about buying the shares.'

'Thanks for offering, it gives me a chance to do something else.'

'You're happy about your decision to change your career?' Clive asked.

'Before I burn out like some of our staff.'

That evening, Tom called just as she parked outside the house. 'Zoe, there's something …'

'What?' she was immediately apprehensive.

'It's Matt …'

'What about him?'

'He's not well.'

She froze. 'In what way?'

'The doctor thinks he's having a breakdown.'

'My God.'

'Sr. Teresa called me.'

'Have you seen him?'

'No, but I'm going around now to talk to him and I'll see the doctor.'

'I'll go as well.'

'Have you been there before?'

'No.'

'Do you want me to pick you up?'

'No thanks, I'll call a taxi.'

'Would you like to meet somewhere adjacent?' he asked. 'There's usually quite a crowd around the place and so I'd prefer to walk in with you.'

They arranged to meet in a nearby pub.

When she arrived at the bar Tom was already there.

'I'm very worried about Matt,' she admitted.

'I hope he improves.'

'He has no one to support him, and I'm not a lot of use. If only he could come home,' Zoe said.

'His life is lonely.'

'I've talked to my father, and asked him to meet Matt, but he didn't want to. I think he's afraid.'

'It's understandable, when you read the letter.'

'It bothers me that Matt has been made into a pariah because someone wasn't prepared to tell the whole truth …even if it is his father …our father.'

'Has Matt made any comment about the letter since you gave him a copy?'

'No, not a word.'

'Maybe this upset has some connection?'

Zoe stared at him, horrified. 'My God, is it my fault then?'

'I'm sorry, perhaps I shouldn't have suggested that.' A look of regret swept across Tom's face.

'No, I would have come around to that way of thinking myself, don't worry. When I gave him the letter I just wanted him to have it because it was addressed to him and he had every right to know the contents particularly when it related to his conviction.'

'It's possible then ...' Tom said slowly.

There was a queue of people outside the shelter, although Tom phoned when they arrived and a back door was opened for them.

A dog ran up to them as they passed through the yard. 'Hi Rex?' Tom leaned down to pat the excited dog. 'This is Matt's dog.'

'He told me about him. He's lovely and friendly.' She bent down and ran her hand along his back. 'So cute.'

Tom ushered her inside and the dog followed them in.

'No Rex,' Tom said, and the dog immediately stopped and backed out.

'He's very well trained.' Zoe gasped.

'Matt takes good care of him.'

'It's nice that he has a dog.'

'But this week he seems to have lost interest in him which is a pity.' Tom closed the door behind them. 'We'll go into Sr. Teresa.'

They walked through the building and down a corridor. He knocked on a door.

'Come.'

They went in to see a woman sitting at a desk. She smiled, put down the phone which was in her hand and stood up. 'Sorry, I'm trying to find some beds for tonight.'

'Sr. Teresa, this is Matt's sister, Zoe,' Tom introduced her.

'How lovely to meet you.' The woman came around the desk and shook her hand.

'Thanks so much for what you've done for Matt.'

'It's not enough I fear, and particularly at the moment.'

'Can I see him?' Zoe asked anxiously.

'The doctor went in to him a short time ago, I'll call him and ask him how Matt is. Sit down. I won't be long.' She left for a few minutes and returned as she had promised. 'He'll be over after the next patient.'

'He's an amazing person to give so much of his time. He's in surgery all day and then spends evenings here,' Tom said. 'You're very lucky to have him, Sr. Teresa.'

'All of our volunteers are wonderful. We have a barber who comes around a couple of nights a week to cut the men and women's hair. It means so much to them. Gives them confidence so they feel more normal. And then we've a dentist as well and a chiropodist,' Sr. Teresa added.

The door opened and the doctor came in.

There were more introductions made.

'Thank you very much for looking after Matt,' Zoe said.

'He's improved a lot since I saw him last night, Zoe. I threatened to send him to hospital if he didn't let me check him out.'

'I'm so relieved to hear that.'

'Anyway, he wasn't very well, dehydrated, blood pressure raised etc., so rather than go into hospital he agreed to start eating and drinking again. He's in better shape this evening.'

'Why did he stop eating?' Zoe asked.

'I've seen it before when men come out of prison, if they haven't much support then they become depressed.'

'I feel guilty, I should have done more for him.' Zoe was upset. There were tears in her eyes.

'You couldn't have known it was going to happen,' Tom reassured.

'Does he need medication?' Zoe asked the doctor.

'Refuses to take any,' he replied and shrugged.

'What's going to happen to him?'

'I'll keep an eye on him. He's much better today, physically that is.'

'But mentally?' Tom asked.

'That's the problem, he needs a lot of help.'

Zoe was silent for a moment. 'Can I see him?'

'I'll ask him, give me a minute.'

They waited.

'Continue on with your calls, Sr. Teresa, don't let us delay you,' Zoe said.

'Thank you, I will.' She lifted the phone again, and glanced at the list of names in front of her. Zoe listened to the nun as she made call after call enquiring if there were any beds, and could see the disappointment on her face as her requests were refused by the various hostels. She was astonished to realise that the nun had such trouble finding beds for people. She knew about homelessness from media reports, but somehow hadn't quite realised how difficult it was. Now faced with the problem, she was shocked.

Matt had probably lived like that when he first came out of prison and she was indebted to Sr. Teresa for helping him. As they waited, Zoe longed to go to Matt and hold him close. Anguish at this delay burned through her. Let me go, she cried inside, her heart tortured. She wanted to comfort him and tell him that she loved him. Remind him that he wasn't alone in the world and that she was there too, and would always be there. Was it her fault that he had become ill? Should she have given him the letter at all? Was it too soon for his sensitive nature to grapple with such an astounding revelation?

She trembled, her hands clasped tightly in her lap. The door opened and the doctor came in again. 'I think it might do him the world of good to see you, Zoe, so go on ahead.'

'Thank you,' she smiled, delighted.

'Now I must continue with the surgery, nice to meet you.'

'Thanks for looking after him.'

'No prob.'

'Matt?' Tom called, pulling back the curtain.

Zoe found it difficult to stop herself rushing in to him.

'Your sister is here, Matt …' Tom said. Then he ushered her past him, but moved away then leaving them alone.

She stood there, trembling, looking down at his dark head, half hidden by the sleeping bag. 'Matt?' she whispered.

There was no reply.

She knelt down on the floor, put her hand on his head and stroked his dark hair gently. He turned and reached towards her, his face wet with tears. She wrapped her arms around him then and rocked him like a child, in tears also. 'You'll be all right, Matt, don't worry. I'll look after you.'

He gasped. Incoherent gulps.

Zoe pulled the sleeping bag away from his face, and dried his tears with a tissue. He clasped her hand. Held it tight in his. Hot and sticky with sweat. She stayed there holding him for a time. How was she going to help him?

She needed to have him home. Not the home he always knew but the place where his family now lived. Was that what he wanted?

'I'm sorry,' he said, his voice was husky.

'Can I get you anything?' she asked.

He shook his head.

'A drink?' She picked up the glass of water which was on a tray beside the bed.

He nodded, and took it from her.

'Are you feeling better?' she asked.

'Now that you're here,' he smiled. 'Thanks for coming. I've felt responsible for things which have happened …'

'What do you mean?' She was puzzled.

'For everything.'

'Don't be crazy, just concentrate on getting well.'

He nodded.

'Promise me?' She kissed him. 'I'll see you tomorrow. Love you …'

Outside, Tom waited.

'Could we bring Rex in to him? I'm sure it might help him, he is very fond of that dog,' she asked.

'We'll ask Sister.' He led the way back to her office and when she had a moment he put the suggestion to her.

'Let's do that, I don't know why I didn't think of it myself,' she agreed immediately.

'Thank you so much, Sr. Teresa.' Zoe was glad.

'Go and get him, Tom.'

They went out to the yard.

'Hi Rex?' Zoe rubbed his fur and he leaned against her.

'Come on boy.' Tom undid the lead from the hook in the wall and they brought him in.

'You take him.' He held back the curtain around the bed.

'Matt?'

He opened his eyes and looked at her.

'I've brought someone to see you.'

The dog rushed towards the bed and leapt up on it.

'He's happy anyway,' she laughed.

'Rex.' Matt put his arms around the animal and hugged him, and was licked enthusiastically.

'He's a lovely dog, you're lucky to have him.'

'Thanks for bringing him in.'

'And he can stay with you, just take him out so he doesn't dirty the place.' Sr. Teresa came in behind them.

'Thanks …' He ran his hands through the dog's coat.

'Goodnight, love,' Zoe said and kissed Matt. 'Take care. I'll see you soon.'

He smiled as they left.

'Matt seemed much better after your visit,' Tom said.

'I'm so glad.'

'You're very special to him. He's lucky to have you.'

'He's very vulnerable.'

'And it was a great idea to bring the dog in.'

'I only hope that he'll pull through.'

'He will,' Tom reassured.

'Thanks for all you do for him, I appreciate it.'

'I like Matt, he's a good person who has had a tough few years.'

She felt guilty. Why hadn't she made contact earlier?

'You're very important to him. He needs you.'

'I need him,' she said, thinking how he had been left out there in the dark on his own like an abandoned orphan. What must it have been like for him? Probably the only person in the prison who didn't have a visitor. Most prisoners had family visits. But how did Matt feel as he waited for someone week after week, month after month, year after year?

'Would you like to have a drink?' Tom asked as they made their way up Grafton Street.

She looked at him, surprised. 'Thank you, that would be nice.'

'How about *The Duke?*'

'Sure,' she smiled, unexpectedly shy and very much taken aback by this unexpected turn of events. She thought about Russell. He had always made the arrangements whenever they were going out, and they usually met up with his friends at their favourite eating and drinking places. It was only now she wondered about her acquiescence. And perhaps that was her mistake. He had taken her for granted.

The pub was very crowded and they only managed to squeeze into a space at the bar. There was something intimate about the way he stood back allowing her to slip in beside him. Her body close to his.

'What would you like?'

'Gin and tonic, thanks.'

'*G & T* and a pint of *Guinness*,' he ordered. Then he turned, looked into her eyes and drew closer. She was taken aback when his lips touched hers. Warm. Moist. So intimate. Her pulse raced as she responded, oblivious of the people around them.

Chapter Forty-nine

It was late when Zoe went home. A mix of emotions in her heart. She was desperately worried about Matt, wondering what had caused his breakdown and blaming herself for not doing enough for him. And very grateful to Tom for doing so much. But she didn't know how she felt about him personally. What an evening, she thought. Going over what he said. Seeing his eyes. Feeling the touch of his hands on her face, soft, sensitive. Remembering the scent of his skin, imbued with a hint of aftershave. The experience was so short and intense she could barely keep up with it. Her heart thumped with excitement and already she knew that her feelings were out of control. She was in a crazy twisting dizzying vortex which took her along a road of wild imaginings and in her deepest self she was shouting *I love you*. And that shocked her. Shocked her totally. How could this have happened so quickly? To fall in love with a man she hardly knew?

And then the question of whether he was single or had a partner or a wife hadn't even been asked. She clasped her hands tight praying that he wasn't tied up in some complicated relationship with a lot of baggage. Or was he the type who flitted from woman to woman. She closed her eyes and made a wish that it wasn't the case. But then the possibility that he might have a family and children pushed into her mind. That wouldn't let go and kept nagging at her. If it was the case then she didn't want to go down such a road, realising how difficult it would be.

With Matt she had a much longer relationship. A sibling blood bond which went back to her childhood. But because all that ended over twelve years before she hadn't known where to find herself or Matt either. She was in a lost twilight world.

She visited him each evening for the rest of that week and by Sunday her brother had made a good recovery.

'He's up and about, sorting the clothes at the moment. We can't believe how much he has improved,' Sr. Teresa told her when she arrived.

'Maybe I could give him a hand,' she offered. 'I have time.'

'There's no need for that, but thanks for offering. Come with me.'

Zoe was amazed at the numbers of men and women who were there, and shocked that there were even some with young children too.

'How will those families find somewhere to stay tonight?' Zoe asked Sr. Teresa.

'I'm sure you heard me phoning around looking for beds. It's like that every night.'

'And do you find them?'

'Not always.'

'And then?'

'We will put them here but when we run out of space they have to sleep rough. Find a doorway and cover themselves up with cardboard.'

'But the children?'

'I usually manage to get beds for the families, but it isn't easy.' She sighed. Her narrow shoulders hunched as she continued walking along the corridor where people sat on benches by the wall. 'This is Matt's section.' She pushed open a door.

Zoe followed her.

The queue of people extended from the door to the counter where Matt was searching for clothes to suit each person.

'What size are you?' he asked.

'Medium,' the man muttered. 'Or used to be.'

'Right,' Matt smiled and went to the racks behind. Pulled out a pair of blue jeans and checked the size. 'Do you think these will suit you?'

He held them up.

'Thanks.

Matt noted it on the computer as the man left the queue and the next took his place. He looked up and caught sight of Sr. Teresa and Zoe. He smiled.

'I'll take over for a few minutes while you go and talk to Zoe.' Sr. Teresa went inside the counter. 'Go into my office.'

'Thanks Sister.' He walked back with Zoe.

'How are you?' she asked, concerned.

'Much better today,' he said sheepishly.

She hugged him.

'It was great to see you this week. I don't think I could have managed without you. And it was wonderful to see Rex.'

'I only wish I could take you home,' she said softly.

He shook his head.

'It will happen, one of these days, I promise you. And you must always let me know if there's anything up with you. You know I travel a bit and I mightn't manage to see you, but we can always chat on the phone.'

'Thanks, appreciate that,' he smiled.

'Have you any idea why you felt so bad?' Zoe ventured. Anxious to know the reason.

'No.' His response was abrupt but she continued on speaking.

'I thought it might be as a result of the letter from Dad. That must have been very difficult for you.'

He didn't reply. And moved towards the window through which he stared, his hands pushed into his pockets. She followed him. 'Talk to me, Matt.' She touched his shoulder gently.

He turned back to her.

'What do you want to do with your life?'

'What opportunities are there for me?' he flashed, a touch of anger in his voice. 'An ex-criminal?'

'You've done your time, all those years spent behind bars.'

Matt shrugged.

'You shouldn't have to carry the weight of that burden around with you.'

'It's a fact of life, Zoe. People look at me as if they recognise what I am. It's painted on me … *criminal*.'

'Don't say that.'

'You're not me, you can't understand the way I feel. The word screams at me over and over, morning and night.' There were tears in his eyes.

Zoe put her arms around him and held him tight. 'Try and put it out of your head, Matt, you must rise above it, and not let it dominate you.'

'I don't know that I can do that.' He wiped the tears with his hands. 'I'm a fool.'

'No, that's not true. I won't allow you to think that way.' She stared into his eyes. 'Look at me.' She gripped his arms with her hands. She forced him to meet her gaze, moisture in her eyes as well. 'You will make your way, I promise you. And I'll be beside you,' she whispered. 'To help in any way I can.'

Tom called and invited her out to dinner. She accepted immediately. No hesitation this time.

They went to a restaurant on Nassau Street, a favourite of his.

'There's a good selection of food here,' Tom said as they looked at the menu.

'Lots of vegetarian, that's great.' Zoe was delighted.

'Are you vegetarian?' he asked.

'Not really, but I like plenty of choice.'

'I'm a steak man myself.'

The waiter arrived to ask about drinks.

'What would you like?' Tom asked.

'Glass of wine would be lovely. I deliberately left the car at home.'

'Red or white?'

'Red for me.'

'Do you like French, or Spanish wine or what would you like?'

'Let me have a look.' She moved closer to him. 'How about a *Rioja*, that one there perhaps?' she pointed.

He ordered it.

They spent a while going through the menu and finally made their choices.

The wine arrived and the waiter poured. Tom raised his glass and they clinked. 'To …' he said with a grin.

She giggled. 'The future.'

'This is a nice place, small and intimate,' she sipped another glass of wine when the waiter had removed the dishes. They talked at length. She told him where she was at. About Russell. The marriage which had never happened. Although he didn't tell her much about his own life.

When the coffee was served, she took a deep breath. 'There is something I've wanted to ask you …I must ask.'

'What is it?' he smiled. His hazel eyes meeting hers with that delicious warmth in their depths.

She took a deep breath. This was harder than she expected. 'I just wondered …if you are married or have a partner?'

He laughed.

She was surprised at his response.

'Do you not think I would have told you that already? I'm hardly going to ask you out to dinner if I have a wife waiting for me at home?'

'It happens,' she murmured.

He didn't answer, but there was a look of concern in his eyes.

'We don't know each other that well …'

She was floundering around now.

'And there I was wondering the same about you, and couldn't imagine that you would actually be free until you told me tonight. And I'm not the sort of guy who plays around. I'm not married. I've never been married. I had a long relationship with a girl when I young but it never even went as far as living together,' he smiled at her. 'I live alone.

A rather solitary life. I enjoy my work and I put all my energy into that. You are the first woman I've felt attracted to in a long time,' he leaned across to kiss her gently.

She drew closer towards him, suddenly feeling amazingly happy.

Chapter Fifty

'I've been looking up flights for London, weekend after next, say Saturday morning. Do you think you would be free?' Gail asked as she sprinkled herbs on the chicken, and then lifted the roasting tin into the oven.

'I don't know, we're very busy and I …' Zoe hesitated as she peeled the potatoes. Tom had taken up more and more of her life since that night in *The Duke*. Their relationship had escalated at such a pace in a very short time she hardly knew where she was.

'Well …?' Gail prompted.

'I'm sorry, I know I said I might come over but now I'm not sure.'

'Come on, Zoe, my friends want to plan an evening, they're all looking forward to meeting you.'

'Are you going to meet Pierre?'

'No, that's all over. I haven't responded to any of his emails or texts recently and I'm hoping he'll give up eventually.'

'You're amazing,' Zoe said, in genuine admiration. 'But there's something I have to tell you …' she felt embarrassed.

'What is it?'

'That man I mentioned …'

'Oh, that guy you fancied?' Gail smiled knowingly.

Zoe couldn't help giggling.

'Are you dating?'

Zoe nodded.

'Congrats,' Gail screamed and threw her arms around Zoe.

'Thank you,' she smiled.

'Who is he? Tell me?' Gail demanded.

'It's Tom, Matt's Probation Officer.'

'How did you connect up with him?'

'Through Matt.'

'Has he got any baggage?'

'No, he's single.'

'That's so unusual, he must be unique,' Gail said excitedly.

Zoe regretted telling Gail about Tom, particularly as she was trying to get over Pierre.

'It didn't take you long to replace Russell,' her sister laughed.

'It just happened …so fast I don't even believe it.'

'Have you fallen madly in love?' Gail had a teasing glint in her eyes.

Zoe blushed.

'I'm delighted for you. But I'm going to have to meet him and give him the once over. You know, family approval, all that jazz.'

'We'll organise an evening, I hope you'll like him.' She put the vegetables into the steamer.

'I'm sure I will. It's so exciting. Now how about our weekend in London, can you bear to leave him for forty-eight hours?'

'Stop messing, of course, we're not joined at the hip …yet,' she said with a grin. 'But it's just that Matt hasn't been well for a while and I want to be here as much as I can just in case he needs me.'

'You're putting him before me?' Gail asked, a resentful tone in her voice.

'He needs help.'

'I don't know how you can spend so much time with him, he's a bastard, an evil bastard.' Gail shuddered.

'He deserves to be forgiven.'

'I'll never forgive him.'

'What about Dad's letter?' Zoe asked.

'He doesn't know what he writes, it's all rubbish, means nothing.'

'He knows exactly. And that full letter was dated two thousand and twelve and then he was in full possession of his faculties even if he does seem a little confused these days.'

'We keep coming back to that letter. Over and over. And we don't even know if there's any truth in it.'

'I feel it is true, and I want it to be true, for Matt's sake.'

'He admitted his guilt, he's been in prison, what does it matter now.'

'If there is new evidence, he will be cleared of guilt.'

'What new evidence could there be?' Gail gasped.

'In the letter Dad referred to knowing something which he hadn't admitted during the trial.'

'How could he have any new evidence?'

'I don't know, but I'm praying I'll be able to persuade him to tell me,' Zoe whispered, a look of longing on her face.

'It's far too late to produce new evidence, the law would never admit it,' Gail snapped.

'I was reading about the *Innocence Project* online.'

'What's that?'

'It's a project which was set up to clear the names of people who have been wrongly accused. Years ago there was an Irish man who was executed for a crime he didn't commit and he received a posthumous pardon from the State after those people interceded for him.'

'And you think that Matt …you're crazy.'

'Our brother deserves it …'

'I haven't got a brother.' Gail was dismissive.

'If there is only one tiny bit of evidence which could be produced to clear his name then I want to give it to him. I don't know how you can say such a thing.'

'But you go on and on about it and I'm tired of listening to you.'

'I'm sorry, but each time I see him I …'

'You're a softy, he can see right through you and is taking advantage.'

'He's not like that.'

'So he's changed radically?'

'Yes, and you should meet him, get to know him again,' Zoe urged.

'I don't want to, he's past tense Zoe, can't you see that? He did a terrible thing and he disappeared out of our lives. I want him to stay there and I never want him back. Let him rot. Anyway, I have to think of myself and rebuilding my career.'

'I'm sure you're going to do really well,' Zoe said gently, hating the fact that her sister was so aggravated.

Gail began to lay the table. Knives. Forks. Spoons. Positioned carefully. Gail was like that. Precise in everything she did.

'We must talk about him.' Zoe took the roast chicken out of the oven and basted it.

'I don't want to.' Gail filled a jug of water and put it on the table.

'I'll call Dad.'

They sat at the table and began to eat.

Zoe didn't quite finish, and left some of her food behind. She wanted to talk about Matt and felt very nervous about doing it. As soon as the others had finished, she took a deep breath. 'Dad, we've found a letter you wrote to Matt.'

'What letter?' Feargal looked puzzled.

'I'll get it for you.' She went to her handbag, took the sheet of paper and handed it to him. 'It's a photocopy.'

He stared at it.

'Do you remember writing it?'

He said nothing. There was a cold blank look on his face.

Zoe could feel a sense of malice emanate across the table from Gail.

'I don't mind that you wrote the letter but I just want to know what is the secret you mention. Something which would have saved Matt from being imprisoned. What does it mean?'

'Zoe, why are you doing this?' Gail hissed.

'We must find out,' she insisted.

Suddenly Feargal stood up, threw the sheet of paper at her and stumbled out of the room. They could hear him go down the corridor to the study and bang the door.

'You've really upset him now,' Gail accused.

Chapter Fifty-one

Feargal leaned breathlessly on the wooden panels of the door. A sense of panic swept through him and he rushed over to his desk. Staring down at the usual mess of papers strewn upon it. He searched among them as if he was looking for something in particular but grew more and more frustrated as he seemed unable to find it.

He leaned his hands on the table. Zoe's words echoed in his mind. She had shown him a letter. But he had written so many. She had only read one, what about all the others? Now she wanted him to talk to Matt. To tell him what happened. To confess. But how could he go back to that night. That night. He almost screamed out loud.

'You must tell them.'

Her voice echoed.

'No.'

'You must.'

The voice was soft, steadfast, and whirled around his head insisting that he listen.

There was a knock on the door.

He stared at it. Terrified. How could he reveal the events of that night? What would happen to him?'

'You must pay the price.'

He looked around. Was she there? In reality. 'Where are you?' he asked vaguely. 'Why can't I see you? Are you a ghost come back to haunt me from some place?'

'I'm here. I've always been here but you can't see me.'

'How is that possible?' Now he was beginning to believe that she actually did exist. He looked around, hoping to see her but he couldn't. There was no one there. 'Where are you Rachel? Where are you?'

'I know that anything is possible and you must believe what I am saying.'

'Dad?' The door opened and Zoe came in.

'Tell her, Feargal, do it for me.'

He couldn't look at Zoe, so ashamed.

'Please tell me what happened,' she asked softly. 'I'll forgive you, no matter what, you're my father.'

He compressed his lips, very nervous. His eyes filled up with tears.

'Don't forget I'll always love you.' She put her arm around his shoulders.

He looked up and saw that Gail stood in the doorway.

'Tell us,' Zoe insisted.

The atmosphere was unbearable for him.

'Go on Dad, just explain what happened …why did you hold back information which could have helped Matt,' Zoe urged.

He sank into a chair. 'Matt …didn't kill …'

They were silent. Tension built up in the room.

'What are you saying?' Zoe asked, her voice shaking.

'I …pushed her …' he said. Suddenly he felt like he was going to drown. He couldn't catch his breath. He would choke. 'I'm sorry.'

Zoe stared at him. 'You killed Mum and all you can say is *sorry?*' Her face was white, eyes wide in shock, lips parted.

Gail let out a wild scream which seemed to go on and on.

Chapter Fifty-two

Matt felt a lot better since meeting Zoe. Her confidence had bolstered him up, and his low self-esteem drifted away somewhat. He thought about the other people in the shelter and decided that his own situation wasn't so bad and that many of the other men and women he met on a daily basis had lives which were far worse than his. These people had their hands stretched out to him for help. How could he help them? He was useless and had never imagined that he might be anything more than that since he had been imprisoned.

He watched their faces as they accepted the weekly bundle of food. It helped them stretch out the money they received each week and they were very glad to get it. The food was donated to the shelter by various supermarkets and along with two other volunteers he packed it into bags which were then stored in the room in which he slept. He threw himself into the work. And most mornings he ran with Rex, loving the company of his dog. At night he worked on the website for Pierce. It gave him something to do which he really enjoyed. As regards the games which Zoe had uploaded he didn't think he could do anything as good and didn't see himself creating games which would be of any use to her.

'How are you feeling?' the doctor asked, looking at him keenly.

'Not so bad,' he replied without meeting his eyes.

'Sleeping?'

'A bit better.'

'Glad to hear that.'

He took his blood pressure. Heart rate. Pulse. 'You seem all right. I'm not so worried now,' he said with a grin.

'Thanks.'

'But I'll be keeping an eye on you, and if you notice any symptoms I want you to tell me, make a note of whatever it is.'

'I will,' he agreed.

'I don't want to find you in the same state as I did that last time.'

Matt nodded with an air of submission. He found it hard to argue with anyone, especially someone who had authority. He wondered if he would ever be able to do that. It was a hang-up from his time in the prison system. That deference which was beaten into him had left a harsh imprint. As if he had been branded on his back by a hot iron with an owner's name. Identified as his property like a slave.

Now he tried to persuade himself that it was good to be alive, and that he was no longer possessed by anyone. He would be healed by God. It was his salvation. In his heart he prayed that one day he would be forgiven. And possibly even loved. Otherwise what was left of his life would be a tragedy.

Chapter Fifty-three

'It was an accident, I was arguing with Matt and she stepped between us …I didn't mean …' Feargal covered his face with his hands.

A black shadow descended on Zoe. A terrible anguish seized her. A physical pain pierced through her heart. The agonising loss of her mother was fresh. As if it was happening now.

Gail pushed past her and stood over their father, her arm raised as if she would exact revenge. 'You're a murderer.'

'No, no …' he tried to avoid her.

'I could kill you …' she spoke through clenched teeth, moving ever closer to him.

'Please don't,' he burst into tears, his body quivering.

Zoe held her arm. 'Gail …'

'He killed Mum …' she threw herself into Zoe's arms and they clung to each other, sobbing.

'It's incredible to think that Dad let Matt take the blame,' murmured Zoe after a while.

'He's …a …bastard,' Gail still cried.

'I can't believe you would do such a thing, Dad.' Zoe gazed at Feargal, so shocked her mind was barely able to cope with what she had heard.

Gail suddenly swung towards her father, leaned over him, grabbed his jacket and shook him hard. 'You let us think it was Matt all along?'

'We lost our brother …all those years he was kept a prisoner,' Zoe screamed at him.

She couldn't believe what her father had said. He had actually been involved on the night in question and let Matt be arrested and tried for a crime which he didn't commit. Was this the man she called her father? Her Dad? Was this the man she loved and had always loved? Looking at him as he sat in the armchair, shoulders slumped, a crumpled broken figure, she almost didn't recognise him.

Suddenly, a tide of dark emotion seized her. Her soul was in torment. She put out her hand and touched his arm. Searching for the man she knew. But she could only feel a sense of loathing for him. How could he have done this horrendous thing. She turned from him and put her arms around her sister and they held each other. How long they stood there Zoe didn't know but gently she disengaged herself and looked at her father who still sat in the chair, equally distressed.

She brought Gail through into the kitchen and sat her down. Like an automaton she made a pot of tea, poured a mug and handed it to Gail. Then she took one into her father and put it beside him. 'Drink that, Dad,' she murmured. The terrible state of anger against him still burned like fire within her. There was a dryness in her mouth and she found it difficult to speak properly, her words slurred like she was drunk. But she lifted the mug and made sure that he held it steadily, her normal caring nature overcoming her antipathy towards him. 'Dad, can you hear me?'

He didn't reply and she was worried then that he might have had some sort of attack.

'Come on, take a sip,' she encouraged.

He did so, and she was relieved. 'Drink all of that. I'll be back in a minute.'

She went out to Gail and found that she was calmer now. 'Are you feeling any better?'

She shook her head.

'Why don't you go to bed?' Zoe suggested.

Gail nodded. She put down the mug and stood up.

'I'll check on Dad.' Zoe went into Feargal's study again. He made no response when she came in, but she noticed he had finished the tea. She took him to bed then and sat by him for a while until he eventually drifted off. Sitting there, she was able to think more clearly about what had happened. Her suspicions about the letter her father had written were now confirmed. But what she had heard was much worse than anything she had imagined.

The house was quiet then. A sense of waiting in the silence. A holding of breath. After a while she went into her own room and called Tom. They chatted for a moment but she found it impossible to hide her distress.

'What's wrong?' he asked.

'I can't tell you …' Tears rushed into her eyes.

'I'll come over.'

'Please …'

'I'll call you when I'm nearby.'

In Tom's car, Zoe put her arms around him and clung tight, tears drifting down her cheeks and dampening his blue shirt.

'It was awful, Tom, to hear him tell the truth after all this time. You know I thought there might be something insignificant which he didn't tell the Gardai, but to know that he killed Mum ….' She explained what Feargal had said to herself and Gail.

'Oh my God,' he whispered. 'My poor love.' He held her close and kissed her. 'Have you told Matt yet?'

'No, I'll call him now.' She pressed his name in her contacts list. He answered immediately. 'Hi Matt, how are you?'

'Busy, just getting stuff ready to go over to O'Connell Street.'

'I won't keep you then, can you meet me tomorrow?'

'Love to. What time?'

'The evening …eight …I'll collect you.'

'Thanks.'

'Look forward to seeing you then.'

She turned off the phone, feeling guilty that she was so curt. But she didn't want him to sense her upset.

'I'm hoping that Gail will come with me,' she said to Tom.

'That could be difficult, do you want me to be there?' he asked gently.

'Thanks for offering but the fact that Gail hasn't met him in years could be a problem, and she hasn't met you either. I'm going to have to introduce you,' she smiled. 'But it's been such a roller coaster between us it's even hard for me to catch my breath. You've swept me off my feet.' She kissed him.

'I'm so glad you feel that way.'

He put his arms around her, and for a few minutes they held each other.

Zoe was comforted.

Neither Gail or Zoe went into work early the following morning and stayed home to talk.

'I'm shocked,' Zoe murmured. 'I never expected to hear such a thing.'

'My mind is going around in circles.'

'To think that he let Matt take the blame. What sort of man is he? I thought I knew my father.'

'What is Matt going to say?'

'I couldn't tell you.'

Gail shook her head. 'I feel bad that I didn't believe there was any truth in the letter. I don't know how I'm going to face Matt.'

'He won't blame you, he's not vindictive.'

'I feel sad that I never really knew him when we were in our teens.'

'He was older than us.'

'Not by much.'

'He was his own worst enemy at that time.' Zoe had to admit.

'I was afraid of him and kept out of his way as much as I could. It seems a terrible thing to say about our brother.'

'There were times I felt the same,' Zoe agreed.

'There's something else, Zoe, although I probably shouldn't say this, but I wondered if Dad was making everything up for some weird reason?' Gail looked at her, eyes puzzled. 'Maybe it's the dementia?'

'But that means he would have had some dementia in two thousand and twelve, and I saw no signs of it then.'

'Maybe the date on the letter wasn't correct.'

'He's not lying, I feel sure of it,' she insisted. 'But how are we going to tell Matt? It's all I've been thinking about.' Zoe was caught between her father and brother. Both of whom she loved. She dreaded taking this thing to another level. A sudden thought swept through her head. What if her father changed his mind by the morning? Or by the following? Denied that he ever admitted he had anything to do with Matt's trial? Then her brother's name would never be cleared.

'Are you all right? You look pale as death.' Gail stared at her.

'I'm fine.'

'Is Matt going to meet us?'

'Yes, tonight. I said I'd pick him up at the shelter.'

'We'll have to go somewhere private, we can't talk in a bar.'

'Tom suggested his apartment. He gave me a key.'

'Will he be there?'

'He offered, but I thought it would be better if it was just the three of us.'

Gail nodded. 'I don't know how I'll face Matt. Is he aware that I didn't believe what was in the letter?'

'No and I never said you would be there this evening.'

'Thanks be to God,' she sighed.

'I hope it won't be difficult for you.'

'I'm not looking forward to it.'

Zoe hugged her.

Chapter Fifty-four

Feargal lay on the bed. He heard the door open a couple of times but kept still with his eyes closed, each time a rush of emotion sweeping through him. He felt so guilty and questioned himself as to why he had done such an evil thing. He couldn't find an answer.

'That was a good decision, Feargal.'

He sat upright and stared into the dimness of the room. It was her again and she terrified him.

'But you'll have to talk to Matt, explain to him.'

'No, I couldn't.' Terror swept through him and he curled up in a ball on the bed. Grabbing hold of the sheet and duvet and trying to pull them up over his head to get away from her voice.

'You must.'

'No, no,' he cried.

'You're nearly there, it's just one more step.'

'I'm too ashamed.'

'You will have to face it.'

'But the Gardai might be involved.'

'You will have to clear his name.'

'How can I do that?'

'By confessing.'

'Don't make me.'

'You have to do this yourself.'

'I can't.' He shook his head.

'I'll be with you.'

'I'm so afraid.'

'He's your only son, you owe it to him.'

Feargal got out of the bed and sat on the edge of it. He couldn't imagine how he was going to confess to Matt. It had been bad enough telling Zoe and Gail but the idea of facing his son was almost impossible.

Chapter Fifty-five

Matt stood behind the counter with the other volunteers serving lunches. He knew some of the men by sight, and it was pleasant to meet them as they came in regularly. But the next man actually addressed him by name. 'Matt Sutherland?'

His eyes widened in shock as he stared into a familiar pair of curious eyes. It was a while since anyone had addressed him by that name. Everyone here knew him as *Matt Smith.*

'Fancy seeing you here,' the man said.

'How're you?' Matt continued filling his plate. He knew the guy from school.

'Not bad, it's strange to see you in a place like this.' His voice was husky. He had a runny nose and a vacant look and was one of those boys who had introduced him to drugs.

'I just help out,' he said hoping the guy would move on.

'Maybe you could help me out?'

'Sorry.'

'Surely you could spare a few euro for an old friend? Haven't seen you in years.'

'I've been living rough myself.'

'Move along.' The next person interrupted.

Matt didn't say anything and began to fill another plate. That guy was the last person he wanted to see.

'Do you know who's giving out the food?' the man shouted suddenly. The people around stared at him.

He hated that they were all looking at him and cringed.

The man pointed towards Matt. 'He's a murderer. This fucker murdered his mother.'

Voices rippled through the room as people heard what the man had shouted and responded.

'Who wants to be in the same room as a killer?' The man continued.

Matt stared at him, horrified. He wasn't able to utter a word.

Danielle took the plate he was holding out of his rigid hand. and pushed him. 'Get out of here, Matt,' she murmured in an insistent undertone. 'Now.'

'Are you letting him off?' The man yelled again and ran inside the counter after Matt.

But one of the other volunteers blocked his passage, and grabbed hold of him. Then a security man they had on the door burst in, pushing his way through the queue of men and women which had broken up into disarray now. Some people rushed to tables hanging on to their plates of food as if they thought they were going to be taken away from them. Others stuffed food into their mouths and hugged corners in the hope that they wouldn't be seen.

Matt ran the gamut of the volunteers serving food until he reached the doors, and flung through them to meet Sr. Teresa coming towards him.

'Matt?' She stopped.

In his haste he tried to avoid her.

But she held out her hand and reached to catch hold of his arm.

He slowed down.

'What's happened?' She stopped his frantic rush to get out of the place. 'Come into the office.' She turned and led the way down the corridor.

At that moment, the security man came out of the canteen dragging the man who had shouted at Matt. 'What'll we do with this one, Sister?' he asked, holding the wriggling man tight with one arm.

'Let him go.' She turned to the man. 'You stay out of here in future.

If I see you again I'll call the Gardai,' she warned him. 'Are you listening to me?'

'But he's a murderer, how can you let him in here?' He pointed at Matt who turned away, unable to face him.

The security man took him to the front door, and closed it behind him.

'Who is that man, Matt?' Sister asked.

'Someone I knew when I was young,' he explained, his voice trembling.

'Is this the first time you've met him since then?'

He nodded.

'I'm so sorry that he behaved like that towards you.'

'I deserved it. It's going to follow me for the rest of my life,' he said bitterly.

'No, Matt. You've paid your penalty.'

'I'll never do that.' He shook his head, unconvinced.

'You have to be positive, Matt, and take no notice of that man. He's gone now anyway. Take a walk, get some fresh air,' she encouraged.

'Thanks for everything you do for me, Sr. Teresa, I don't know what I'd do without you.'

She smiled.

He took her advice, and with the dog he headed out towards Howth. The day was cloudy and rain threatened, but he took no notice. Just glad to get out on his own, and escape those awful few moments back at the shelter when the man had recognised him and reminded of those terrible days. It had been his worst nightmare and now it had come to pass.

His earlier confidence had been obliterated. His heart was gutted. A darkness overshadowed him. How could he ever face anyone? What if someone else accused him? He was crushed by the thought of that.

As he ran along by the sea, he thought about what had happened.

The man was a friend of his in school. He had been in the Leaving Cert class when he left and this was the first time he had seen him since then. He jogged on until he came to Howth. It was late evening now but he didn't want to go back to the shelter. He wanted to hide. So that he didn't have to look anyone in the face ever again. Or hear what the man said. *Murderer. This fucker murdered his mother.* The words repeated over and over in his head and pierced his soul. Bringing such shame that it was impossible to confront the terrible deed he had committed. Fear and anguish tormented him.

He walked through Howth, stopping at a small supermarket and buying a roll in a plastic box, two bottles of water, and some ham. Outside, he used the box for the water for the dog, and gave him the ham, munching the roll as he went along, following the narrow road up around the head. It was some climb but he was used to it. Eventually, the Baily Lighthouse came into view. The sea was steely grey, streaks of silver light breaking the late evening sky. He climbed up towards the summit, taken back in time to Ballystrand when his father worked at the lighthouse. So much a part of his childhood he could hear the foghorn sound a warning. That dreary moan always full of foreboding.

Staring down at the lighthouse, the sea beckoned. Offering solace. Was that the answer to his misery. Should he turn his back on life? He stood up and walked nearer the edge and stared down into the water which splashed up against the rocks. With a crazy detachment he felt it was welcoming him, back to the place he knew best.

Rex whined, pulling against him.

Matt felt the tug on the lead which hung around his wrist.

The dog whined again. And then barked.

His phone rang. He knew it was Zoe. He was about to answer it but couldn't, unable to speak to her. He took it out of his pocket and turned it off.

He had arranged to meet her at eight o'clock but in such darkness of spirit he decided that she would be glad he was gone. Free from the shame of knowing him. A ghastly killer.

Chapter Fifty-six

Zoe stood around the corner from the shelter and rang Matt. She listened to the phone ringing out, wondering why he didn't answer. Perhaps there had been a misunderstanding about their arrangement? She continued to wait, assuming he was delayed. Fifteen minutes passed. Thirty minutes. By then she was worried and decided to go in.

She felt guilty passing the queue of people, but the security man allowed her in immediately. Inside she asked for Sr. Teresa and was directed to her office. She knocked on the door.

'Come ...'

'Sr. Teresa?'

'Zoe?'

'I'm worried about Matt. I was to meet him this evening but there's no sign of him.'

A shadow passed over the nun's face.

'Is something wrong?' Zoe immediately picked up on that.

'There was a problem today during lunch. Some man shouted at Matt and he was very upset.'

'What did he shout?'

'I didn't hear it. I've asked the volunteers but no one wants to talk about it.'

'My God.' Zoe was horrified.

'I suggested he go for a walk and so far he hasn't come back. But I was glad about that, he very seldom takes any time off and is always here.'

Zoe didn't know what to say.

'Have you called him?' Sr. Teresa asked.

'I've been ringing since eight but there's no answer.' Zoe was desperately concerned now. 'Where would he go?'

'He doesn't go drinking as far as I know so he's hardly sitting in a pub.' The nun seemed as worried as Zoe.

'Let me know if he turns up, will you.' She gave her a business card. 'Thanks Sister …' She shook the nun's hand and left. As soon as she was back in the car she rang Tom to explain the situation and then went to collect her sister from his apartment.

When Zoe told Gail Matt wasn't coming she was angry. 'Let's hope he's not reverting to type,' she said, a sarcastic tone in her voice. 'Unreliable bastard.'

'It's the first time this has happened, he's always on time. But he could react badly if someone said something, then you wouldn't know what he might do,' Zoe defended him.

'It's annoying, I was building myself up to apologise that I hadn't believed what was in the letter, now I'm deflated,' she grumbled.

'Come on, I'll drop you home.'

'What are you doing?'

'Tom has gone over to the shelter to see if Matt has come back, and I'm going to meet him.'

'Best of luck to you.'

Zoe leaned across and kissed Gail. 'See you tomorrow.'

'Sorry I was annoyed.'

'Don't worry. I'm sure he'll turn up later tonight.'

She nodded, and opened the car door. 'Send me a text.'

'Will do.'

'Mind yourself.'

Zoe waited until Gail had disappeared into the house and then headed back to the shelter where she met Tom.

'Any sign?' she asked.

He shook his head.

'Have you any idea where he might have gone?'

'I don't know love.' He reached to kiss her.

'I've been racking my brains to try and remember anything he said which would give us some idea of where he might be.' She stared down the dark street in the hope of spotting him. 'I've just thought …' She looked at Tom. 'He mentioned that he runs out as far as Howth with the dog. He enjoys the sea and the Baily Lighthouse. It reminds him …'

'Perhaps something happened to him and he couldn't get back?'

'Let's take a drive that way.' Tom ushered her into his jeep.

'Thanks a mill for doing this,' Zoe was grateful.

'Why wouldn't I?' Tom gave a low laugh. 'Don't you know I'd do anything for you and Matt too?'

Zoe hugged close to him.

'Right, let's start searching out that way,' he said.

Tom drove slowly towards Howth. There were very few people walking along the road at this time of the night.

'Who's that?' Zoe exclaimed.

'Where?' Tom slowed down and peered out through the window of the jeep.

'No, it was just a shadow. Where are you, Matt?' she murmured.

'He could be anywhere.'

They continued driving.

'Let's head through Sutton and on to Howth, there's more going on there. Plenty of eating places and bars.'

'Maybe we'll see him, there should be a lot of people around.'

'Hope so.'

'Should we ring the Gardai?'

'They won't do anything for twenty-four hours. And I'd rather not, his situation is awkward.'

Zoe nodded, realising immediately what he meant.

They drove around Howth and up to the summit, but it was dark now and there was no one around. They climbed out of the jeep and went down one of the narrow paths, but it was extremely windy.

'It's late, Zoe, and quite dangerous here. We'll never find him.' He took her arm. 'Anyway, I don't know if there's much point continuing to search. He might already be back at the shelter.'

'Sr. Teresa said she'd call me if he came back.'

'She's gone home by now.'

'And whoever is on the door tonight mightn't pass any comment when he comes in. But why didn't he phone to say he couldn't meet me? That's puzzling. It's not like him.'

'Maybe he lost his phone, or it needs to be charged, could be anything.'

'I'll try it again.' Zoe pressed Matt's name in her contacts list. 'Can't get through. Sounds like the phone is off altogether. I hope he's not sleeping rough, it's cold tonight. That reminds me, he usually goes around to O'Connell Street and gives out food to the homeless, let's head that way.'

They parked and made their way to the GPO, but couldn't see Matt among the people there.

'There's another group further up, let's go.' Tom put his arm around Zoe's shoulders.

There was a long queue of men waiting for food, and others sitting and standing around eating.

'There's one of the volunteers I know, so this is Sr. Teresa's shelter. We're in the right place.' They waited until they had a chance to talk to him, but he said that he hadn't seen Matt tonight.

'What time do you finish up?' asked Zoe.

'Somewhere between one and two.'

'So he could still arrive, it's only twelve-thirty.'

'He may do.'

'Thanks.'

He nodded, and continued serving soup to the men and women.

'Let's go back to the shelter,' suggested Tom.

'I pray he'll be there.'

'We'll find him, don't worry.'

They drove back and Tom parked outside.

'What can we do?' Zoe appealed to him.

'I think you should go home and get some sleep, I'll stay here and wait.'

'No, I don't want you to do that, you have to work tomorrow. Could we go into the shelter and wait there?' Zoe wondered.

'Yes, I'm sure we could. Let's do that,' Tom agreed.

They went back inside and the security man allowed them to sit in the office.

'At least it's warm in here.'

'Thanks for staying with me.' They sat close together, and she drifted off to sleep. Hearing noises, people's voices, doors opening and closing, and early the following morning she woke up and saw Tom in the chair beside her heavily asleep, his head on her shoulder. She smiled and watched his relaxed face, so still and peaceful in the early morning light which drifted through the thin fabric of the net curtain. She felt a sense of knowing him now. Like they were two people alone in a strange alien place. To see him sleep like a child was to understand the honesty of this man she had met such a short time before. To remove the mask we all show to the world and see what lay beneath.

He opened his eyes and caught her looking at him. He smiled and put out his hand to catch hers. 'Morning my love,' he whispered.

She leaned across and softly touched his lips with hers. They were caught in a spell of time which lasted only a few seconds before the realisation of why they were here hurtled back into Zoe's mind.

'I wonder has Matt come back?' she murmured.

'Let me check,' he said.

'I'll go with you.'

Tom stood up and went outside, followed by Zoe. They talked to the security man and when he confirmed that Matt still hadn't returned she turned to Tom, clung on to him and burst into tears.

He held her close.

'I'll get us some breakfast …' he said. 'What would you like?'

'Just a cup of coffee …' She wasn't hungry.

'Go back into the office and I'll be with you in a few minutes, and try to relax, love.' He kissed her again.

She sat there, her mind a blank. Where was she going to find her brother? She simply didn't know.

Tom came back in, carrying a tray with coffee and toast. 'Thanks.'

He put the tray down.

She picked up a slice of toast and bit into it.

'What are you going to do?' Tom asked.

'I might go back out towards Howth, other than that I simply don't know where I might go.'

'Do you want to go home for a while to rest, you must be very tired.' He took her hand and held it.

'I want to find him, that's all.'

'I have appointments this morning, unfortunately,' he said. 'But as soon as I'm free I'll see you.'

'I'm not going to work today, I intended to put in a few hours at home so nobody's expecting me.'

'I'll call you as soon as I can meet you.'

'I'll go back out to the Howth area.'

'Take care, my love.'

Chapter Fifty-seven

Matt was awakened by Rex licking his face and he pushed himself up from the cramped position among the bushes where he lay all night. The wind blew strongly, particles of icy water in the gusts. The sound of seagulls cawing echoed as they whirled and dived in search of food. He shivered in the cold morning air, rubbed the shiny coat of the dog and then put his face close and breathed in his scent, so comforted by the warmth of another body. He felt hungry then and realised that the dog probably needed something to eat as well. He hadn't expected that he would still be here this morning. His dark thoughts of the night before hadn't taken him as far as this. Now he faced the day which stretched ahead with nothing at the end of it. A dull grey day without promise. When he was released from prison he had been hopeful that his life would change. That he might be forgiven by those who used to love him. And now he had rejected the one person who had stretched out her hand to him. He felt wretched. The dog whined and looked up at him. His brown eyes warm. He held him close, and whispered goodbye.

Matt walked down towards the cliff. Struggling against the gale which tore at his clothes and almost sent him reeling as he stared down the rocky incline which stretched to where angry waves crashed. He was going to Ballystrand. Going home. He let go the dog's lead. It lay curled in the grass. Slack.

'Bye Rex ,' he said and continued walking.

Chapter Fifty-eight

Zoe drove out against the early morning traffic. Somehow she couldn't go anywhere else. It was the only place Matt had ever mentioned and she prayed to her mother that she would help her find him. Her phone rang and she replied immediately in the hope that it was Matt.

'Zoe?' Gail's voice was sharp and echoed around the car. 'Where are you?'

'I'm searching for Matt.'

'Where?'

'Howth.'

'What makes you think he'll be there?' Her sister's voice held accusation.

'He mentioned he used to come out this way …to the lighthouse.'

'Have you been up all night?'

'No, I grabbed a couple of hours on and off.'

'With Tom?'

'Yes, but not the way you think. We sat on chairs in the shelter, not very comfortable.'

'Not very romantic either I'd say.'

'Actually, there was a moment …' Zoe smiled.

'I want you to introduce me to this man, when is it going to happen?'

'Soon. In the meantime we must find Matt …'

'I can't look for him, I'm working today.'

'How's Dad?'

'I left him in bed, although Mrs. Moran will be around later.'

'She'll keep an eye on him.'

'Text me if anything happens, will you? And sorry for being so sharp last night, it's just ...'

'I know, you're predisposed to reacting that way, it's understandable.'

'I felt bad about it afterwards.'

'I'll let you know if I find him.'

Now she was back in search mode. Driving slowly and glancing left and right. Needing to see the tall figure of her brother jogging with the dog alongside. But didn't. Occasionally she pulled in, and sat watching. There were more people walking now. Going to work probably. A couple of women taking their early morning run. Groups of teenagers on the way to a nearby school with bags slung on their backs.

She continued on. Stopping. Starting. Until she reached Howth, driving around the Head. The sea held harsh memories of her childhood. Even now, she felt uncomfortable as she drove along, her eyes still peering around her in search of Matt. Her phone rang. Her heart began to thump in the hope that it could be him. She answered it.

Any sign of Matt, Zoe?' Tom asked.

'No, I'm still looking. I'm going up to the summit.'

'I've talked to Sr. Teresa and she'll call me as soon as he appears. I'm sure he just needed time out, Zoe, and when he's got himself together he'll come back,' Tom reassured. 'Try not to worry too much, my love.'

'I hope so,' she sighed. Thinking that the timing was terrible. She had been so anxious to tell him that their father had admitted that it was he who killed their mother and now wondered if Matt had known that, would he have left the shelter? If only she had had a chance to talk with him. To explain that their father had confessed and seemed to feel very guilty that Matt had spent so many years in prison.

Questions burst out of nowhere. But she was in such a frenzy, she had no immediate answers, and needed more time to ponder. To think outside the box. Like she was trying to complete a cryptic crossword.

She drove up to the summit, parked, and climbed out of the car. She followed one of the narrow pathways which zigzagged over the summit and had to watch her footing in shoes which weren't ideal for walking in such a place. The lighthouse was over to her right and she went in that direction. It was deserted up here on such a stormy morning as this and her coat was dragged and pulled by the wind, her hair constantly blowing into her eyes and preventing her from seeing clearly. She searched in her shoulder bag for a clip, rooting in and out of the various pockets until at last she found one, pulled back her hair and continued on.

Suddenly, she heard the sound of a dog barking and wondered where it was coming from. She looked around but couldn't see a dog anywhere. But the barking continued. Harsh. Insistent. Was it possible that it was Matt's dog? Excitement swept through her and she tried to identify the direction of the sound. It seemed to be coming from below. She left the path and went closer to the cliff edge, peering over to see other levels further down. And it was then she saw him. Her heart began to beat. The dog was barking at him. And she saw him grip hold of his jeans and pull against him.

'Matt?' she screamed, waving madly. 'Matt?' But her voice whirled away on the breeze and she knew he couldn't hear her. With a terrible sense of foreboding, she climbed further down, trying to keep her footing on the rough slope and prevent herself from falling.

Chapter Fifty-nine

Matt was buffeted by the wind now and it had begun to rain. His ears were filled with the cacophony of the sound of the seabirds whirling above and below him. He blessed himself. 'Forgive me,' he whispered.

Rex barked insistently.

He turned around and pushed the dog away.

But the dog resisted and suddenly leapt at him with a growl, his teeth catching the cloth of Matt's jeans at his ankle and dragging on it.

'No Rex, stop.' He tried to get him to release his grip, but he pulled against him, hanging on.

In his despair something made him hesitate from making that last move, reluctant to take Rex with him. He bent down closer to the dog but he wouldn't release the hold he had on his jeans. 'Let go, Rex.' He tried to pull the denim from his mouth but he growled again and hung on even tighter. As Matt dragged at his collar, he saw someone out of the corner of his eye and looked up. A woman was leaping down the steep slope towards him, and in his confused state, it took a moment before he realised that it was Zoe. What was she doing here in Howth? Rushing down the hillside towards him? He stared at her in puzzlement. Then turned to look out to sea again, the lighthouse in the distance, a grim reminder. In his mind the shadow of darkness returned, an unyielding urge to carry through his plan, so that Zoe could live unfettered for the rest of her life, and not have to carry the weight of his shame.

'Matt?' she screamed his name. Carried on the wind her voice had a sing-song childlike ringing sound and he turned back to see her totter down the steep slope, almost lose her balance and fall in her attempt to reach him. A logical thought unexpectedly occurred in his head. If he didn't stop her then both of them would fall over the edge into the abyss. And the blame would fall on him. And all the promise of her beautiful life lost. Endless days of happiness. Loving. Sunshine. A perfect radiance around her. And she was so deserving of that it was imperative that he prevent something terrible happening.

She was coming closer. Covering those last few metres. And in that instant he put out his arms and broke her lunge as she threw herself on him, in tears. Her arms wrapped around him and they swayed as the wind wrenched at them and the seabirds screamed. 'Don't do it, Matt, please, I beg you, don't …' she cried, while the dog still snarled and kept his teeth dug into the end of the leg of Matt's jeans which was in tatters by now.

He held her tight and steadied himself, preventing either of them from losing their balance. Then he grabbed her hand, turned and drew her back up the incline. The dog let go of his jeans, and barking loudly followed them, jumping excitedly beside him. When they climbed back up to the path, Zoe put her arms around him. 'My God, Matt, I can't believe you were going to … promise me you will never do that, please?' Zoe begged. 'Promise?'

He looked down into her clear honest eyes. He couldn't tell a lie.

In the car, Zoe called Tom, and he asked her to put Matt on.

'Hey Matt, how are you?' Tom asked.

'I'm fine …' He said the words but didn't believe himself. All he knew was the humiliation of his attempt to take his own life. He had even failed in that.

'I'll talk to you later.'

Matt nodded and handed the phone back to Zoe.

'Tom, we'll go with the original plan. See you later,' Zoe said.

Matt stared out the car window. Pedestrians strolled. Mothers pushed buggies. Children walked along holding on to their parents' hands. Vehicles came in the opposite direction. Life was continuing for all of those people. But he was trapped. His life was going nowhere. The dog whined and pushed his head into his hands.

'Your dog seems to be able to understand what's happening,' Zoe said. 'Was he trying to stop you from …?'

He nodded. 'He was trying to rip my jeans into pieces.'

'Has he ever done that before?'

He smiled down at Rex, stroking his head.

'Tom gave me the key to his apartment so that we can talk in private,' Zoe explained to Matt as she drove towards it. 'I'll call Gail, she wants to see you.'

'I didn't think she wanted to have anything to do with me again. I can't believe that she has changed her mind. It will be wonderful to see her.'

'Something has happened.'

'What?'

'It would be best if we tell you together.'

Zoe swung into the gates of the apartment block and pulled into the carpark. Then she led the way into the foyer and they took the lift up to the second floor. Zoe walked along the corridor followed by Matt and Rex. His hands were sticky and he was very nervous. He didn't know what to expect. Zoe inserted the key into the door and pushed it open. 'Sit down, I'm sure you must be hungry,' she said. 'There's cereal, bread, eggs, or would you fancy a slice of pizza?'

'Pizza sounds good,' he smiled.

'Best breakfast you could have,' she laughed.

She went to the fridge. Took it out of the plastic packaging and put it into the microwave oven.

'Thank you. This is a nice place.' It was awkward now. He didn't know what to say.

'Tom is very generous and said we could come here to talk. It's more relaxed.' She heated plates and set the table.

'Could I use the bathroom? I feel grimy after spending the night outside.' He stood up, wiping his hands on his jeans.

'Sure, it's just down the corridor. Second door on the right.'

He went in and stared at himself in the mirror, and had to admit he looked pretty rough. He took a pee, pulled off his shirt. Splashed hot water and doused his face and hair. Scrubbed his hands. Towelled himself dry. He looked again in the mirror and stared at himself. What a useless bastard, he thought. He should have jumped when he had the chance and ended it all. It would have been better for everyone.

'I'm looking forward to this meal. Can I help?' He wanted to do something to assuage his feeling of worthlessness.

'You relax, Gail is on her way over.'

After what seemed like a very short time, the doorbell rang. He stared nervously towards it.

'Why don't you answer it?' Zoe asked with a smile.

He looked at her, uncertain. Then he moved slowly towards the door.

'Go on,' Zoe encouraged.

The bell rang again.

He turned the handle and opened the door to see Gail standing there looking at him.

His mouth was dry. Tears filled his eyes.

'Matt ...' she whispered and ran towards him, arms opened wide to clasp him close to her.

He was so happy to see her.

'Forgive me for not wanting to meet you before now,' Gail was emotional.

'Don't worry,' Matt said.

'I couldn't get past my stupid self,' she admitted.

'It's so good to see you,' he whispered and held her close.

After a moment she looked at him. 'You've changed ...'

'Older ...' he smiled.

She hugged him tightly.

'I'm so sorry about everything, I know I can never make it up to you,' he said.

'It's so good to have you back, Matt, as a family.' Zoe embraced him also, the three of them standing close together. 'Now, let's eat,' she said after a few minutes.

'The reason we wanted to meet was to tell you that we've talked to Dad about his letter,' Zoe explained.

'She never gave up,' Gail said.

'I had to find out why he wrote to you.'

He gazed at her, he hadn't expected this.

Zoe went on to explain what their father had said.

Matt couldn't believe what he was hearing.

'Why did you plead guilty?' Gail asked.

'At first I pleaded not guilty, but when they showed me the photographs I had to assume it was me. It was terrible. All that blood.' He was shaking.

'How could you plead guilty to a crime if you couldn't remember?' Zoe asked.

'I was on drugs at the time …spaced out.'

'What sort of drugs?' Gail asked.

'Weed. Cocaine. I was a drug dealer and an addict myself, so if I'm truly honest I didn't know where I was a lot of the time.'

'So why do you think Dad didn't admit that he killed Mum?' Gail asked.

'I don't know.'

'The worst part was blaming you,' Zoe said slowly.

'When I read the letter I just assumed Dad had some small piece of evidence which might have meant my sentence would have been a bit shorter, but this …is unbelievable. Are you sure he's telling the truth?'

'Well, we have been thinking he could be verging on dementia these days, but the letter was written in two thousand and twelve and when we talked to him he admitted that he was involved.'

'Would he talk to me, do you think?' Matt asked.

'We don't know. He's been very upset since. He won't get out of bed, although Mrs. Moran has been looking after him,' Gail explained.

'I want to see him …' Matt insisted.

Chapter Sixty

'How is your Dad?' Tom asked.

'Not so good. He seems very depressed.'

'It must be difficult for him.'

'I feel sorry for him. We don't know the reason why he did such a terrible thing, and what it's done to him over the years since it happened.'

'Have you thought of what might be the next step?' Tom entwined his fingers with hers.

'Matt is anxious to see Dad and as soon as he seems a bit better we'll suggest it to him.'

'Good idea. If your father admitted the truth then it would mean Matt might be able to clear his name.'

'He would have to do that legally, and open the case again?'

'Yes.'

'But would Dad have to go to prison?'

'Probably, if he was found guilty.'

'But surely …at his age?'

'It mightn't be very long but he could still get a custodial sentence.'

'Remember we talked about the length of time since it happened and that the case might not be admissible.'

'That's also a possibility.'

'But it's Matt's right to take it further if he wants, isn't it?'

'The legal route will be a tough road, and costly.'

'I realise that.' She was downcast.

'You just have to leave it up to Matt.'

'He actually didn't believe it.'

'I'm not surprised. Cheer up, my love. Hopefully it will all work out for Matt. It must be a relief to him to know what happened.' He put his arms around her and drew her close. His lips clung to hers tenderly.

She lay in his arms longing to give herself to him completely. This situation between her father and Matt tormented her. She could see no way out of it without the most terrible hurt to those she loved. Her father and brother, and Gail too. Her feelings were intense and she longed to explain to Tom exactly how she felt, but couldn't.

'I want you with me, Zoe.' His fingers twirled through her hair, and the delicacy of his touch caused her heart to beat unbearably fast, every nerve ending so finely tuned the extent of conflict within her seemed almost impossible to bear.

She pressed her lips on his and let him know that she wanted the same thing. Sharing their days and nights. Their lives. Knowing that he was there for her.

'It's what I want too, Tom, but at the moment I just can't …'
She ached for the magic he offered but she couldn't accept.

'I understand.' He cupped her cheek in his hand. 'I'm not going to rush you into making a decision, I know how things are at the moment. But please believe me when I say that you can depend on me. I will love you always.'

Chapter Sixty-one

Feargal couldn't get up out of bed. He just couldn't. He didn't want to eat or drink either, but Zoe and Gail had asked Mrs. Moran to come in more often so that she could cook his meals as Zoe was working in the office this week, and Gail had to travel to Cork.

Mrs. Moran was a pleasant middle-aged woman and he did like her, but even she wasn't able to persuade him to get up out of bed, although he did take some food. When Zoe arrived home, she managed to persuade him to get up and come down to eat.

'Dad, I made your favourite fillet steak, eat it quickly now before it gets cold.' She put his plate in front of him, and sat down herself to a piece of salmon.

'Thanks,' he muttered.

'I was going to ask Matt around at the weekend,' she said when they had finished, glad that Feargal had eaten most of the dinner.

He stared at her, his eyes wide.

'He needs to come home, if you saw his living conditions you would be shocked.'

'Oh …'

'You're worried about meeting him again, aren't you?'

He nodded.

'He wasn't angry when we told him what you said.'

'You told him?' The blood drained out of his face.

'We had to,' she said gently.

'I feel so guilty.' His lower lip trembled. 'He must hate me. Gail said she hated me.'

'She didn't really mean that.'

'She shouted.'

'Gail was in shock.'

'You must all really detest me and I don't blame you.' He pulled out his handkerchief from his pocket and dabbed his eyes.

'Look I'll bring Matt around and we'll have a nice lunch all together.'

'I'm afraid.' He shuddered.

'You're going to have to face up to it.'

'She said that too.'

'Who?'

'Your mother.'

'Mum?'

'She talks to me.' Tears dribbled down his face.

'How?'

'I hear her, she told me to tell you what I had done.'

Zoe took a sharp intake of breath. 'Where does this happen?'

'In the bedroom. She wakes me up sometimes.'

She didn't know what to say.

'I'm glad I got up, thanks for making me, I was afraid up there.'

'Afraid?'

'She's very annoyed with me.'

'I'd love to talk to her …if only for a minute,' Zoe admitted. 'Although I can't imagine such a thing. It would be a miracle.'

Chapter Sixty-two

Matt struggled. The power of his father still bore down on top of him. His anger corrosive. He was dragged back to those times when he railed against him. To those dark days of aggression. When he refused to obey Feargal and allowed himself to be alienated, a wall raised between him and all who lived in that house in Ballystrand.

So much had happened since he had been released from prison. Reading that letter which his father had written to him. Meeting Gail and Zoe together, and hearing what his father had told them about that night. It was all too much and he felt that he had to get away. Even for a short time.

He called the Abbey and enquired about staying there for a couple of days. Relieved when the brother he spoke with said that he would always be welcome whenever he decided to visit them.

He took a bus to Dungarvan and walked the rest of the way to Ballystrand. He went to say a prayer at his mother's grave, and brought flowers again. Then he walked back to stand staring for a while at the lighthouse on the rocky promontory and turned towards the monastery on the hillside. In his mind, his mother and father, and his two sisters, were here with him. Walking up from home to attend Mass at Christmas or Easter, special days which they celebrated in this beautiful peaceful place. Now he opened the gate, and followed the same road which led up to the grey buildings on the hillside.

He was welcomed by an elderly monk who wore a black and white cassock and introduced himself as Brother Brendan. He brought him into the office of the Abbot who sat him down and chatted about life in the Abbey, explaining how the monks passed their days in prayer for the world. 'It is time for liturgical prayer now, and this is followed by *Benediction*. Would you like to take part?'

'Yes, I would.' Matt nodded.

The monk led him through cool silent corridors towards the church and he knelt in a pew listening to the monks chanting. This was followed by *Benediction*, something which he hadn't experienced for many years and was reminded again of his childhood and visits to the monastery by the sound of the frail singing voices of the elderly monks. He stared around him. A diffuse light filtered through the stained-glass windows in the small church and added a magical dimension which increased that sense of peace and wonder which had descended on him as he walked in through the gates.

His room was small and painted white. It contained a simple bed with a white cover, a table, a chair, a wardrobe. The small window looked out over the sea and the lighthouse and that was everything to him.

On the table was a book of prayer, and the schedule of the day. He read through it and heard the bells chiming. Then he went to join with the monks in *Vespers*, and later in the evening, *Compline*. At other times, the monks could be seen sitting at a window, or walking in groups or alone in the cloister praying. Matt was especially conscious of the signs on the walls which had the word *Silence* printed on them. He was too shy to acknowledge any of the monks, although they often nodded to him as he passed and that made him feel that he was somehow a small insignificant part of this community of men who had chosen to renounce the world.

Work and prayer. That was what the Abbott said. 'In prayer we come to know and love God. Through prayer we surrender the life of materialism.'

That was emphasised when he went to see the farm which was run by local workers, as most of the monks living in the monastery were elderly and no longer able to work there. Although two of the monks in their seventies still tended the vegetable garden, producing what was needed for the monks themselves.

He was in bed just after nine, which was extremely early for him. And for the first time since he had left prison he didn't remember anything at all during the night. No dreams or nightmares disturbed his sleep, until he awoke to hear the chiming of the bells calling the monks. There was a discreet tap on the door. He had asked Brother Brendan to give him a call at three-thirty.

After he had taken a quick shower and dressed, he joined the other monks as they made their way along the corridors of the Abbey to the church. He listened to *Vigils* which consisted of psalms and lessons from scripture as the community watched for the dawn. He stayed there, caught up in that ancient ritual.

He went back to his room and sitting on the end of his bed he watched the magnificence of the dawn breaking over the sea. The golden globe of the sun climbed up from the horizon and the sky glowed with an ethereal light. Next was *Lauds,* prayers at daybreak, and was a reminder to dedicate the day to God. Now he understood that each of those parts had their own precise significance. From the dawn commitment to God until sunset when sins were confessed.

Matt left the following morning. Regretting that he was saying goodbye to this peaceful oasis. A place where he had found solace for the first time since he had left prison.

That terrible craving for drugs which had returned to press upon his soul had diminished, and he could breathe again without its weight bearing down upon him demanding satisfaction.

He remembered something the Abbott had said. It was a quotation from St. Benedict.

Let everyone that comes be received as Christ.

But in Matt's heart he was the least of those who would ever be received. The greatest of sinners.

Chapter Sixty-three

As they had arranged, Zoe collected Matt on Sunday. To her surprise he mentioned that he had been at Mass.

'You go to Mass?'

'Occasionally.'

She pulled away from the kerb, and headed through the quiet city streets. 'I have to say that I don't go anymore,' she admitted. 'All that stuff about the priests put me off, and most of my friends too.'

'It's up to everyone to make their own decision. I have to make amends for …' He stopped talking and there was an awkward silence.

Zoe thought that her brother had really changed. The person she knew when she was young had gone. That wild aggressive individual who had frightened the life out of them with his behaviour certainly wasn't the man sitting beside her. 'Did you finish that website design?'

'Yes, it was enjoyable.'

'Have you got paid?'

'I have, but I didn't like to charge too much. They're a charity and don't have a lot of money.'

'Bet you got a kick out of doing it?'

'I did.'

'Any luck with the gaming?' She had been wondering about that.

'I have a few ideas floating around.'

'Any fascinating characters?'

'I was trying to pin it into an alien world, something strange. But I haven't done much lately, I'm sorry about that, particularly as you gave me the computer. But I'm hoping to get back to it.'

She flashed a smile at him. 'We're nearly home now.'

'I dread meeting Dad.'

'He feels the same.'

'When I saw him at Christmas I thought he looked quite old.'

'You haven't seen him for many years, he's changed a lot.'

'We've all changed, I suppose. Although Gail and you don't look so different.'

'Thanks,' she laughed.

She drove into the estate saying a silent prayer to her mother for help. Most of all, she didn't want a row to erupt between her father and brother the way it had on Christmas Eve.

'Have you seen Tom?' she asked.

'I met him on Monday.'

'You remember I mentioned we've been out together a few times.'

'I gathered as much from Tom, he had a big smile on his face every time he mentioned your name,' Matt laughed.

'What do you think?' she asked, suddenly needing approval from her brother.

'He's a nice guy, I'm happy for you both. When I heard that you broke up with your partner and cancelled your wedding, I felt a bit guilty.'

'Why would you feel like that?' She stopped the car.

'I thought it might have been because of me.'

'What do you mean?'

'People have all sorts of attitudes about someone like me.'

'Don't you even think about that. We broke up because we were not getting on, and I can tell you I'm a lot happier now with Tom.'

'I'm glad.'

She leaned towards him and dropped a kiss on his cheek.

'I hope you'll both be very happy.'

'I hope so too.'

They climbed out of the car and nervously Zoe put the key in the door, opened it and ushered Matt in ahead of her. After a moment, Gail appeared into the hall. Rushed towards Matt and threw her arms around him. 'It's so great to see you home at last, *big bro.*'

He hugged her. 'Thanks.'

'Let me take your jacket.' He shrugged out of it and she hung it up.

'Dinner is almost ready, we're eating in the dining room, Matt, just because it's a special day. Come on, Dad's already inside.'

A look of apprehension passed across Matt's features, and he hesitated outside the door.

Zoe opened it and went in first. 'Dad, Matt's arrived.'

Gail put her arm around Matt and they went in together.

Feargal looked up.

Matt went towards him. 'It's great to see you, Dad,' he murmured.

The old man put out his hand.

Matt gripped it. Then he leaned forward and patted his shoulder.

'Son …' He burst into tears.

'Dad.' Matt put his arms around him.

'I'm so sorry,' Feargal said huskily, tears choking his speech. 'I should have told them, should have …but I left you there.'

'I'm not even sure what happened,' Matt said softly.

'It's a long time ago.'

'It was my fault, I caused the row.'

'No, Matt, not your fault.'

'It was all me, since I was a boy, you know that.'

Feargal shook his head in denial.

Matt kept holding him.

'Dad?' Zoe put her arm around him. 'Are you all right?'

He didn't reply.

'Right, dinner's ready,' Gail announced.

'Matt, you sit here at this end.' Zoe pulled out a chair.

Gail appeared with a tray, and put the soup tureen in the centre of the table. Then poured soup for each of them. The girls sat down. 'Hope you enjoy.'

Matt blessed himself.

Zoe noticed and wondered. This was a side to her brother she would never have expected.

They began to eat.

No one talked.

Zoe and Gail served the main course of roast lamb, and for dessert Gail had baked a pear crumble. Then tea and coffee. Afterwards, they cleared away and put everything into the dishwasher.

'What do you think?' Gail looked at her sister as they stood in the kitchen.

'I don't know. Let's leave them on their own for now. Give them space.'

'It would be so good if they could make up.'

'Is it possible after all these years?'

'It's brought it all back, Zoe, Mum dying so suddenly. There was no warning, and the shock did my head in. I couldn't grasp what was happening at the time and tried to forget.' Gail was emotional. 'But I couldn't. Her image was always there in the background, smiling at me, and her voice too. And the thought that Dad says he can hear her scares me ...'

'Maybe we should have talked more. It might have made it easier. When we were sent to different schools in Dublin I really missed you.' Zoe was tearful.

'And I never knew where Matt had gone,' Gail said slowly.

'Or about the court case?'

'Packing us off to Auntie Peg made sure about that. Until I looked up the papers I didn't find out exactly what had happened.'

'Did the girls in your new school know?'

'I don't think so. No one said anything and I had only one year to do anyway.'

'I went to London just to get away.'

'Maybe we should have gone together.' Zoe put her arms around Gail.

'We missed those years.' She was gloomy.

'I suppose Dad thought he was doing the best for us, but I still can't believe that he caused Mum's death, it's just too hard to get my head around it.'

'Can you forgive him?'

'I don't know, it's all too soon. Some days I want him to stand up in court and face the law, and others I feel I don't want to put him through that at his age. And I often wonder if it would be what Mum would want. Still, for Matt's sake maybe he should pay the penalty.'

Gail nodded, but said nothing.

'I was so glad when you came back. Now we're a family again.' Zoe put her arms around Gail.

'And Tom and yourself?' she smiled.

Zoe giggled.

'You're an item now. When are you moving in with him?'

'Don't know, I have to think of Dad.'

'Did I hear the door opening?' Gail asked walking into the hall and standing for a moment. 'No. They're still inside.'

'They've been in there over an hour, are they talking?'

'Let's hope so.'

'They need to get to know each other again.'

'If that doesn't happen then they won't reconcile with each other. Dad feels so guilty it would be far better if he got it off his chest. What do you think of this business of talking with Mum?'

'It's probably his imagination. Hearing voices from the past can happen, particularly if there's some dementia.'

'I hope that he's not heading that way. It would be dreadful.'

'It won't. It can't.' Zoe clasped her hands together. A whispering prayer whirled around her heart. But there were questions too. Did their father deserve understanding after what he had done? Did he deserve forgiveness?

Chapter Sixty-four

Feargal sat staring at the tablecloth. It was white linen with an embroidered flower design in pink and green. He remembered Rachel had made it. The woman he loved. His heart blazed with longing and he wanted her back. To tell her how sorry he was that he had been the one who …murdered her. Pushed her out of his way until she fell. He could see her lying there. A widening pool of blood underneath her head.

'Rachel?' he called her.

'Feargal?'

He looked around. And could see her sitting in her comfortable easy chair opposite him. Holding an embroidery ring with the linen stretched across it, a fine needle threaded with pink silk held in her thumb and forefinger. For the first time he could see her. Looking as beautiful as ever. He put his hand out but was unable to reach her. 'Forgive me, I took your life from you,' he said. 'I'm so sorry.'

'Did you say something, Dad? I didn't catch it,' Matt said.

'Your sorrow should be for Matt, Zoe and Gail, they all need your help, especially Matt.'

Had he done enough? Would she be satisfied or was she going to insist that he go to the Gardai and confess. His shaking hand clenched and unclenched. The sinews and blue tinged veins were raised in the pattern of brown spots on his skin. Now smooth, and then flaccid as he dug fingernails into his soft palm and pressed tight.

'Talk to Matt, Feargal.'

His son sat opposite him at the table but he couldn't look at him. The silence between them lengthened. There was something terrifying about it. The guilt in Feargal grew and grew, until it almost exploded.

'Tell him what happened.'

'I can't,' he whispered.

Matt looked up as he spoke.

'Do what I say, Feargal.'

His heart pounded rapidly. He began to perspire. His skin was sticky. He shivered.

'Explain why. He must know.'

He shook his head.

'Otherwise he will never forgive himself.'

Feargal raised his head and his eyes met Matt's. Almost identical blue. Shape. Expression. Although a generation apart they had the same genes. A father. A son. So alike. 'I didn't mean …it was all in the heat of the moment,' he muttered.

'I understand,' Matt said.

'I loved your mother. I want you to know that.' He pressed his hand on his forehead. His jacket sleeve slid back to reveal a very thin arm, the skin in folds, ivory white with a scattering of brown mottling as on his hands. 'The worst thing was to blame it on you. I can't believe I did such a thing. Every day I castigate myself. Every day it gets worse and my life has turned into a nightmare which never ends. Over the years I have tried to apologise to you, writing notes in an effort to explain. Starting with a few words and then tearing them up, very seldom able to finish, only managing odd words, half sentences, which never went far enough to free you from the burden you had to carry.'

'There's no need to tell me everything, Dad …' Matt said softly, getting up from his side of the table and pulling a chair close to Feargal.

'I must. She wants me to.'

'She?' Matt repeated, puzzled.

'Your mother.'

The younger man's shoulders slumped suddenly. 'What does that mean?'

'She speaks to me.'

'How is that possible?' Matt whispered, a look of intense puzzlement on his face.

'I'm telling you it happens. Even a minute ago she told me to explain to you. She was here. You heard me talking to her.'

'It's a long time ago, there's no point in bringing it up now. It happened. It's over.'

'I was afraid to tell you,' Feargal muttered.

'There's no need now.'

'But you were only a boy. You had your life ahead of you and I robbed you of all those years.'

'Maybe it did me good.'

'How could that be?'

'In prison I managed to get off drugs and drink, and even cigarettes too. I think I'm a much healthier person now,' Matt said, smiling.

'Where did your youth go? Your twenties. The best time in a young man's life?' Feargal insisted.

'If I hadn't gone into prison I could be dead by now.'

'I should have helped you. Instead I made sure you were locked up.'

'If I had continued the way I was going I would probably have taken an overdose one day.'

'Not if you got the help you needed.'

'I didn't want help back then, Dad. Did you not notice that?'

'There are ways. I should have found them.'

'Let's forget about it now. I want to look forward and put the past behind me.'

'You must go to the Gardai.'

Feargal looked around him, fear on his face.

'Clear Matt's name.'

'No, I can't do that.'

'What do you mean, Dad?' Matt asked.

'Your mother …she wants me to go to the Gardai …'

'You're imagining it.'

'No, I'm not, she's there,' He pointed across the room. 'Sitting there, sewing.'

'You don't have to go to the Gardai.'

'But the family, people you knew, they all think …how can you face them?'

'I've already faced one person who knew me back then, but you, Zoe and Gail are the only people who matter to me.'

'Your name must be cleared, that's what your mother wants.'

'And what will happen to you then?' Matt asked.

'I don't care.'

'You'll never survive in a prison. You'll die there.'

'If it just means there's a headline in the paper which says that you are innocent then that will mean everything to me. That's all I want. My life is over either way.'

'You've still a lot to give,' Matt persuaded.

'If you saw me over these last years you wouldn't say that. I've been like a man of a hundred. A shell. Dragging myself around.'

'You're not very agile, I can see that, but your mind is as sharp as ever, you could have a very full life.' Matt put his arm around the hunched shoulders.

'And I want yours to begin at long last,' Feargal said. 'And I know it's what Rachel wants.'

'Mine will take its natural course.'

'You must know who you are, that's the most important thing. A man who is acquitted by the courts, walks out, his head held high, blameless, above suspicion.'

'And have you incarcerated in my place, no way, Dad, that's not going to happen. The time has been done. Society has been paid,' Matt said with certainty.

'You don't want me to pay for my crime?'

'You've already paid by the sound of it. Done every year of that sentence on the outside, carrying your guilt.'

'My God, Matt, how could you be so forgiving?' He laid his head on his son's shoulder, tears drifting down his weathered cheeks.

'It's easy. You're my father and I love you.' Matt kissed him.

Chapter Sixty-five

'I'm resigning, Russell,' Zoe announced, standing opposite him.   He looked up at her, his mouth open, a shocked expression on his face.

'What?' he gasped.

'You heard me.'

'But …'

'I'm selling my shareholding. Clive is interested in buying it.'

'But that means he'll own even more.' He stood up with a jerk. His face flushed.

'Work that out between the two of you, he is your father,' advised Zoe.

'Why didn't you tell me before this?'

'I've just decided,' she laughed.

'Bloody hell, what is it with you?'

'You don't like the thought of me leaving?' she asked.

'Of course I don't.'

'I seem to remember at a recent meeting that you said you wanted me gone.'

'I didn't mean that,' he grimaced.

'You've got your wish now. I'll have a chat with the accountant.'

'Why are you resigning, just when we are doing so well in our expansion projects into the east. I thought you wanted to handle that. You made a big issue out of it.'

'I'm going because I am sick of looking at you.'

'You can't leave …' he shouted.

She turned back at the door and glared at him. 'Can't I?'

Then she went into her own office and sat down at her desk. She looked around the room. This place in which she had worked for the last few years. Giving this business her all. And seeing it expand at an incredible rate, beyond their wildest dreams really.

And now she was turning her back on it. She had resigned. Given up this entity which she had created with Russell. She couldn't believe it. Now she felt free to make her own decisions. She hadn't realised how heavily this whole situation with Russell had weighed on her since Christmas.

'I admire you, Zoe, you've got a lot of guts. It's not easy to give up something which was very much a part of yourself. You loved this business,' Clive said.

'I have to admit I did. It was my life. But as you know I've had doubts lately and now that I've made the decision I feel much better.'

'There are very few people who would give up a successful business because of the social implications, although my hands are tainted as well.'

'I'd never say that to you.'

'Thanks,' he smiled.

'It's time to change my life. And since I've met Tom, everything is different.'

'You are lucky. I'm happy for you.'

'And I'm keen to do something with Matt, give him a chance to set himself up in a web design business,' Zoe told him. 'I've had a look at what he's done so far and it really is excellent. I had asked him to try to design a game but he hasn't done much on that and seems to prefer web design.'

'There are a lot of people in that business but you have so many contacts you shouldn't have much problem setting yourself up.'

'I hope not. Anyway, I'll have a few euro to tide me over in the meantime.'

'You'll do very well whatever it is, I'm certain of that,' Clive smiled at her. 'By the way, I'm hoping to have a chat with Matt sometime soon. We might meet for a drink and maybe you would come along as well?'

They met one evening, and Clive didn't waste any time getting to the point. 'Matt, there's something I want to mention to you. Zoe has told me that your father has confessed his involvement in the death of your mother.'

'I hope you don't mind that I mentioned it to Clive?' Zoe asked immediately.

'No, no.' Matt shook his head.

'My brother is a barrister like myself, although he's still working and didn't change career like I did. Back in two thousand and six both of us were aware of your case, and now he would be willing to talk to you about what could be done.'

Matt looked at him, puzzled.

'I don't know whether you would be interested in doing that, but I just felt that you should be aware of it.'

'I don't think so.' His immediate reaction was firm. 'But thank him.'

'It might mean you can clear your name,' Clive said.

'But that would mean I'd have to involve my father? Go to the Gardai?'

Clive nodded.

'I can't imagine doing that.'

'It's your right.'

'I've talked to my Dad about that, and assured him that I won't be involving the law.'

'If you were found not guilty it would mean there would be no restrictions on your life. You know, travel, work, banking, borrowing, these are all aspects of everyday living which can be affected by the fact that you have served a prison sentence.'

'Thank you for offering me the chance, and please tell your brother that I do appreciate his interest.'

'Are you concerned about the cost?' Clive asked.

'No, it's not that. Although obviously it would be a factor if I wanted to go down that route,' Matt smiled.

'My brother would be prepared to act for you *pro bono*, he said to make that clear.'

'That's so generous, I can't believe it.' Matt was taken aback. It was obvious in the expression on his face.

'I'm astonished as well,' Zoe added. 'Will you tell him we're really grateful? Maybe you might let us have his address and we can send him a card to say *thank you*.'

Matt nodded in agreement.

'I will of course.'

Zoe was amazed at the change in her brother since that day he had met his father. There was a brightness in his eyes which hadn't been there before, and his quiet smile belied the horror of his life in prison.

Chapter Sixty-six

Zoe and Gail tried to persuade Matt to move into the house in Donnybrook.

'We want you home,' Zoe insisted. Determined to let her brother know that they really wanted him.

'I'm fine staying at the shelter and there really isn't space here. Dad mightn't be keen to have me around,' he argued. 'And there's the dog too.'

'Dad wants you to come home, and we all love dogs so it will be lovely to have him. We have four bedrooms and we'll just clear out the box room. You don't mind sleeping in the smaller one?' Gail asked.

'I don't care where I sleep,' he smiled. 'Maybe I'll come back …if Dad really doesn't mind.'

'We want you home and that's it,' insisted Zoe. 'You can't be living in a homeless shelter.'

'Thanks.' He hugged both of them.

The last three months of Zoe's tenure at *RZ Gaming* went by with such rapidity she couldn't catch her breath. There was a lot of work to be completed so that she could hand over to the person who would be taking her place. An enthusiastic girl who she felt couldn't wait to get her out of the way, as did Russell himself once he had accepted her decision. Only then Zoe felt she could take that step back from the company and start all over again in a new business. She would start with web design, and work with Matt and was looking forward to the challenge.

It was a strange feeling to have made the decision to quit *RZ* and all the people she knew so well. There was a big celebration on the day she left and they all got together that evening in a nearby hotel, although Russell was conspicuous by his absence. But she didn't care, and was almost glad that he wasn't there, happy to spend time with all the other people who had joined her to say goodbye. It was an emotional evening and Zoe enjoyed it, so grateful to all her colleagues and particularly for the exquisite gold chain and matching bracelet they presented to her.

'You should take a break,' Tom advised. 'We could go away for a few days. I can't take a long holiday now but maybe at Christmas.'

'I have that voucher I received from the travel agency because of the cancelled ...' she hesitated. 'Although maybe you mightn't want to use that?'

'I don't care ...' he laughed.

'It might be better to leave it until Christmas, it's October now so there's no point going anywhere in Ireland, the weather is so uncertain at this time of the year, we could be blown out of it,' she laughed.

'How about the Christmas markets in Budapest, something like that?' he suggested.

'That's hardly your thing now, is it?'

'Not really.'

'We're not doing that then. Anyway, hanging around now just wouldn't do me any good. You know I'm a workaholic.'

'You don't have to tell me that,' he smiled.

'Do you think you'll be able to put up with me?' she asked with a grin.

'I'll put up with you any way you are.' He held her close. 'Good, bad, indifferent. You might drive me crazy but that's what I want.'

'You're a very special person, Tom Sheridan.'

'And you don't know how special you are, I can't believe that I've fallen in love with you, I thought I'd be a loner for the rest of my life, becoming more crusty and cranky with every year that passed.'

She couldn't believe that this man felt so passionately about her. She felt cherished by him. A feeling she had never known before.

On this first Monday without a job she was forced to look at her life critically. It felt very strange to find herself without a schedule for the first time in years. No plan. No arrows pointing left and right to send her off in the correct direction. She yearned for what she had lost. Disappointment settled in her stomach. A heavy stone lay there. She felt she was in a swamp, being dragged down into the mire unable to save herself.

She hadn't expected that her reaction to resigning would be so extreme. Was the company she had established with Russell so imbued in her heart and body that she couldn't live without it? She refused to accept that. She was going to go on and establish another business. Carve out a new career. But what was that first step? She would have to recreate herself. As she sat at her laptop staring at the screen her mind was blank. Automatically she clicked *inbox* and checked her emails. Most of them were business emails, and it was tough for her to reply and redirect people she had known for years to her replacement in the company. That took time and eventually she came to the end of the list. She dreaded the thought that every day there would be more emails and that she would have to reply to them too. Using the same words. Over and over. A refusal of what once had meant so much to her. She struggled through the morning, heard her father get up, shower, and go downstairs. But she stayed in her room. She didn't expect him to understand what was going on with her, since she hardly knew herself. Tortured with indecision, she wondered how her life would be now.

Perhaps an ill-defined thing which she couldn't even grasp as she groped around in darkness like someone who had lost her sight. Tears moistened her eyes and she thought about Tom. He gave her so much love she knew that whatever she chose to do in her life then she must have him beside her. Just thinking about him made her pick up the phone and call. He answered immediately.

'That was quick,' she managed a smile.

'I was waiting for you.'

'You knew I'd call?'

'I hoped.'

'You're not busy?' she asked.

'I have work to do but you're more important.'

'Thanks,' she whispered softly.

'How's it going?'

'Not good,' she had to admit the truth to him. There was no point in lying. 'I suppose I feel like someone at a crossroads, and I don't know which way to turn.' It felt good to unburden herself.

'You're bound to feel at a loss initially, it's like a sudden change in the pace of your life, an anti-climax,' he said.

'I hope it doesn't last, I hate this feeling.'

'You need to give yourself some time.'

'But what can I do?'

'Why not just relax? You've been going at such a pace for the last few years your body needs to chill out. Your clients are going to arrive thick and fast as soon as it gets out that you're in business. I'll put a sign around my neck asking that anyone who needs a great website designer should make immediate contact,' he said.

She was aware of the smile in his voice and couldn't help but laugh. No matter what happened Tom always seemed to come out with something funny which raised her spirits. 'Thanks for that.'

'You're going to be so busy you won't believe.'

'I don't know about that ...' she said with a grin.

'You just need a start,' he insisted. 'And it will be good for Matt to get his teeth into something.'

'It's nice to have him living at home.'

'I don't think he ever expected it.'

'And he and Dad are getting on well.'

'It is such an amazing turn around. Unbelievable really. Oh, there's my other phone, I'll have to take it, will I see you this evening? Let's have dinner to celebrate?' he asked.

'Thanks, love to.'

'I'll pick you up about eight.'

'Matt, will you manage to find the time to work with me if I get any clients?' she asked him.

'I don't know that I'm good enough.'

'From what I've seen of your work already, you're well qualified.'

'But I've no experience, all I've done are two websites, that's nothing.'

'But we'll work together and your confidence will soar the more experience you get,' she persuaded. 'I'm looking forward to working with you.'

'Thanks for your belief in me.'

'You're on for it then?' she asked with a smile.

'Of course, I couldn't refuse you.'

'We'll be in business together, on our way to success and hopefully make some money as well. Any ideas on a company name?'

He shook his head.

'Give it some thought, and we'll sit down tomorrow and make a decision ...' She hesitated then. Something had occurred to her this afternoon as she contemplated her rather empty life and she wanted to run it past Matt and get his opinion. 'Because I'm not busy at the moment I wondered if I might do something to help Sr. Teresa.'

'What were you thinking of?' Matt was immediately interested.

'Opening a charity shop,' she announced with a wide grin, excited.

'That would be fantastic.'

'I'm thinking of a designer shop. The clothes I can get from my friends and I've a lot of stuff which I don't need. So the first thing to do will be to locate a premises somewhere in the city which hopefully will not be too expensive.'

'I'll put it out on social media and see what happens, you might be surprised at the result.'

'And mention that we're looking for volunteers to run it as well.'

'Will I say that you'll need stock? I'm sure people would donate to help Sr. Teresa.'

'Not yet, otherwise we could be out the door with clothes and have nowhere to store them. I'm sure I'll have enough to start off. I'll try and rent a pop-up shop somewhere in town. I'll have money from the sale of the shares eventually, and I'll be able to afford it.' She couldn't hide her enthusiasm.

'What about setting up a *Fund-it* campaign, we might manage to cover some of the rent for the first year?'

'That's a great idea.' She began to feel better. There was a definite plan now.

Her phone rang. 'Do you mind?'

Matt shook his head.

'Zoe here.'

'It's Sylvia,' she murmured to Matt, and then continued to listen. 'Yes, sure I could meet you tomorrow. Will I call to the salon? Ten o'clock? Look forward to seeing you then.' She ended the call. 'That was Sylvia, who is a friend of mine and a wedding planner.' She hesitated for a few seconds but then continued on. 'And she wants to upgrade her company website. How about that?' Zoe couldn't believe her luck. It was extraordinary that just out of the blue someone should call.

Now she was energised. This was the first website she would design with Matt. And she was so happy to grasp at this opportunity. She was in a new world. To take on this challenge would mean that she could attack life with even greater dynamism. And to bring her brother along with her meant so much. He needed confidence to tackle the difficulties which stood in his path and she wanted to give it to him.

The days with Russell had drifted away and didn't matter to her any longer. Tom filled her life with love now. He was the one on whom she could utterly depend in this new universe. All she had to do was to put out her hand and he would always be there to hold it tight and reassure her, no matter how she felt. An aura of happiness surrounded her. She couldn't believe how much he meant to her. How much her life had changed.

Zoe and Matt met with Sylvia, and they discussed her requirements in detail.

'Thanks so much for giving us the opportunity to work on your website.' Zoe hugged Sylvia.

'Sure who else would I ask?' she smiled. 'The one we have at the moment is out of date and needs a lot of work.'

'We'll design something beautiful that will really show off your bridal service, make the site more client friendly and so increase your business.'

'Thank you, I really appreciate it, and I'm looking forward to seeing the new look.'

After that Matt had to go into the shelter to work and Zoe talked to Sr. Teresa about her idea.

'My goodness, I'm absolutely astonished. A shop?'

'All my friends have so much designer clothes they never wear they're going to be delighted to donate them.'

'It's amazing. Thank you so much.' She blessed herself.

'Matt was thinking of setting up another campaign to raise funds on social media to cover the rent. Would that be all right?'

'Of course, it's a wonderful idea.'

'And we thought of asking for volunteers to work in the shop as well,' she added.

'Maybe some of our people here might be prepared to help.'

'That would be great.'

'I can't express how much I appreciate your generosity, Zoe. I'm really grateful to both you and Matt.'

'I'm only glad that I've got the time, Sister, it was really through

Matt that the idea occurred to me.'

'We are so lucky to know people like yourselves and we depend on you for our very existence.'

'That night when I came in I was shocked to see so many people here needing help. It was then I decided I must do something for you.'

Chapter Sixty-seven

Matt couldn't believe how much his life had changed. While his father had admitted his involvement in the death of his mother he still couldn't believe it. To be able to gaze into his father's eyes without rancour for the first time since he had been a boy was something so beautiful his heart beat with elation. But with that feeling there was guilt too. In his soul came memories of the clash of their wills. His father wanted to bend him. Force him to accept his bidding. And Matt was obstinate. Always refusing to follow his orders. His face dark. Bitter. In resistance. Antagonism reigned. Matt felt incompetent. Never reaching Feargal's high standards and suffering because of it. He tried hard, and when his efforts fell on hard ground and achieved nothing, then he railed against the man who demanded more.

But Matt wanted to know his father now. Understand him. And they talked at length.

'You've written a lot.' He indicated the notebooks on the desk.

Feargal nodded, and handed him one.

Matt opened it.

'I hope you can understand my writing,' Feargal said. 'At times it's a bit of a scribble and I can't even read it myself.'

'I'll have no problem, it's fine. I'm really looking forward to knowing the story of your life.' Matt began to read.

'Good luck,' Feargal said with a grin. 'I'm glad that you want to know more. You're the first person to read my journals, the only person I want to read them.'

Matt was immediately engaged by the account of a storm which threatened the lives of the sailors on board a ship which was caught on the rocks. He was engrossed in the events described and while his father continued writing at his desk Matt relaxed back in an armchair and continued reading.

Time passed. There was an unexpected harmony between the two men of which Matt was only vaguely aware. But occasionally he lifted his head and his eyes caught sight of his father as he gripped his pen and let it dig into the notepaper. An air of rigidity about him as he transferred the musings in his head into hard fact.

'This is fascinating,' Matt murmured. 'Thank you for letting me read it.'

Feargal said nothing, just picked up another and handed it to him.

They remained there, each in their own world. One writing. One reading. A subtle drawing together through the links of the past. He felt grateful to his father for allowing him to step into his space and have access to something so precious. He turned the pages carefully. Some had been torn. Others were creased. The handwriting was illegible in places. But he still managed to understand this depiction of his father's life. Something he had never been able to do before. He searched for the truth among these lines and empathized with the man who had given him life.

Matt turned a page, and was shocked to see a letter written to himself.

'Dear Matt, this is another attempt to apologise to you for the terrible cruelty I've exacted on you. Please forgive me for letting you take the blame for your mother's death. I detest myself. The guilt clouds my very existence. I only hope that one day we will be able to look at each other once again like father and son without this shadow looming over us. I pray every day that God will grant me this wish.'

Matt looked up at his father and their eyes met.

301

In warm recognition, Feargal reached out his hand and grasped Matt's, holding it tight.

'Why don't I put your writing up on the computer and then you can read it more easily?' Matt suggested.

Feargal stared down at the notebook in front of him and ran his hand across the closely written page. Then he smiled and nodded. 'I'd like that ...'

Chapter Sixty-eight

'We've found a shop,' Zoe said as soon as she arrived at Tom's door, almost about to burst with excitement. 'I couldn't get you on the phone to tell you.'

'Sorry, I was at a meeting. But that's fantastic news.' He hugged her.

'A woman responded to Matt's *Twitter* message and as her tenant has just left she is willing to give it to us for the first year free of charge, can you believe it?'

'Where is it?'

'Ranelagh.'

'Good footfall. What size is the unit?'

'Fairly big. And it has a store-room at the back, kitchen and bathroom.'

'What was the previous business?'

'Fashion, so the fact that we're selling the same product will be an advantage. People mightn't even realise that the shop has changed,' Zoe explained. 'You know how the public are, they sail past and don't even notice the name,' she laughed.

'That could stand to you,' Tom agreed. 'And let's hope they walk in the door in their droves.'

'And I've got three more calls to quote for our web business which is now called *Ballystrand Web Design*. What do you think of the name?'

'Sounds good. Different.'

'Matt suggested that so I went for it immediately.'

'Congratulations.'

'Thank you.' She was thrilled now.

'I'm so glad you're in good form, I can see it in your eyes my love. I was worried when you left the company, and wondered if you mightn't survive without it.' He seemed very concerned.

'We've been busy working on Sylvia's website and I have to say it's looking really great. I can't believe how things have begun to fall into place, there's no comparison with how I felt a few weeks ago, you've no idea ...' She felt emotional and there were tears in her eyes.

He held her tight. 'I was frustrated that I could do so little to help you.'

'Just having you close is everything to me.' She leaned against him, just letting go.

'You mean that?' Tom seemed surprised.

'Yes.' A huge rush of thankfulness swirled through her, and reminded how much he meant. There was an enchantment between them. A mysterious fascination which sparked an attraction and drew them towards each other.

'I can't believe it. You know how much I had hoped that you and I would...' His eyes glowed and enticed.

'I'm sorry it's taken me so long to ...'

'I've endless patience.' His voice was warm and comforting. 'And I'm prepared to wait as long as it takes for you to decide to be mine.'

'I am yours, how could you think anything else,' she giggled.

Suddenly he moved, and knelt down on one knee. 'Zoe Sutherland, will you marry me?'

She burst out laughing.

'Don't keep me in suspense for an answer,' he smiled broadly, stood up and stretched his arms wide. 'Just tell me you'll marry me?'

'Yes my love, yes.' A feeling of intense happiness swept through her.

He smiled. 'This has to be the best day ever.'

His lips pressed softly on hers and she responded. They were silent for a few moments, just standing in close embrace. She was radiant.

So complete within the trusting love he offered to her. What had gone before had faded into obscurity. Joy surged in the brightness of her heart and Zoe knew that she would give him the rest of her life.

Chapter Sixty-nine

Sister Teresa's Designer Store in Ranelagh was packed with people the evening it opened. They had invited everyone they knew and there was an amazing response. Zoe was so glad that her father was interested. Some of the staff at *RZ Gaming* and of course, Clive. To her surprise Jean arrived as well and as she hugged Zoe it was nice for her to know she was forgiven. Clive had been a great help as they tried to get the shop ready for the Christmas trade. Generous too, in that he covered the cost of the expenses, insurance, cash register, computer, and shop fittings. Zoe was so grateful to him. Her own clothes which she had donated and those of her friends hung on rails and were much admired.

'I love that blue silk,' one girl exclaimed. 'Will you put my name on it and I'll be around tomorrow to try it?'

'Sure, I'll do that now.' Zoe put her name on a card and did as she asked.

'And I love this black …' another said. 'Will you do the same for me?'

Zoe smiled, delighted. She could see a number of sales already.

The champagne corks popped loudly, and Tom poured the fizzy liquid into flutes and handed them out to guests.

'To *Sister Teresa's Designer Store,*' Zoe yelled triumphantly and raised her glass.

'Doesn't it look amazing,' Gail looked around.

'What do you think, Sr. Teresa?' Zoe asked the nun.

'It's wonderful, I'm so grateful to you, Zoe, and Matt too.' She gently pressed her arm. 'And the clothes are beautiful. I wish I could wear some of those dresses myself,' she giggled like a young girl.

'You can choose anything you like,' Zoe offered.

'I wouldn't dream of doing that, every item must be sold and not on my back.'

'And I hope that there will be lots of sales after tonight.'

A man pushed his way through the crowd, followed by a photographer. 'I'm from the *Times,* could I have a word with you, Zoe?'

'Sure, I'd be delighted. But I have a Press Release which you might be interested in reading.' She picked one up from the counter and handed it to him.

'Thank you, but I would like to know why you are so involved?'

'I came to know about Sr. Teresa and decided to help by setting up the shop. The homeless people really need so much.' She didn't want to go into too much detail.

'Let's take some photographs,' he suggested. 'Perhaps with Sr. Teresa and yourself?'

She brought the nun over and they posed.

'Where is Matt?' Sr. Teresa turned, and looked at Zoe. 'He should be in the photographs, but I can't see him.'

'I'm not sure where he's gone.' She couldn't see him either.

'Smile ladies please …' The photographer clicked his camera.

When they had left, Zoe went over to Tom. 'Have you seen Matt?'

'He took your Dad home, he was tired.'

She was relieved. Always worried about Matt since that day in Howth.

'And we must go too.' Sr. Teresa embraced her.

'I'll let you know how we get on. I'm really looking forward to doing business here, and I hope we'll be successful.'

'You will be, I'm sure.' The nun smiled.

'Thanks for asking some of your volunteers to help.'

'They were delighted.'

'I'm hoping the publicity will bring in customers.'

'I'll pray for our success.' She took Zoe's hand and held it gently.

Slowly the shop emptied of guests.

'Tom, thanks for serving the drinks. You're a pet. And for helping to get the shop ready, I couldn't have done it without you. And Clive, thanks a million for everything, you're so generous.'

'No problem, I enjoyed it.' He was putting used glasses into boxes along with Gail.

'Let's finish up here and go somewhere to celebrate,' Tom suggested. 'I'll bring these boxes out to the car.'

To Zoe's delight, her friends who put their names on outfits all came back the following day and made their purchases. Sr. Teresa and Zoe's photo was in the newspaper and that brought a few more people in, some to browse, and others to buy.

Zoe spent the day there herself. To her delight, a woman who lived locally and had many years of retail experience offered her services on a part-time basis and was prepared to run the business day to day with the volunteers. Zoe could cover it the rest of the time.

'I can't get over how well Dad is looking,' Gail said to Zoe. 'I thought he'd collapse altogether when Matt came home. I never thought he'd be so happy. It's extraordinary.'

'He's like a man ten years younger, and the writing, that's amazing.' Zoe looked across the room to where Matt and Feargal sat.

'The fact that Matt is putting all his notes on the computer gives him so much confidence, he'll have a book out of it soon.'

'I even heard them discussing a title for it yesterday, they're so enthusiastic.'

'Dad, how is the book going?' Zoe asked. 'Have you reached the end yet.'

'We're nearly there,' Matt said.

'How about finding a publisher?'

'As soon as we've finished, we're going to put it out there,' Matt explained.

'Or go online.'

'Maybe.'

'Online?' Feargal grinned. 'How about that?'

'You'll have a bestseller, Dad,' she added.

'*Memoir of a Lighthouse Keeper*. It will be a number one.' Gail was animated.

Chapter Seventy

Matt walked the beach with his father, followed by the dog, Rex, who waited expectantly for Matt to throw another ball into the sea for him. Zoe and Tom followed and in his arms he carried their two-year old daughter, Rachel. It was a warm bright afternoon in June, and the waves crashed up on to the shingle, sucked it back into the sea, and flung it up again with a swish swash sound. He was reminded of that day when he stood overlooking the rocks in Howth and thought about taking his own life. If he had done that then he wouldn't be here now, holding the arm of his father, having found him again.

'I wish you weren't going ...' Feargal said slowly.

'I'm sorry ...' Matt bent his head to hear what he said.

'I wish you weren't going away,' he repeated.

'I'll just be here in Ballystrand.'

'But we won't see you again.'

'I'm not sure how long I'm going to stay, they might throw me out as unsuitable,' Matt smiled.

'I'm sure that won't happen.'

'Who knows.' He shrugged.

'Your mother told me she's happy for you.'

He stared at him, shocked.

'She came back last night ...'

Matt took a deep breath.

'And told me it will be the last time I'll hear from her.'

Matt didn't know what to say.

'She said you'll be fine now,' Feargal murmured.

He couldn't believe what his father was saying.

Together they went in the direction of the lighthouse. He held on to his father as they climbed up on to the rocks, and around the circular red and white striped building. He stretched out his hand and reached to touch the cold concrete, pressing against the uneven roughness. For a few seconds he closed his eyes.

His father stood there too, staring up. Matt put his arm around him. 'Takes you back?' he murmured.

Feargal nodded.

They stayed there in silence for a while, each of them caught in a world of their own.

Tom put Rachel into Matt's arms. He held her close and she gave him a wet sticky kiss.

'Look after this little one, she's very precious,' he said, his voice husky.

'We will, don't you worry,' Zoe assured him.

'Rex …' He bent to ruffle his black fur.

He hugged Zoe, Gail and Tom. And lastly, his father. 'Love you all,' he whispered, and then turned to walk towards the gates.

Tears flooded his eyes as he headed in the direction of the huddle of old grey buildings around the church spire on the hillside. He didn't look back until he reached the entrance and only then he turned to see the small group still standing there, the little girl waving her hand energetically, and the dog barking.

'Welcome Matt,' the Abbott said.

The tall priest ushered him inside and they sat down.

'Thank you for accepting me, I'm very grateful to you and the community.'

'I'm glad to see you and hope that you'll find living here with us rewarding. You can stay as long as you like.'

Matt swallowed, unsure of what to say. He had made his final decision to come back to the monastery the previous year, but had stayed on with the family until his father's book had been published. Gail had gone back to London, Zoe and Tom had got married and had their daughter, Rachel, and then moved into the house in Donnybrook to live with Feargal. *Ballystrand Web Design* was doing really well, and Zoe could hardly keep up with the demand for their services, and found that running the business, and Sr. Teresa's Designer Store as well as looking after little Rachel, took every minute of her time, but she was happier than she had ever been, and Matt was very glad for her.

When he had visited the Abbey on that previous occasion, he found the atmosphere calm and peaceful. A sense of holiness in those silent passageways. He was still haunted by the death of his mother and even though his father had admitted what had happened on that terrible day, Matt still held himself responsible.

He walked into the cloister with the Abbott and heard the bells chime for *Vespers*. As they came near the church, he could hear the voices of the monks echoing and immediately said a silent prayer that in this Holy place he would be able to make reparation to his mother at last.

TO MAKE A DONATION TO
LAURALYNN HOUSE

Children's Sunshine Home/LauraLynn Account
AIB Bank, Sandyford Business Centre,
Foxrock, Dublin 18.

Account No. 32130009
Sort Code: 93-35-70

www.lauralynnhospice.com

Acknowledgements

As always, our very special thanks to Jane and Brendan, knowing you both has changed our lives.

Many thanks to both my family and Arthur's family, our friends and clients, who continue to support our efforts to raise funds for LauraLynn House. And all those generous people who help in various ways but are too numerous to mention. You know who you are and that we appreciate everything you do.

Grateful thanks to all my friends in The Wednesday Group, who give me such valuable critique. Many thanks especially to Vivien Hughes who proofed the manuscript. You all know how much we appreciate your generosity.

Special thanks to Martone Design & Print – Brian, Dave, and Kate. Couldn't do it without you.

Grateful thanks to Transland Group for transporting our books.

Thanks to CPI Group.

Thanks to all at LauraLynn House.

Thanks to Kevin Dempsey Distributors Ltd., and Power Home Products Ltd., for their generosity in supplying product for LauraLynn House.

Special thanks to Cyclone Couriers and Southside Storage.

Thanks also to Irish Distillers Pernod Ricard. Supervalu. Tesco.

Many thanks to Elephant Bean Bags – Furniture - Outdoor.

And in Nenagh, our grateful thanks to Tom Gleeson of Irish Computers who very generously service our website free of charge.Walsh Packaging, Nenagh Chamber of Commerce, McLoughlin's Hardware, Cinnamon Alley Restaurant, Jessicas, Abbey Court Hotel, and Caseys in Toomevara.

Many thanks to Ree Ward Callan and Michael Feeney Callan for all their help.

And much love to my darling husband, Arthur, without whose love and support this wouldn't be possible.

MARTONE DESIGN & PRINT

Martone Design & Print was established in 1983 and has become one of the country's most pre-eminent printing and graphic arts companies.

The Martone team provide high-end design and print work to some of the country's top companies. They provide a wide range of services including design creation/ development, spec verification, creative approval, project management, printing, logistics, shipping, materials tracking and posting verification.

They are the leading innovative all-inclusive solutions provider, bringing print excellence to every market.

The Martone sales team can be contacted at (01) 628 1809 or sales@martonepress.com.

CYCLONE COURIERS

Cyclone Couriers – who proudly support LauraLynn Children's Hospice – are the leading supplier of local, national and international courier services in Dublin. Cyclone also supply confidential mobile on-site document shredding and recycling services and secure document storage & records management services through their Cyclone Shredding and Cyclone Archive Division.

Cyclone Couriers – The fleet of pushbikes, motorbikes, and vans, can cater for all your urgent local and national courier requirements.

Cyclone International – Overnight, next day, timed and weekend door-to-door deliveries to destinations within the thirty-two counties of Ireland.

Delivery options to the UK, mainland Europe, USA, and the rest of the world.

A variety of services to all destinations across the globe.

Cyclone Shredding – On-site confidential document and product shredding & recycling service. Destruction and recycling of computers, hard drives, monitors and office electronic equipment.

Cyclone Archive – Secure document and data storage and records management. Hard copy document storage and tracking – data storage – fireproof media safe – document scanning and upload of document images.

Cyclone Couriers operate from Pleasants House, Pleasants Lane, Dublin 8.

Cyclone Archive, International and Shredding, operate from

11 North Park, Finglas, Dublin 11.

www.cyclone.ie   email: sales@cyclone.ie Tel: 01-475 7000

SOUTHSIDE STORAGE
Murphystown Road, Sandyford, Dublin 18.

FACILITIES

Individually lit, self-contained, off-ground metal and concrete units
that are fireproof and waterproof.

Sizes of units : 300 sq.ft. 150 sq.ft. 100 sq.ft. 70 sq.ft.

Flexible hours of access and 24 hour alarm monitored security.

Storage for home
Commercial storage
Documents and Archives
Packaging supplies and materials
Extra office space
Sports equipment
Musical instruments
And much much more ....

Contact us to discuss your requirements:

01 294 0517   -   087 640 7448
Email: info@southsidestorage.ie

Location: Southside Storage is located on
Murphystown Road, Sandyford, Dublin 18
close to Exit 13 on the M50

Transland Group is one of Ireland's most reputable and innovative transport and logistics companies. We provide a daily pallet distribution service within Ireland through our membership of PalletXpress, and a consistently reliable UK and European import / export service through Palletways, Europe's largest pallet network. Our palletised distribution network offers unbeatable coverage in over 20 countries.

Transland Group is committed to creating innovative, technology-driven supply-chain solutions. Our pioneering low-cost online booking facility enables customers to avail of special discounted rates for early booking, saving them time and money. Customers can also track their consignments online from collection through to delivery, and receive POD information automatically upon delivery. This facility is especially beneficial for small to medium sized companies, who can manage all their transport requirements through one system.

Customer satisfaction is at the core of Transland's business. Our mission is to provide the highest level of service to our clients in all areas of our operation, and respond proactively to customers' requirements.

Transland has offices in Ireland (Dublin) and the UK (Lichfield), and is a member of the IIFA, BIFA and CILT. For more information, please visit www.translandgroup.com.

ELEPHANT BEAN BAGS

Designed with love in Co Mayo, Ireland, Elephant products have been specially designed to provide optimum support and comfort without comprising on stylish, contemporary design.

Available in a variety of cool designs, models and sizes, our entire range has been designed to accommodate every member of your family, including your dog - adding a new lounging and seating dimension to your home.

Both versatile and practical, our forward thinking Elephant range of inviting bean bags and homewares are available in a wealth of vivid colours, muted tones and bold vibrant prints, that bring to life both indoor and outdoor spaces.

Perfect for sitting, lounging, lying and even sharing, sinking into an Elephant Bean Bag will not only open your eyes to superior comfort, but it will also allow you to experience a sense of unrivalled contentment that is completely unique to the Elephant range.

www.elephantliving.com

THE MARRIED WOMAN

Marriage is for ever ...

In their busy lives, Kate and Dermot rush along on parallel lines,
seldom coming together to exchange a word or a kiss.
To rekindle the love they once knew, Kate struggles to lose
weight, has a make-over, buys new clothes, and arranges a
romantic trip to Spain with Dermot.

For the third time he cancels and she goes alone.

In Andalucia she meets the artist Jack Linley. He takes her with him
into a new world of emotion and for the first time in years she feels
like a desirable beautiful woman.

Will life ever be the same again?

Available now online
McGuinness Books
www.franobrien.net

THE LIBERATED WOMAN

At last, Kate has made it!

She has ditched her obnoxious husband Dermot and is
reunited with her lover, Jack.

Her interior design business goes international and TV
appearances bring instant success.

But Dermot hasn't gone away and his problems encroach.

Her brother Pat and family come home from Boston
and move in on a supposedly temporary basis.

Her manipulative stepmother Irene is getting married
again and Kate is dragged into the extravaganza.

When a secret from the past is revealed Kate has
to review her choices ...

Available now online
McGuinness Books
www.franobrien.net

THE PASSIONATE WOMAN

A chance meeting with ex lover Jack throws Kate into a spin. She cannot forgive him and concentrates all her passions on her interior design business, and television work.

Jack still loves Kate and as time passes without reconciliation he feels more and more frustrated.

Estranged husband Dermot has a change of fortunes, and wants her back.

Stepmother, Irene, is as wacky as ever and is being chased by the paparazzi.

Best friend, Carol, is searching for a man on the internet, and persuades Kate to come along as chaperone on a date.

ARE THESE PATHS TO KATE'S NEW LIFE OR ROUNDABOUTS TO HER OLD ONE?

Available now online
McGuinness Books
www.franobrien.net

ODDS ON LOVE

Bel and Tom seem to be the perfect couple with successful careers, a beautiful home and all the trappings. But underneath the facade cracks appear and damage the basis of their marriage and the deep love they have shared since that first night they met.

Her longing to have a baby creates problems for Tom, who can't deal with the possibility that her failure to conceive may be his fault. His masculinity is questioned and in attempting to deal with his insecurities he is swept up into something far more insidious and dangerous than he could ever have imagined.

Then against all the odds, Bel is thrilled to find out she is pregnant. But she is unable to tell Tom the wonderful news as he doesn't come home that night and disappears mysteriously out of her life leaving her to deal with the fall out.

Available now online
McGuinness Books
www.franobrien.net

WHO IS FAYE?

Can the past ever be buried?

Jenny should be fulfilled. She has a successful career,
and shares a comfortable life with her husband, Michael,
at Ballymoragh Stud.

But increasingly unwelcome memories surface and
keep her awake at night.

Is it too late to go back to the source of those fears
and confront them?

THE RED CARPET

Lights, Camera, Action.

Amy is raised in the glitzy facade that is Hollywood.
Her mother, Maxine, is an Oscar winning actress, and
her father, John, a famous film producer. When
Amy is eight years old, Maxine is tragically killed.

A grown woman, Amy becomes the focus of John's
obsession for her to star in his movies and be as
successful as her mother. But Amy's insistence
on following her heart, and moving permanently to
Ireland, causes a rift between them.

As her daughter, Emma, approaches her eighth
birthday, Amy is haunted by the nightmare of
what happened on her own eighth birthday.

She determines to find answers to her questions.

Available now online
McGuinness Books
www.franobrien.net

FAIRFIELDS

1907 QUEENSTOWN CORK

Set against the backdrop of a family feud and prejudice
Anna and Royal Naval Officer, Mike, fall in love.
They meet secretly at an old cottage
on the shores of the lake at Fairfields.

During that spring and summer their feelings for each
other deepen. Blissfully happy, Anna accepts Mike's
proposal of marriage, unaware that her family have a
different future arranged for her.

**Is their love strong enough to withstand
the turmoil that lies ahead?**

Available now online
McGuinness Books
www.franobrien.net

THE PACT

THE POINT OF THE KNIFE
PRESSES INTO SOFT SKIN ...

Inspector Grace McKenzie investigates the
trafficking of women into Ireland and is
drawn under cover into that sinister world.

She is deeply affected by the suffering of one
particular woman and her quest for justice
re-awakens an unspeakable trauma in her own life.

CAN SHE EVER ESCAPE FROM ITS
INFLUENCE AND BE FREE TO LOVE?

Available now online
McGuinness Books
www.franobrien.net

1916

On Easter Monday, 24th April, 1916, against the
backdrop of the First World War, a group of
Irishmen and Irishwomen rise up against Britain.
What follows has far-reaching consequences.

We witness the impact of the Rising on four families,
as passion, fear and love permeate a week of
insurrection which reduces the centre of Dublin to ashes.

This is a story of divided loyalties, friendships,
death, and a conflict between an Empire
and a people fighting for independence.

Available now online
McGuinness Books
www.franobrien.net

LOVE OF HER LIFE

A MAN CAN LOOK INTO A WOMAN'S EYES
AND REMIND HER OF HOW IT USED TO BE
BETWEEN THEM, ONCE UPON A TIME.

Photographer Liz is running a successful business.
Her family and career are all she cares about since
her husband died, until an unexpected encounter
brings Scott back into her life.

IS THIS SECOND CHANCE FOR LOVE DESTINED
TO BE OVERCOME BY THE WHIMS OF FATE?

Available now online
McGuinness Books
www.franobrien.net

ROSE COTTAGE YEARS

THE HOUSE IN THE STABLE YARD IS AN EMPTY SHELL
AND FANNY'S FOOTSTEPS RESOUND ON HER POLISHED
FLOORS, THE RICH GOLD OR WOOD SHINING.
THE HAUNTING SOUND OF ANNA'S PIANO AND THE
SPIRITS OF THE PAST ARE ALL AROUND HER.

Three generations of women, each leaving the home they
loved. Their lives drift through the turmoil of the First World War,
the 1916 Rising, and the establishment of the Irish Free State,
knowing both happiness and heartache in those years.

BINA CLOSES THE DOOR GENTLY BEHIND HER. THE CLICK
OF THE LOCK HAS SUCH FINALITY ABOUT IT. AT THE GATE
SHE LOOKS BACK THROUGH A MIST OF TEARS, JUST ONCE.

Available now online
McGuinness Books
www.franobrien.net

CUIMHNÍ CINN
Memoirs of the Uprising

Liam Ó Briain

(Reprint in the Irish language originally published in 1951)

(English translation by Michael McMechan)

Liam Ó Briain was a member of the Volunteers of Ireland
from 1914 and he fought with the Citizen Army of Ireland
in the College of Surgeons during Easter Week.

This is a clear lively account of the events of that time.
An account in which there is truth, humanity and, more
than any other thing, humour. It will endure as literature.

When this book was first published in Irish in 1951, it was hoped
it would be read by the young people of Ireland. To remember
more often the hardships endured by our forebears for the
sake of our freedom we might the better validate Pearse's vision.

Available now online
McGuinness Books
www.franobrien.net